The Right Fit

Also by Sinead Moriarty

The Baby Trail

The Right Fit

sinead moriarty

WASHINGTON SQUARE PRESS

New York   London   Toronto   Sydney

Washington Square Press
1230 Avenue of the Americas
New York, NY 10020

This book is a work of fiction. Names, characters, places and
incidents are products of the author's imagination or are used
fictitiously. Any resemblance to actual events or locales or persons,
living or dead, is entirely coincidental.

ISBN-13: 978-0-7434-9678-0
ISBN-10:   0-7434-9678-7

First Washington Square Press trade paperback edition March 2006

10 9 8 7 6 5 4 3 2 1

WASHINGTON SQUARE PRESS and colophon are
registered trademarks of Simon & Schuster, Inc.

Manufactured in the United States of America

Designed by Davina Mock

For information regarding special discounts for bulk purchases,
please contact Simon & Schuster Special Sales at 1-800-456-6798 or
business@simonandschuster.com

For Mum and Dad

acknowledgments

Sincerest thanks to all at Atria Books, in particular my editor Greer Hendricks for her enthusiasm and encouragement, and to Suzanne O'Neill for all her help.

Thank you also to my agent Emma Parry for her loyal support.

Thank you to the fantastic team at Penguin Ireland and to all at Penguin UK.

A big thank you to everyone at Gillon Aitken Associates: the dynamic Sally Riley, Ayesha Karim, and most of all, Gillon himself.

I owe a debt of gratitude to Catriona Kirwan for her kindness and patience in talking me through the adoption experience. Thanks also to Helen Kingston for her humorous insight into the home visits.

Thanks to Lis Leigh for her help and guidance.

Thanks to Paul White for his legal advice.

Thanks to my friends for cheering me on.

Thanks to Mike and Sue for being so enthusiastic and supportive always.

The book is dedicated to Mum and Dad with deep gratitude for being such wonderful parents.

My biggest and most heartfelt thanks go to the two men in my life—Troy, for his unwavering encouragement, love, and support (and his significant input into the book!), and Hugo, for giving me the precious gift of motherhood.

*H*i, my name's Emma. I'm a thirty-five-year-old makeup artist. Three years ago I married James. Things were going swimmingly in our "happy ever after" marriage until we decided to try and have children.

That was two years ago. Since then I've attempted post-sex handstands, headstands, and any other upside-down positions I could conjure up; spent hours with my legs in stirrups being prodded internally by all manner of specialists; taken mountains of hormone-inducing drugs; had one failed IVF attempt and I'm still not bloody pregnant.

To be honest I was becoming a bit obsessed about it—completely and utterly manic, to be precise. It was time to look for another solution. I was driving myself and everyone around me insane, so I made the decision to stop all treatment and go the adoption route. James had agreed to it—after a small amount of arm twisting—and we are now embarking on this, phase two, of attempting to become parents.

Adopting a baby is the perfect solution to our problems. And it's bound to be much easier than the natural route . . . isn't it?

chapter ONE

I WOKE UP THIS MORNING without a pit in my stomach. It felt fantastic. My first thought wasn't—"What day is it in my cycle?" or "What injections, hormones, or tests do I have to take today?" Nor did I have to worry about having sex. I realize this may sound odd, but believe me—having to have sex every month on day eight, ten, twelve, fourteen, sixteen, and eighteen of your cycle, with a couple of extra rides thrown in to be on the safe side, is not all that much fun.

Now that we were going to adopt, I was looking forward to getting back to a spontaneous sex life that wasn't ruled by my temperature and didn't end up with me standing on my head for twenty minutes in a lame attempt to aid the sperm by adding my own version of gravity to the equation.

I looked over at James, who was heading out to the shower.

"Isn't it great?"

"What?" he said, looking around suspiciously.

"The fact that now when you shower, you can masturbate to your heart's content. Your sperm can swim freely. You no longer have to keep them all in for baby making. So liberate them, let 'em flow . . . ," I said, waving my arms about over my head. I had previously banned James from masturbating because I had read somewhere that the male's sperm needed to be kept in for as long as possible so they would be chomping at the bit during sex and charge up and fertilize the eggs.

"Thank you, darling," said James, grinning at me. "It's wonderful for a man to have his wife's blessing to play with himself. I may be a while!"

I went downstairs to make breakfast. I was feeling very Doris Day–esque as I whisked the eggs and fried the sausages. This was a new day. A fresh beginning. I had a really good feeling about it. No more stress about trying to get pregnant. No more doctors and hospitals and drugs. We were going to adopt. We were going to give a child a happy home. I pictured some poor little mite in a war-torn country gazing at me through the bars of her iron cot. Dressed in rags she looked up at me, her huge blue eyes begging me to take her away to a safe, warm place. I bent down to hold her hand, and slowly, she began to smile at me, her pinched face lighting up.

"That's the first time Svetlana has ever smiled," gasped the director of the orphanage. I beamed back at the beautiful little girl. I was special, she was special. We were made for each other.

I imagined James holding Svetlana in his arms as we burst through the arrivals gate in the airport. Our families, gathered to greet us, were holding WELCOME HOME SVETLANA banners and big red CONGRATULATIONS balloons. I saw them oohing and aahing when they first met our gorgeous, smiling daughter. James and I beamed at each other, proud parents at last. Fast-forwarding twenty years, I saw myself cheering as Svetlana won the best actress award at the Oscars for her portrayal of a deaf musician fighting against the odds to become a world-class pianist. In her acceptance speech she thanked everyone, and then, pausing for maximum effect, she said, "But most of all I want to thank my mother for saving my life. If it wasn't for her I wouldn't be here today. This Oscar is for you, Mum, you are the person I love and admire most in the world. I owe everything to you . . ." I nodded and bowed my head as the audience rose to its feet to applaud me.

"Emma, what on earth are you doing? The sausages are burning." James pushed me aside and pulled the pan off the stove, staring at his blackened breakfast. "Are you all right? What's going on?"

"Nothing," I snapped, embarrassed at being caught bowing and waving to the cream of Hollywood.

James shrugged and took over the cooking. He was used to finding me daydreaming. When he was halfway through his scrambled eggs and burnt sausages, I announced that I was going to call the adoption people.

"Today?" he asked

"Yes today. No point in wasting any more time, we might as well get going."

"Okay, well will you get them to send us out all the relevant information so we can go through it before making the final decision."

"What do you mean final decision?"

"I'd just like to know a bit more about the process before plunging in, that's all."

* * *

James had been a bit reluctant at first about the whole adoption thing. He was worried about the child's medical history, its family medical history, abuse, AIDS. . . . But I said that everything was a leap of faith. Having kids of your own was scary too. Then I brought up his mad uncle Harry who had a fetish for exposing himself to people, but who had three sons who were completely normal and well balanced. Who could tell what genes and mental or medical foibles were going to be passed down? It was unknown and mostly inexplicable territory, but we couldn't live our lives in fear. After much discussion and debate, James had agreed to the adoption, so I was none too pleased with this "final decision" comment.

"James," I said, trying to be patient. "We discussed this—at length. We agreed to go ahead with it. I'm not ringing up to ask for an information pack, I'm calling to put our names down on the list."

"All right, fine, but will you ask them to send us some guidelines, I just don't think it's as straightforward as you seem to."

"Don't be silly, every time you turn on the TV there are orphaned children staring out at you, desperate for good homes. Besides, after the last two years, it'll be a piece of cake," I said brimming with confidence. There was no way this could be more difficult than trying to get pregnant. Adoption was going to be a walk in the park compared to the last two years. I couldn't wait to get started.

Later that day when James had gone off to practice, I called the Adoption Board. James had been promoted from assistant coach to manager and head coach of the Leinster rugby team. Leinster had lost in the semifinal of the European Cup to Toulouse the year be-

fore, and James had gone into mourning for weeks. So he was determined to win the cup this year and was giving the team his un-
divided attention and putting in even more time than ever at work.
I just hoped his practice schedule wasn't going to clash with our
adoption schedule.

"Hello" snapped a grouchy voice at the end of the phone.

"Oh hello, I'm ringing to adopt a baby," I announced.

The woman sighed. "Hold the line."

"Hello," snapped an equally grumpy-sounding colleague.

"Yes hello, I would like to adopt a baby please."

"Have you filled out the Intercountry Adoption Form?"

"The Inter what?"

"The form. Have you filled it out?"

"No, I haven't filled out anything," I said, beginning to feel a
bit grumpy myself. What was wrong with these women? Why were
they being so rude? And what on earth did she mean by 'intercountry'? Maybe I had misheard and she meant intercounty. Yes that
must be it; she needed to know what county I was from in Ireland.

"Address."

"Sorry?"

"I need your address so I can send you the Intercountry Adoption Form."

"Did you say intercounty?"

"No dear, I said intercountry. As in Ireland and China—not
Dublin and Cork."

"But why would I want one of those forms? Isn't it easier and
quicker to get an Irish baby? There must be hundreds of young
teenage mothers who give up their babies for adoption."

The woman snorted. "Single mothers, give up their babies?
Where have you been for the last ten years? Irish baby, ha ha, that's
the best I ever heard."

I was now really angry. How dare this old boot laugh at me? Sure, I had fantasized about adopting a child from a war-torn country, but realistically it'd be a lot easier to get a local baby.

"So what are you saying—I can't adopt an Irish child?"

"There are no Irish babies up for adoption. There were four in total last year. Four in the whole country, and we have thousands of parents looking to adopt and a huge backlog. Intercountry is the only option. Do you want a form sent out or not?"

"Yes, please," I said, feeling utterly deflated.

"Address?"

I gave her my address and hung up. I was reeling. Four Irish babies in the whole country! A huge backlog of parents, with the only option being intercountry. What did that mean? How big was the backlog? What countries were involved in intercountry? Did it include England? With James being English, maybe we'd have a good chance of getting an English baby. But if the single mothers in Ireland were keeping their babies, the single mothers in England were probably doing the same.

I had imagined I'd ring up and they'd say, "Thank you for calling. What a wonderful person you must be to want to adopt a child. When can we meet you? We have hundreds of children waiting to be placed." I never imagined I'd be barked at, laughed at, and then hustled off the phone.

As I sat there lurching between wanting to cry and wanting to call back and tell the woman exactly what I thought of her and her attitude, the phone rang. It was my mother.

"Who were you on to? I've been trying to get through for the past ten minutes."

"The adoption people," I said without thinking.

"What?"

I wanted to bite my tongue in half. How on earth could I have been so casual? Telling my mother that we were gong to adopt a baby required buildup. It should have started with lots of subtle hints about the wonders of adoption. Throw in a few stories about people she had heard of who had successfully adopted—Mum loved Mia Farrow and thought her multiple adoptions were wonderful. She was always saying how it was the Irish blood in Mia (her mother was the famous Irish actress Maureen O'Sullivan) that made Mia such a good and charitable person. After a series of long discussions about Mia's successful adoptions, I should then have just hinted that we were thinking of going down that route ourselves. Never, but never should I have pounced the news on her as I had just done. And let's face it I had thirty-five years practice— well, I only started talking at three, but you get the idea—so it was a very stupid and fatal mistake on my part.

"Adoption people? What on earth are you at, Emma? Lord save us you've only been trying for a family for a short while, what in God's name are you rushing into that for? I'd say they laughed you out of the place."

"No, actually they didn't. They're sending me out the application forms today. Furthermore, I've been trying to get pregnant for two years, which is not a short time. It feels like an eternity to me."

What the hell, I had landed myself in it now, I might as well ram the point home.

"Pffff—eternity my eye. You young ones expect everything to happen instantly. Life's not like that. Application forms? I never heard the like. It takes time to get pregnant. Rushing out and adopting the first child that comes along is foolish. What does James think of all this madness?"

"He is one hundred percent behind me. He thinks it's fantastic, in fact it was his idea," I lied.

My mother thought James was the bee's knees and the cat's pa-

jamas. He could do no wrong in her eyes. The fact that I had managed to marry someone who was stable, extremely attractive, and
successful had thrown her completely. You couldn't blame her
really, because before James there had been a string of unstable, un-
attractive losers. The icing on the cake was the fact that James was
English—she seemed to think I'd married a young David Niven.
The fact that James looked and acted nothing like the actor was irrelevant. He sounded a bit like him, and that was good enough for
Mum. She loved telling all her bridge cronies about her wonderful
"English" son-in-law. Don't get me wrong. I loved my mother, but
now that her three children were all grown up, she had too much
time on her hands. My younger brother, Sean, had been living in
London for over ten years and my sister, Babs—my parent's after-
thought—was now a bolshie twenty-three-year-old student who ignored her. So Mum's spare time was spent focusing a lot on me, my
marriage, and my attempts to get pregnant. It now looked as
though we would be adding adoption to the list.

"I somehow doubt that James had anything to do with this
harebrained scheme to adopt. You should—"

"So, Mum, what did you call for?" I said as firmly as I could
without being short.

"Well, I was just calling to tell you about Francis Moran."

"Who?"

"You know Francis well; you used to play together when you
were kids."

"I have no idea who she is."

"Oh for goodness sake, you used to pal around with her and
sure isn't her brother the managing director of that mobile phone
company . . . what's this his name is? Greg . . . no . . . Gary . . .
no . . . Gerry is it?"

"I've no idea who you're talking about."

"Well anyway, didn't Francis go to Turkey on her holidays and get engaged to a waiter out there. Her poor mother is beside herself."

"Well, if she's happy what's so terrible about it?"

"Happy? With a Turkish waiter she met on a week's package holiday? Sure everyone knows he's only marrying her to get a visa to come over here."

"Maybe it's true love," I said, defending my childhood pal who I had no recollection of ever meeting.

"Come on now, Emma, don't be ridiculous. Francis was always a bit wild. I remember when you used to . . . oh, actually now that I think of it, it wasn't you she was pally with at all, it was Sean. I better go and ring him to fill him in. Okay, bye."

"Bye," I said into the empty receiver.

When James came home later that evening I told him about the adoption people being rude and not having any local babies and having to adopt abroad.

"I hate to say I told you so," he said, saying it anyway, "but I did warn you that this wouldn't be easy."

"I don't understand why it's so hard. I mean Mum's school friend saw a documentary one time about the orphanages in Romania, and the next day she hopped on a plane. A week later, she came back with a kid under each arm. They were delighted to let the children go."

"First of all, I doubt very much it happened quite like that, and second of all, that was ten years ago—times have changed."

James was one of those guys who never let you get away with exaggerating. I like to exaggerate, I like to say it took me three hours to get home when it actually only took an hour and ten minutes. I think it makes for a better story. James on the other hand likes facts to remain facts and not turn into fiction. When he pulled other people up on it, I thought it was smart and funny, when he did it to me I wanted to poke his eyes out.

"That is how it happened actually. I've seen pictures of her carrying the two babies out of the orphanage. She was carrying her little girl in her arms and holding the little boy's hand. They looked as if they were a normal family—except for the fact that the kids look nothing like her. Anyway the point is, we'll have to go abroad to adopt because there are no Irish babies."

"I expected that actually. I read an article recently which said that something like eighty percent of all adopted children in Western Europe are foreign."

"Well next time don't keep the statistics to yourself, share them with me so I don't go making a fool of myself. So what do you think?"

"About having Ling Su Wong as a daughter? I dunno, but if she looks like Lucy Liu from *Charlie's Angels,* I'm okay with it," he said, finding himself very entertaining.

chapter TWO

A WEEK LATER I called over to Lucy's flat. Lucy is my best friend. We were in school and college together, and she is an all-round fab person. Until last year she was single and beginning to get a bit fed up with it, but then I set her up with Donal—the captain of James's rugby team. Donal is a bit rough around the edges—there is a touch of the caveman about him—but underneath it all he's a really good guy. After a rocky start they fell madly in love and have now decided to move in together.

I arrived at Lucy's apartment, which looked as if a bomb had hit it. For someone who was normally so organized both at work—she had one of those ball-breaking management-consultant-type jobs—and at home, Lucy was looking unusually frazzled. I sat down on her bed and watched her sift through her belongings.

"I just don't know what to bring and what to leave behind. What happens when you move in? Where do I put my Tampax? Do we have sex every night? Do I need to wear hot underwear

every day? Help, Emma," said Lucy as she sifted through her gorgeous La Perla underwear. Looking good was not going to be a
problem for Lucy, I thought as I picked up a beautiful midnight
blue lace bra. Apart from her gorgeous underwear, she was tall,
slim, and stunning with long, thick, black hair. Lucky Donal.

I, on the other hand, was five foot four, a redhead and a little
chunky around the hip area. I'm not saying I didn't scrub up well,
but first thing in the morning I was not a pretty sight. Poor old
James was subjected to my Marks & Spencer cotton underwear
and was lucky if the colors matched. As for garters, I hadn't worn
them since the first time we had sex to conceive—as opposed to
"just for the sake of it" sex. Maybe I should get new underwear. It
couldn't be pleasant to have to look at my big white ass in sexless
cotton knickers. I'd have to make more of an effort, I'd look up the
Victoria's Secret website when I got home and put in an order.
Spice things up a bit. No sex toys or anything, just some hot lin-
gerie to detract from my flabby thighs.

"Relax, it'll all be fine. You'll just find your own rhythm. And
no, you don't have to wear garters every day. Well, I don't anyway."

"I'm very glad to hear it," said Lucy. "Seeing someone twice a
week is manageable. You get your hair blow-dried, you put on your
best underwear and it's all great. But on a daily basis it'd be hard to
keep up. What about sex though? On the one hand I'm worried
he'll be gagging for it twenty-four/seven and on the other I'm worried he won't want it at all. I keep reading about couples who move
in together and their sex life dies. They go from not being able to
keep their hands off each other to only having sex once every few
weeks."

"To be honest, Lucy, my sex life has been so regimented over
the last two years I can't remember what we were like before that.
Maybe you should ask Jess?"

Lucy looked at me and raised her eyebrows. We giggled. I had forgotten about the night Jess confessed to not having had sex for eight months after the birth of her first child. Jess was our other best friend. She was married with two children and was finding it hard going. The good news was, that she had got back to having sex only three months after her second child was born.

"I'm going to miss it here, it's been a real haven for me," said Lucy, looking around her lovely cream and beige apartment. "Donal's place is a bit smelly and bare. It's a real bachelor pad."

"Just think of all the fun you'll have doing it up and making your mark," I said, doing my best Pollyanna impression.

"God, Emma, I'm really scared," admitted Lucy, in a rare display of vulnerability which made my heart melt. "What if it doesn't work out and I end up on my own again?"

"Hey," I said, giving her a bear hug, "you're going to be fine. Donal worships the ground you walk on. I've never seen you this happy with a guy. You're made for each other."

"Yeah, but it's not just the two of us is it?" said Lucy, referring to Donal's niece, Annie. Five years ago when Annie was ten, her parents—Donal's sister, Paula, and her husband, Tom—were killed in a car crash. Paula had named Donal as legal guardian to Annie. So Donal had moved back to Ireland from the UK where he was playing rugby professionally, to look after his niece. She was in boarding school now and only visited one weekend in six, but little orphan Annie had reacted very badly when Donal told her that Lucy was moving in. She clearly didn't want another woman taking Donal away from her, so Lucy was understandably nervous about dealing with a fifteen-year-old who hated her.

"Don't worry about Annie, she'll come around. She obviously just has abandonment issues, being an orphan and all that. She'll love you when she gets to know you. Speaking of orphans, I called the Adoption Board and they told me I have to go overseas to adopt a baby, so we could end up with the united colors of Benetton!"

"What happened to all the Irish babies?"

"There are none. It's weird actually that you will be kind of adopting Annie—well, being lumped with her—at the same time that I'm trying to adopt a baby."

"God, that is a bit weird. You can come over and practice your parenting skills on Annie if you like, she's out in three weeks. Come on, I better get all my stuff moved in before she has a chance to change Donal's mind."

A few days later Lucy was unpacking her boxes in Donal's house when he strolled into the bathroom and saw his cupboard—which used to hold a bar of soap and a toothbrush—crammed full of bottles.

"What's all this?" he asked

"Oh, it's just stuff for my hair. I'll need to buy a new medicine cabinet for my other products, there's no room in here."

"Hair products?" said Donal, gazing down at the numerous bottles cramming up his sink. He picked one up. "*Kerastase Aqua-Oleum, Nang-Nutrition—nourishing recharge.* . . . What the hell does that mean? Is it in Chinese? *Frizz-ease, mirror image heat activated laminator,*" he read. "Laminator! For your hair? Whatever happened to shampoo? *KMS Silker leave-in treatment, detangles and controls static and flyaways* . . . ah Jesus, Lucy, you've got to be kidding me. Is there one product for each hair on your head?"

"Donal, it takes time, energy, money, and good products for a girl's hair to look good, so buzz off and leave me to it."

Donal shook his head and walked into his bedroom. Lucy heard a roar.

"What the hell?"

She followed him in and saw him staring at his wardrobe, which was now filled with her shoes—just the fifty pairs.

"How in God's name could anyone in their right mind need all these shoes. You have—one, two, three . . . eight pairs of black boots in here."

"They're all totally different," said Lucy.

"Fifteen pairs of little strappy shoes! We live in Ireland, not Barbados."

"I wear my Jimmy Choos every Saturday night. I'll let you in on a little secret, women suffer to look good."

"Jimmy what?"asked Donal

"Choo, he makes amazing shoes."

"What's the story with all the Chinese stuff? Hair products and now shoemakers. Whatever happened to Head and Shoulders and Clarks shoes?"

"Some of us actually moved out of the seventies. It's really quite liberating, you should try it."

"All the Chinese wear is those old flip-flops, so why would I want them to make my shoes? Hey," said Donal, staring at the wall, "where's my poster gone?"

"If you are referring to that tacky picture of Pamela Anderson in a thong, it's in the bin."

"What? I love that picture. It's good for the soul to wake up to a beautiful sight every day. I open my eyes in the morning, and there she is, winking at me. It's fantastic."

"You're joking!" said Lucy looking appalled. "If you think that I'm going to have those plastic boobs staring down at me every morning, you've got another thing coming."

"They may be plastic but they look fantastic. Seeing Pammie helps me get motivated in the morning. She gets me going. Right, where's the poster?"

"Donal, it may have escaped your notice, but you are now in your thirties, it's time to take down the teenage posters. Not to mention the fact that you are about to embark on a new living arrangement, which includes me, your girlfriend, sharing your bedroom. If you want to look at someone's breasts, look at mine."

Donal looked down at Lucy's chest. "Lucy, it may have escaped your notice that two fried eggs do not have the same impact as two large melons."

Lucy's first night living with Donal was spent alone in his bed, while he slept in Annie's room. When she woke up the next morning Donal was standing beside the bed with a tray.

"Breakfast in bed," he announced as he placed the tray on her lap. "As you will see to the left, we have a mound of shredded paper that was formerly the lovely Ms. Anderson with the horrible big plasticky boobs. To the right we have two perfectly rounded, beautifully shaped fried eggs and a rose. You have to say you forgive me, because I can't spend another night in that tiny bed, my legs were frozen. I'm an athlete, and we sportsmen need our limbs to be kept warm at all times."

"You're a world-class idiot all right," said Lucy smiling. "You're forgiven—this time."

Donal hopped into the bed and snuggled up to Lucy. Placing his hands on her fried eggs he asked, "Any chance of some action?"

Lucy elbowed him sharply in the ribs.

"Ouch"

"Don't push your luck, sunshine. You're lucky to be allowed to lie beside me. Sex is not on the menu this morning. You'll have to do a lot more groveling first."

Donal hopped up and knelt in front of her. "I'm so sorry, Lucy,

I will never mention Pammie again. You're the most beautiful girl in the world, not only have you a sensational body but you are also a beautiful person inside. You are the woman I have dreamed of meeting all my life. I had given up all hope of meeting someone special until I met you. You, Lucy, have changed my life, I cannot believe how lucky I am. Now can we have sex?"

What the hell, thought Lucy, she was only depriving herself as well.

chapter THREE

A WEEK LATER I RECEIVED an official-looking letter addressed
to Mrs. Hamilton. I still hadn't got used to being called Mrs.
Hamilton. Mind you, I had been delighted to be able to change to
Hamilton, because my maiden name was Burke. When your name
is Burke, you have to try harder to fit in than other people with
nice normal-sounding surnames. "Oi Burke head" was the highly
amusing nickname that Sandra Teehan called me on my first day in
middle school. The first day at a new school is difficult enough
without being singled out during roll call and sniggered at by the
entire class. Although Lucy, my best friend from down the road,
joined the school at the same time as me, she was in a different
class—the one with all the other geniuses. I was in the class with
the just-about-average girls, only one class up from the real thickos.

Sandra made my life fairly miserable in the first few months of
school. She was the "cool" girl in the class, in the way that at twelve
years of age the loudest girl in the class always is. She had a group of

mates who laughed at everything she said, and a lot of their time was spent poking fun at me and my stupid name. Meanwhile, I was sitting beside the class supernerd Fiona, who constantly followed the teachers around, trying to befriend them and regularly snitched on her fellow classmates. The last thing I needed was to get lumbered as a fellow nerd. I was desperate to be in with the "cool" gang, but they were having none of me. Lucy, meanwhile, was hanging out with her classmates and having a ball. All the clever girls stuck together, even at lunch break. Lucy, I'm sorry to say, gave Judas Iscariot some stiff competition—she completely disowned me. As if that wasn't bad enough, after blanking me during school hours, she'd come around to my house at the weekends to hang out with me.

And so I spent my lunch breaks being ignored by my so-called best friend, trying to avoid Sandra and her gang, and also running away from Fiona, so as not to be tarnished with her geeky reputation, which left me pretty much alone. I used to take refuge in the bathroom, and read *Little Women*, feeling a great kinship with the main character, Jo. I, like her, was an outsider. I felt very sorry for myself indeed. I lay awake at night dreaming up different ways of torturing Sandra. I wanted to inflict pain on her, I wanted her to suffer. I agonized over how I could get out from under her when it suddenly came to me—if I studied hard every night and did really well on my Christmas exams, I'd be moved up a class. Sandra was not the sharpest knife in the drawer, so the likelihood of her ever following me up a grade was slim to none. I lay in bed and grinned; all I had to do was study.

For the next five weeks I studied late into the night. My parents were surprised by the sudden turnaround. No longer was I interested in watching TV and listening to records. I dashed up the stairs after school and didn't reappear. I sat the exams at Christmas, and for the first time in my life I knew the answers to everything.

My results shocked both my parents and me, and I was duly upgraded a class. I was now in the second cleverest class as opposed to the second thickest. My parents were delighted, as was I.

When we went back to school after the Christmas holidays I felt like a new person. Over mince pies and cream in my house, I had confronted Lucy on her disloyal behavior, and she had promised to be an in-school friend as well as an out-of-school friend, as long as I started behaving a bit more normally and stopped hiding in the bathroom at lunchtime.

"I know it's mean, Emma, but everyone thinks you're a bit odd and if I hang around with you I'll get picked on too. So just try to be more normal and hang out with the cool people in your new class. Jess Curran's quite cool, so try and be in her gang."

Harsh words, but good advice. Jess was very cool—she had spiky hair and was going steady with a boy called Mark. We became great friends, so much so that Lucy ended up being jealous of our friendship and felt decidedly left out. After letting her sweat it out for a few weeks, I eventually invited her over to hang out at my house with Jess, and we became the Three Amigos. When Sandra tried to bully me, Jess told her that as she was both fat and ugly—she'd really need to work on her personality or she'd end up an old spinster with a dried-up fanny. Coming from a girl who actually had a boyfriend, this was a crushing put-down. Sandra never bothered me again.

I still occasionally raise this Judas interlude with Lucy over a bottle or three of wine, and she lurches from teary apologies to telling me to get over myself, reminding me that it happened over two decades ago and that she has spent the last twenty-three years making up for it by being a top friend—which is true.

* * *

I opened the letter addressed to Mrs. Hamilton. It was from the Adoption Board thanking me for my inquiry in relation to inter-country adoption and saying it would be processed in accordance with standard procedures. They enclosed two booklets to provide me with some information—James would be pleased with that—and an application form for assessment. Along with this we were required to provide originals of: long-form birth certificates, a long-form marriage certificate, and any documents relating to pre-vious marriages.

The application form was accompanied by three pages of ap-plication guidance notes. I skimmed over them, and most of them didn't relate to us. They were things like—if we were not married then only one of us could apply to adopt, and we had to be a resi-dent in the country for at least a year before adopting—but the last point caught my attention: it was about providing references. The references we chose had to know us both very well and know our families, and at least one of the referees had to have children.

Yikes. The only couples we knew well who had children were James's brother Henry and his awful wife Imogen, who lived in En-gland, and Jess and Tony, who had two kids. The only problem was that I hadn't spent a whole lot of time with Jess's kids. Truth be told, I had kind of avoided seeing them. I found it really difficult to be around babies, so I barely knew little Sally and Roy. As for Imogen's children, her son Thomas was a brat, but I was fond of her twin girls, especially my goddaughter Sophie, although I hadn't actually seen her since the christening, nearly a year ago. By the looks of things, James and I would have to start hanging out at Jess and Tony's to try and bond with their kids. The notes said that our references would have to send in written letters and be visited by a social worker to discuss their relationship with us more thoroughly. Obviously that ruled out Henry and Imogen. I doubted somehow that the Adoption Board was going to fork out for a social worker to pop over to Sussex for a few days to interview them. It'd have to be Jess and Tony, and I'd get Lucy to be the other reference.

I filled James in about the letter over dinner and then told him I'd decided on Jess, Tony, and Lucy. He looked up at me and shook his head.

"Hold on, Emma. Deciding who our references are going to be is not a snap decision, we need to think about it."

"What's to think about? I've just told you who they're going to be. We don't need to analyze it for hours, it's been decided."

"By you, without consulting me."

"For goodness' sake, it's no big deal, they'll be great."

James picked up the form and began to read.

"It says here that the references should know both partners very well. Jess, Tony, and Lucy are all your friends. We need someone who knows me and my family well."

"Like who?"

"Like my brother," said James. "Oh no, actually it says they can't be family members."

"Exactly," I said, pretending I had read the small print. Phew—that totally ruled out Henry and Imogen. Thank God, because I knew that Imogen didn't like me at all. She was one of those loud, overbearing, horsey types, and every time she rang or saw me she'd demand to know why I wasn't pregnant.

"All right then, I'll ask Donal."

"Yeah, right."

"Why not?"

"Because, he's a male chauvinist pig."

"This is the man you set your best friend up with."

"Yes, because Lucy can give as good as she gets. He'd frighten the life out of some poor gentle social worker."

"Apart from the fact that Donal has been my best friend since we met seven years ago, he's also bringing up Annie pretty much on his own. He's the perfect candidate."

"As is Lucy as stepmother to Annie, on top of which she spends all day negotiating and dealing with difficult clients. Lucy can be very persuasive you know, which is exactly what we need. We want the social worker to be convinced that we will be ideal parents."

"Having your two best friends as referees is simply not going to work. It has to be balanced, Emma, it says so here," said James tapping his finger on the form. "The referees need to know both of us very well. What about Paddy and Sarah? They've got kids."

Paddy was the fullback on James's team and was a nice guy, but his wife Sarah was the most almighty bore you ever met and aggressive to boot. I have actually never seen her with her coat off. When we go out, she sits there with a puss on her face, coat on, handbag in her lap, sipping a club soda, unless she's feeling particularly wild, in which case it'll be a pineapple juice. The first time I met her, I had only just started seeing James and was still at the stage where I had to down at least three sneaky drinks at home for Dutch courage before meeting up with him. By the time I met Sarah I had had an additional three drinks on an empty stomach. That's the other thing about the early dates; I wouldn't eat all day in a lame attempt to have a flat stomach. Anyway, James introduced me to Sarah who was, as usual, sitting down with her coat on. I went to sit down beside her in an attempt to be friendly. I was trying to make all James's friends like me so that they'd tell him what a great catch I was.

"Hi, Sarah, nice to meet you," I said in superfriendly mode, trying not to slur my words.

She sort of smiled, in that mean way where the person just

about raises the ends of their lips but shows no teeth. I like to see a set of gnashers myself; I find it a lot more genuine.

"I heard James had a new girlfriend," she said, yanking her coattail from under my bum. "So what do you do?"

"I'm training to be a makeup artist. Isn't that cool?" I was still on a high from having made the decision. I had agonized over it for three years, so it was a huge relief to have finally made the break and resigned from my mind-numbingly boring job as a recruitment consultant. I was thoroughly enjoying my makeup classes, I had finally found something I was really good at . . . if I say so myself.

"Makeup artist?" said Sarah, not exactly whipping out the pom-poms to cheer me on in my new career path.

Thankfully I was so delighted with myself that I didn't really notice—although that could have had more to do with the drink than the happiness.

"What do you do?" I asked politely.

"I work at Jones Kelly and McDonald. I'm the first woman ever to be made a director," she announced, assuming I knew the famous JKM firm. Needless to say, I had never heard of them.

"Good for you," I enthused. "What do they do?"

She looked horrified. "They are the most prestigious public relations firms in the country, everyone has heard of them. Bernard Jones advises the president."

"Well I've never needed publicity, so I'm not up-to-date with the top dogs," I said, beginning to wonder how to make a quick escape. I was clearly wasting my time trying to impress this one. Maybe if I had been the CEO of Lancôme she wouldn't be glaring at me as if I was pond scum.

"So how exactly did you meet James?"

"I picked him up in a bar, took him home, and gave him the

best night of his life," I whooped as I drained my drink in one long swallow. "Oh will you look at that, I need another drink. Well cheerio then," I said, bouncing to my feet.

James told me later that night that Sarah had said I was a live wire. James in his innocence and goodness took it as a compliment. Having grown up with one brother and then gone to an all-male boarding school, James didn't really get it when women were being subtly bitchy, and Sarah was always supernice to him, so he thought she was fine, which really got my goat. Anyway, suffice it to say that Sarah was not my favorite person, and although we were civil to each other, hell would freeze over before she was a referee for this adoption.

"Over my dead body," I said, looking at James with my don't-even-think-about-it face on.

"Well then it's going to be Donal. We'll have Jess and Tony from your side and Donal from mine."

"Okay, but you better warn him to be on his best behavior. I'll get Lucy to pick him out some decent clothes for the interview and check the form before he sends it off. At least she'll be there to keep an eye on him."

"Right then, it's sorted. Now let's have a look at these information books," said James, picking up *Understanding the Assessment Process*. I looked at the clock, *Sex and the City* had just started. Sod the leaflets, I'd let James read them and give me a synopsis.

chapter FOUR

THE FOLLOWING SATURDAY was my sister Babs's graduation dinner. None of us could believe she had actually made it through college. All she had done for three years was strut around in teeny-weeny miniskirts, flicking her long blonde hair, and batting her eyelids at everything in a pair of trousers. Babs was a real head turner, but she had a very large nose—from the Barry Manilow stable of noses—which prevented her from being completely in love with herself. Having spent three years studying social science she was now taking some time out to decide what to do with the rest of her life and trying to persuade Dad to buy her a nose job as a graduation present.

Sean flew home from London for the weekend to come to the family dinner. I went to the airport to pick him up. He bounded over and bear-hugged me.

"Hey sis, good to see you. How's things?"

"Okay. What's going on?"

"What?"

"You practically skipped off the plane, so I know something's up. Come on spill the beans."

"Well, I've met this girl . . ."

Sean was a redhead like me—but more of the carrot and big orange freckles variety—and hadn't had much luck with women. Personally, I always felt he shot too high. I know it sounds awful, but he had a terrible habit of falling in love with stunning model types who were never going to go for him. You have to know your limits, and unless you're a cute, famous, movie star redhead like Eric Stoltz, models are just not going to fall at your feet. Sean was extremely successful. He was a partner in the highbrow law firm of Brown and Hodder and earned ridiculous amounts of money, working a mere nineteen hours a day. He was also the nicest person in the world, and I adored him. There were only eighteen months between us, and we were very close.

"Oooooh, what's she like?" I said, silently praying that she was not a model or an actress like the last girl he had brought home, who turned out to be having an affair with her manager.

"She's lovely, Emma. She's a teacher."

Great, I liked the sound of that. A teacher was perfect. A teacher wouldn't be flighty or hard-nosed or selfish. A teacher would be nice and normal and down-to-earth and sweet-natured.

"She's very pretty, her name's Shadee."

"Cherie? Like Tony Blair's wife?"

"No, Shadee like Shadee," said Sean, just a little defensively.

"Unusual name," I said, prying without prying.

"She's Persian."

Persian? What was Persian? I knew about Persian cats, they were the big furry ones, but I had no idea where Persia was. It sounded exotic and very far removed from Ireland.

"Sorry, Sean, I've no idea where Persia is."

"It's Iran."

Oh my God! Alarm bells started ringing in my head. Iran! Iran where all the women had to be covered from head to toe in black with only a slit for their eyes. Iran, where all the men were total religious zealots. I had seen Sally Field in the movie *Not Without My Daughter* where she was held captive by her mad—but very attractive—Iranian husband. What on earth was Sean doing? Had his confidence dropped so low that he was now going out with a woman whose face he had never seen?

As breezily as I could, I asked if she had been living in England long.

Sean looked at me and smiled. "She is English, Emma. Her parents are Iranian, but she was born and bred in the UK so she's a mixture of both cultures, like so many of the people in England now."

"So she doesn't wear the black sheet?"

"You mean the yashmak? Of course she doesn't, nor does her mother. One of the reasons they fled Iran was because of the Ayatollah Khomeini and the introduction of new laws that were all based on Islam. They were clever enough to get out before the fundamentalists took over."

Shadee was obviously a good teacher. Sean knew his stuff, and judging by his slight prickliness he was expecting some strong, uninformed reactions—he knew his family all too well. He was clearly planning to educate us all on Persian affairs.

"Well good for them," I said. "So how long have you guys been dating?"

"Nearly three months"

"WHAT? I've been on the phone to you loads of times and you never mentioned it."

"I wanted to see if it was going anywhere before I said anything. I'm not expecting Mum to react too well to the fact that
she's not Catholic, Irish, or even European."

"Initially I'd focus on the fact that she's a teacher and then
break the rest of it to her gently. She'll be fine, she'll just be delighted to see you so happy," I lied.

We drove straight to the restaurant where Mum, Dad, Babs, and
James were waiting for us. Babs was wearing a skirt that looked a
lot more like a belt and a plunging top that left nothing to the
imagination. Mum was hissing at her through a fixed smile,
which wasn't very effective. She looked like she had a bad case of
lockjaw.

"You look like a cheap hussy. This is a respectable restaurant,
could you not have worn something decent."

Babs rolled her eyes. "You have to flaunt it while you've got it."

"Hi, Seabiscuit," said Sean, leaning down to kiss Babs while
the rest of us tried to keep a straight face.

"What's a seabiscuit?" asked Mum, at which point I thought
James was going to choke on his drink.

"It's a stupid race horse with a big nose. Sean thinks he's a
fucking comedian," said a very grumpy Babs.

Mum threw her head back and roared laughing.

Dad, James, and Sean then launched into a detailed discussion about the Leinster rugby team's chances of winning the European Cup under James's guidance, and dissected every player on
the team. Babs then got into a snit because it was her night and
they were all talking about rugby. I, on the other hand, was
relieved the conversation was about rugby and not Sean's love life.

But eventually Mum interrupted and asked Sean how work and things were going.

"Good, thanks. I've met a great girl actually. She's a math teacher."

"God, I'd say she's a barrel of laughs," said Babs.

"How lovely," said Mum. "A teacher, isn't that wonderful Dan?"

"Great news," said Dad.

"Tell us all. What's her name? How long have you been seeing her?" asked Mum.

"I've been seeing her for about three months now. Her name's Shadee."

"Shireen?"

"No, Shadee."

"Welsh?" asked Dad.

"No, Scottish I'd say," said Mum.

"Neither," said Sean.

"Sounds more Asian . . . ouch!" said James as I kicked him under the table.

"Well it is actually. She's Persian," said Sean throwing himself in headfirst.

"What's Persian," said Mum, looking confused and a little concerned.

"Persia is Iran" said Dad, looking decidedly worried.

"It's okay, she doesn't wear the gear and she was born and bred in England," I jumped in, trying to break the tension.

"You have to go to Iran to find a girlfriend and you've the cheek to tease me about my nose," said Babs, stirring it up as usual.

"There was a super bloke in school with me from Iran— Johnny Naser. He was six foot five, but a real gentle giant, great batsman too," said James, trying to help ease the tension and failing miserably.

"She considers herself half English half Iranian," said Sean tersely.

"Is she . . . ah . . . religious," said Dad, cutting to the chase.

"No, but her parents are Muslim and she respects the values of the Muslim faith."

"Iran," said Mum. "Did I see a film about Iran?"

I was hoping she wasn't referring to *Not Without My Daughter*.

"Lord," said Mum, wide-eyed. "I did see a film about Iran, and poor Sally Field was trapped there with her daughter and the husband was an awful fellow and he seemed very normal at first. Oh yes, in America he was very charming and then once he got home he turned into a monster. Swear to me you'll never go there, Sean, do you hear me. Never. This girl may seem normal now, but mark my words once she steps foot inside that country she'll be a different person. No, Sean, you'll just have to tell her to go and find someone from her own background and you find yourself a nice Irish girl."

"Don't be ridiculous, Mum," snapped Sean. "That's like her parents forbidding her to see me because I come from Ireland so I could be a member of the IRA. I really like her, so you better get used to the idea."

"Dan, talk to your son," said Mum glaring at Dad.

"Well, Sean, to be fair, our cultures are very different. It could cause problems down the line."

"She's not the bloody ayatollah's henchman for God's sake. Her father's a surgeon, her mother's a teacher, and her brother's an accountant. They're a normal family, just like us."

As if on cue, Babs—who had tied her napkin around her head

so you could only see her eyes roared—"Hey guess who I am? I'm Sean's new girlfriend—Shahreeeeeeee."

I looked at James, whose mouth was twitching, and had to look away before I started to laugh. He leant over and whispered in my ear, "I'm glad we're adopting. Imagine if our children inherited Babs's genes!"

"Or her schnozz," I said, giggling.

chapter FIVE

I SPENT THE NEXT TWO WEEKS standing in long lines waiting to get my birth certificate and our marriage one—neither of which I could find at home. When I called James's mother to send me his birth certificate, she could put her hand right on it, which didn't surprise me. Mrs. Hamilton was one of those superorganized women who always knew where everything was. I was always amazed by the neatness of her house. There didn't seem to be any "stuff" hanging around. No unopened mail, old newspapers and books, tennis rackets in the hall, coats hanging on the end of the stairs, shoes kicked off in the kitchen, crumbs on the bread board, out-of-date cheese in the fridge. Each room was immaculate, and every time we came home from a visit, I'd try to emulate her tidiness. It usually lasted a day. James had not inherited his mother's genes and neatness was certainly not my forte, so by day two we were back to our untidy but familiar surroundings.

I completed the adoption form, filling in our references'

names and at the last minute decided to write a cover letter to send
in with the application, although it didn't ask for one. I was hoping
to appeal to the reader's emotions and help our chances of jumping
up the queue.

> *Dear Sir/Madam,*
>
> *I am writing to apply for an intercountry adoption.*
> *See enclosed a completed application form and the neces-*
> *sary documents.*
>
> *My English husband, James, and I have been trying*
> *to have a baby for two years now, with no success. We*
> *are dying to have a family and give a child a happy and*
> *loving home. We are not fussy at all and are open to*
> *children from any country of any color or creed. If the*
> *child has sisters, brothers, cousins, or even very close*
> *friends—we'd be happy to accommodate them too. We*
> *are prepared to do anything that will help speed up the*
> *process. As we have an intercountry marriage, we feel we*
> *are particularly well suited to an intercoutry adoption.*
>
> *I look forward to hearing from you soon.*
>
> *Yours sincerely,*
> *Emma Hamilton*

I checked it for spelling mistakes and sealed the envelope. I felt
the fact that James was English might give us a more international
feel and make us stand out. Granted he wasn't from deepest darkest
Africa, and we weren't exactly being stoned on the street for our in-
terracial union, but nonetheless it was an intercountry union. I also
thought that stressing our openness to children of different creeds
and cultures would help, and if there were siblings, sure we might
as well take them too and do it all in one go. I hadn't discussed the

possibility of a multiple adoption with James, but I'd cross that bridge if and when I needed to. There was no point in telling him about it yet.

When James came home later, I hid the magazine I was reading and pretended to be studying the intercountry information booklet, which had almost put me into a coma. I had been doing well until I got to page three, which went into detail about The Hague Convention on the Protection of Children and Co-operation in Respect of Intercountry Adoption. At that point I found my eyes being drawn toward this month's *Vogue,* which had been delivered that morning, and had spent a very pleasant hour reading about Botox and the vital knowledge that this year's black was gray. Still, I wanted James to think I was doing as much research as he was, so I stuffed the magazine under my chair.

"Hello, good day?" said James, kissing the top of my head.

"Mmmm yeah, just reading up about the Hague Convention, pretty interesting stuff."

"Absolutely key to the protection and well-being of children, as is the United Nations Convention on the Rights of the Child," lectured James as he opened the fridge. Thankfully he was distracted by the meager sight of a crusty chunk of cheddar cheese and an out-of-date Müller Light yogurt. "Okay, well it looks like it's going to have to be pizza."

"Sorry, I meant to go to the shops on the way home, but Amanda asked me to stay on and do her makeup for some dinner she was going to tonight."

Amanda Nolan was the host of *Afternoon with Amanda,* which was Ireland's version of *Oprah*—except the guests tended not to be glamorous Hollywood stars. Amanda's guests were more often than not members of the Irish Country Women's Association or local politicians and C-list celebs. I had been doing her makeup for the show for the past couple of years. It was regular work, and although some people, including my mother, thought Amanda was a brazen hussy because she had had an affair with John Bradley, the leader of the opposition party, I liked her. She was very direct and always said it like it was, which I found very refreshing.

James ordered pizza and I went off to meet Jess and Lucy for a drink. We caught up on each other's news, which in mine and Jess's case wasn't much. I told them about the adoption application, and Jess told us that little Sally was now beginning to talk and little Roy was crawling. Unlike other friends with children, Jess had no interest in regaling us with the details of Sally's eating patterns or the regularity of Roy's diaper changes. When she was out with us, she liked to switch off and have a laugh. She was also sensitive to the fact that I had been trying desperately to get pregnant, with no success, and that Lucy wanted a family but was still in the early stages of her relationship.

"So Lucy, what's it like living with Donal? Tell us all," said Jess.

"Apart from our first night fiasco, it's been fine. I do find it a bit weird though, sharing everything with someone else. I'm so used to my own space. The bathroom is the hardest."

"Pubic hair in the shower, facial hair in the sink, and wet towels on the floor," said Jess, giggling,

Lucy laughed. "Exactly. But it's also the privacy thing. I like to hang out in the bathroom and shave my legs and put on face masks in peace. But the other day as I was soaking merrily in a big bubble bath with a face mask on, Donal came in and"— Lucy leaned forward and whispered—"peed in front of me!"

Jess and I roared laughing.

"It's disgusting. Is it normal? Am I just being a prude?" asked Lucy.

"No, it's just that I did it in front of James and he's the one who freaked," I said, giggling.

"Tony bolts the door so I can't get in," snorted Jess.

"What do you mean?" asked Lucy, beginning to laugh herself, more at us than with us.

I told her about the time, when I first moved in with James, and he was brushing his teeth one morning, minding his own business, when I walked in, sat down on the loo, and peed. He stopped rigid in midbrush and stared into the mirror. Then, covering his eyes with his left hand, he slowly turned to me and hissed, "What in God's name are you doing?"

"Peeing," I said, smiling up at him. "Oh that's better, I was bursting. You don't mind do you?"

"Mind! Emma, there are certain tasks a man does not want to see his girlfriend performing, and that is one of them. Really and truly it's just too much information," he huffed.

I laughed. "What? Does it really bother you? For goodness sake, it's only natural. I don't mind in the least if you pee in front of me."

"I can assure you that will never happen."

"What about all those years in boarding school with the communal showers and toilets?"

"It was an all-male boarding school. It's totally different."

"Did your mum never pee in front of your dad?" I asked, winding him up.

"Of course she didn't. My mother wouldn't dream of it. She's a lady," he said, going all stuffed shirt on me.

"Oh for goodness' sake, it's no big deal. It's not as if I'm peeing *on* you," I said, winking at him.

"Emma, a man thinks of his girlfriend like his mother. Ladylike, precious, with a little mystery. Having you squatting beside me, pissing like a racehorse when I'm trying to brush my teeth in peace is the most almighty turnoff. I moved in with you because you're my girlfriend. If I wanted to move in with someone who I felt comfortable peeing with, I'd have moved in with Donal."

When Jess and Lucy stopped laughing, Jess told us that Tony had bought a lock for the bathroom door so she couldn't barge in when he was in the shower and pee in front of him. He was of the James frame of mind—toilet habits should be kept secret and private.

"So how come I'm with the only guy who thinks it's normal?"

"Because you're the only one of us who thinks it's gross," I said, laughing. "If Jess or I lived with Donal, we'd spend all day in the bathroom, peeing simultaneously."

"Did you say anything to him?" asked Jess.

"Later on, I said I thought we needed a lock for the bathroom door, and he said 'No we don't, Annie has her own little bathroom, so you don't have to worry about her coming in on top of you.' So, realizing I'd have to spell it out, I said that I thought we needed one ourselves, for our own bathroom for going to the toilet, etcetera. 'Don't worry, Lucy,' he said, 'if I'm taking a shit I'll keep you posted so you don't walk in on me.' I suppose I should be grateful, because at least I'll be spared him pooing in front of me," said Lucy, laughing despite herself as Jess and I wiped the tears steaming down our cheeks.

"Apart from the peeing, how's it going?" I asked.

"Actually very well. He has given me free rein to do up the house—except for Annie's room, which I'm not going to touch for fear of upsetting her, but when she gets out of boarding school next weekend, I'm going to ask her if she wants to decorate it and offer to pay for it as a housewarming present. The place is beginning to look less like a rugby club and more like a home. I've painted it all cream, and I've ordered beige couches. So far, Donal seems to like it. He won't accept any rent money, so it's my way of contributing. It feels weird not to pay my way."

"That's the one thing I hate about not working," said Jess, "having to ask Tony for handouts every time I want to buy something."

"Ooooh that must be hard," I said.

"It's desperate, because all the things you enjoy spending money on like clothes, beauty products, massages and hair, have to be accounted for, and guys have no idea how much things cost. Tony can't understand how my highlights cost a hundred euros every six weeks. So I said, fine then I'll stop getting the highlights, but don't complain when you find yourself married to a mousy brown dog."

"What about clothes?" I said, unable to imagine explaining to James how much money I spent on clothes and shoes. Even now, when I was paying for them out of my own pocket, I lied to him about the quantities. Whenever he asked "Is that new?" I said— "Don't be ridiculous, I've had this old thing for years."

"Well, now that I've finally got back into shape after a mere eight months of starving myself," said Jess, rolling her eyes, "I've started shopping again. But the joy is taken out of it when you have to justify every purchase. I splurged on a Donna Karan dress last week and Tony found the receipt in the bottom of the bag. I felt like I was fifteen again, explaining to my dad that I needed that Benetton outfit, because otherwise none of the guys at the disco would ask me to dance. Tony kept saying how I had to curb my spending because we have two kids now and we need to tighten our belts and money doesn't grow on trees and we are a one-salary family and you never know what's around the corner . . . eventually I said, 'Look, Tony, here's the deal. While you're swanning around in your flashy office, going for liquid lunches in fancy restaurants, I'm at home wearing old tracksuits and covered in baby puke. So if I decide for the first time in a year to buy a dress that not only fits me, but actually looks good on me, then I will buy that shagging dress and not feel guilty about it. You should be delighted to see me taking an interest in my appearance. It can't be much fun coming home to a blob in a tracksuit every day. That's how affairs start. I'm stuck here with no budget for my highlights or clothes, chasing after our children all day. Eventually, I'll end up getting depressed, turning to food for comfort, and putting on forty pounds. Meanwhile you're in the office all day with Suzie and Denise, the secretaries with the bleached hair, tight skirts, and stick-thin bodies. So what's it going to be, Tony? Me, happy in the nice dress, or our marriage falling apart?' "

"You're unbelievable," said Lucy. "I should be taking notes. What did he say?"

"He said he'd love to meet Suzie and Denise, they sounded fantastic, and did I think they'd end up in a threesome."

chapter SIX

A WEEK LATER WE RECEIVED A LETTER back from the adoption people thanking us for sending in our application form and giving us a number—2,527. They said they were currently dealing with applicant number 2,396, so they hoped to get to our application in eight to twelve months. In the meantime they suggested that we do some research into what country we'd like to adopt from. The more information we had, the easier it would be when we came to do the adoption course.

I sat down at the kitchen table and cried. It could be a full year before we started the process, and then what? Another year? Another two years before we got our baby? Why was it so difficult to have a child? We'd already wasted two years trying naturally, and now it'd be another two or three years this way. Maybe we should pack it in. Maybe we just weren't meant to be parents. I blew my nose and looked down at the letter again. Hang on a second, I thought, there may not be any Irish babies available for adoption, but there were definitely foreign children crying out for homes. Every time you turned on the TV there was a war on somewhere, with thousands of little orphans stranded in refugee camps or bleak children's homes. Why the hell was it taking so long? I wasn't going to take this lying down. Feeling sorry for myself wasn't going to get me anywhere. I looked down at the name on the bottom of the letter. Julie Logan. Right—be afraid Julie, I thought as I dialed the number, be very afraid.

The grumpy receptionist put me through to Julie.

"Hello," I barked. "Emma Hamilton here. I've just received a very unsatisfactory letter from you, claiming that I have to wait up to a year until my application can begin. It's ludicrous."

"I know it must seem crazy and extremely frustrating," said a very soft and kind-spoken Julie. "Unfortunately with recent government cutbacks and an increase in people wanting to adopt, we're struggling to keep up. We're trying to reduce the waiting time by a couple of months, but it's an uphill battle. In some areas it's a two-year wait."

She sounded so genuinely sorry and sympathetic that I couldn't shout at her.

"But it's so frustrating," I said, groaning.

"I know. I'm sorry about that. The only thing I would suggest is that you decide what country you are going to adopt your child from and do as much research into it as possible. It will be a huge help when you start the process."

"Okay, but what if lots of people suddenly drop out, or if the finance minister gives you loads of cash in the next budget, will you let me know?"

"I will of course," said Julie, laughing, "but don't hold your breath."

I've been holding my breath for two years I thought glumly. I hung up and sat down. I had two choices: spend the next year feeling frustrated and upset—which is pretty much how I had spent the last two years—or become an expert in my country of choice so that when we got onto the adoption course, we'd fly through it and would be singled out as the most eager adopters and thus get the nicest baby. We needed to pick a country and start doing our homework.

I spent the next two hours on the Internet. I logged on to the International Adoption Association of Ireland website and scrolled down through the information. There was a long piece on the Hague Convention, which I skipped, and then information on the various countries. I chose Russia and China because they seemed to have the most information on those two, and let's face it, they were two of the most densely populated countries in the world. If we couldn't find babies to adopt there, we never would. Besides, if we went through all the countries on the list, we'd never decide.

When James came in I pounced.

"Listen, we got a letter from the adoption people—it's up to a year's wait, which is a total pain. It's because they have no budget. Anyway, in the meantime we have to choose a country—so it's Russia or China. Which one do you want? We need to decide now. We haven't time to be overanalyzing it. We need to do loads of research on the country we choose."

"Hello to you too. If we have a year to wait, why do we need to decide now? It's not a decision to be taken lightly."

"China or Russia—which?" I said, ignoring him.

"Emma," said James, taking me by the arm and leading me to the couch, "calm down. We've loads of time, and we need to look at all our options. What about other countries like Vietnam or South America? Why have you narrowed it down to China and Russia?"

"I knew you'd do this," I roared, taking all my frustrations out on him. "I knew you'd come home and stick your stupid oar in and start trying to introduce other countries to complicate the issue. I've looked at the websites, and they are the two most popular countries and they're jam-packed full of people, plus China has a bilingual agreement with Ireland."

"Bilateral."

"What?"

"I think you meant bilateral agreement."

"I know what I meant. Why are you trying to confuse the issue? It's bad enough to have stupid crappy eggs that won't produce our own baby, without you coming home and trying to force me to adopt a child from some country I've never heard of. Choose—Russia or China?"

"China."

"Why?"

"Because of the bilateral agreement."

"And what about the fact that there are no other Chinese people in Ireland?"

"Did I miss something here—I thought China was one of your two choices?"

"It is, but when Sean announced he was seeing someone from Iran and I saw my parents' reaction, I started thinking about the number of Asian people you see in Ireland. And the bottom line is—there aren't many at all. Dublin may like to claim it's very cosmopolitan, but an Asian child would be in a very small minority."

Despite what people liked to think, the Celtic Tiger had not made Dublin a melting pot of creeds and cultures. A sprinkling of Asian and Romanian immigrants did not add up to a lively multiracial society. Besides, having grown up looking like everyone else, I had still found it hard to fit in sometimes, so God knows how difficult it would be for an Asian child.

"So, Russia or China?" I asked again.

"Let's see, well of a choice of two, you have just ruled out one. So I'm going to go out on a limb here and say Russia."

"Excellent, we agree then," I said, smiling.

"It would appear we do," said my sarcastic husband. "Seeing as how you're being so decisive, who should I play on the wing in next month's European Cup game—Jeff Mooney or William Murphy?"

"Jeff."

"Any particular reason?"

"Nicer legs."

"Now why didn't I think of that?"

"James."

"Yes?"

"Sorry for being a bit hyper, I just didn't want you to start dissecting every country in the world. I want to focus on one country and just get on with our research. And I'm totally wound up about the long wait."

"It's okay darling. Russia's a good choice, so is Jeff."

Later that night I called Sean to see how he was getting on and to tell him that he would soon have a Russian niece or nephew. I also wanted to see how his relationship was going.

"Hi."

"Hey sis, how are you?"

"Good, thanks, you?"

"Great."

"So, how's the romance going?"

"Very well actually. I think it's the first normal relationship I've ever been in, and it feels great. We spend pretty much every night together. I'm thinking of asking her to move in."

Oh God, I thought. How the hell am I going to break this to Mum?

"Wow, that's pretty quick."

"Hardly," bristled Sean. "We've been seeing each other for four months."

"Fair enough. So anyway, we're going to adopt a Russian baby. We were thinking Chinese or Russian, but I think Russian is probably better for Ireland," I said, changing the subject.

"What do you mean? Why not Chinese?"

"I think it'd be difficult for an Asian child to grow up in Ireland."

"Why?"

"Because there aren't that many Asian people living here and they'd always be different."

"God, Emma, that's so parochial. That's the problem with Ireland; everyone lives in the bloody dark ages. It doesn't matter what you look like as long as no one else makes you feel uncomfortable. The problem is not the child being Asian, it's the closed society you'd be bringing it into."

"What are you saying? That we're all a bunch of racists?"

"Basically—yeah. Did you see the way Mum and Dad reacted when they found out Shadee was Iranian?"

"Yes I did, Sean, and I'd say it's pretty much the same way her parents reacted when they found out you were Irish. I wouldn't say they were popping the champagne corks either. Well? Were they?"

"No, they weren't," he grudgingly admitted.

"Mum and Dad want you to be happy and they just feel that adding cultural, racial, and religious differences to a relationship can cause a lot of problems down the line," I said, defending my parents.

"Fine, but it's frustrating when your mother is basing her

knowledge of a society on some stupid film with Sally Field in it. I got a package at work last week. It was the book *Not Without My Daughter* and inside was a note from Mum saying—'Just read it and make up your own mind. P.S. I met young Maureen Doherty last week. She was asking specially for you. She's lost thirty pounds on Weight Watchers and looks fantastic. Plenty of fish in the sea over here for you.'"

We both laughed.

"Look, Sean. They're just worried about you. It's not racism, it's concern. Just like Shadee's parents are worried about her going out with an Irish guy."

"Yeah, I know, but it's frustrating because I really like her, Emma, and I want my family to like her too."

"If she makes you happy, we'll love her. Mum and Dad will get over the fact that she's Iranian in no time. Now, getting back to the Russian child we're going to adopt—what do you think?"

"I think it's great, and I really don't think it matters what country you adopt from, because you'll be amazing parents. The kid will be very lucky."

"Really?"

"Absolutely. Now do me a favor and talk to Mum. I don't want any more packages or notes. She needs to get used to the idea of Shadee."

"Okay, I'll do my best."

chapter SEVEN

THREE WEEKS LATER I was doing the makeup for one of the guests on *Afternoon with Amanda*. Her name was Dorothy Flynn, and she had written a book about gardening with a strong focus on garden mazes—whatever floats your boat I guess. As I applied her makeup, she talked incessantly about her children. She kept telling me how wonderful they were and what joy they brought her and how her life was so complete now. . . . I smiled and nodded and continued blending in her foundation. After twenty minutes, it really began to bug me. I was sick of hearing about how fulfilling she found motherhood—it was making me feel empty and useless—so I tried to change the subject.

"So, tell me about your book," I asked. Even though gardening and mazes left me cold, anything was better than her incessant chatter about the wonder of parenting.

"It's great actually. The kids love the garden. They get such a kick out of the maze I created. I have a picture of them in the maze

in my book," she said, leaning down to open the book. "Let me
see, oh yes here's the page. Look aren't they gorgeous?"

I glanced down at the page, feigning interest. Hang on. The
little girl and boy in the photo were Asian. I looked up at Dorothy.
She smiled and nodded, she had clearly been through this explanation a thousand times.

"Yes, my two little angels are adopted. They were born in Vietnam."

"Oh my God. I'm adopting," I said, suddenly coming to life.
"What's it like? How did it work out? Is it amazing? Are they
happy? Do they feel different? Tell me everything."

Dorothy—who had gone from boring hedge shaper to hero in
three minutes flat—filled me in on her experiences. She said the
adoption process was long and at times arduous, but that she could
see it was important for the Adoption Board to be sure that the
prospective parents were 100 percent committed, as adoption is a
huge step to take. She said that all you can do is love your children to
bits and hope for the best. In her case, her two children were happy
and stable and didn't seem to be affected by looking different at all.
She said the town she lived in had welcomed them with open arms,
and they were never made to feel anything but part of the community.

By the time Dorothy had finished telling me about the day she
picked her babies up from the orphanage and how she had fallen in
love with them at first sight, there were tears streaming down my
cheeks.

"Oh God, it just sounds amazing. I'm dying for that to happen
to me."

"Don't you worry, pet," she said, patting my hand. "It'll all
work out. It's a long and lonely road from trying for your own
baby to adopting, but I promise you it's worth it in the end. You
must be both patient and determined."

We hugged and I finished her makeup through waterlogged eyes. Her blusher was definitely a little off kilter, but thankfully she didn't seem to notice. I went home on a high. It was all going to work out. I just needed patience and determination.

When I got home I logged on to the Internet and typed in "Russian adoption" which brought up 118,316 results. There was information about adoptions from Kazakhstan, Ukraine, Armenia, and other countries I had never heard of. There were sites for Russian language, culture, songs and folklore, orphanages, adoption agencies . . . the list was endless. I eventually found a chat room where several women mentioned a book for those adopting from Russia called *The Russian Adoption Handbook* by John Maclean. I rushed out to buy it.

I went into the biggest bookstore in Dublin and tried to find the section on adoption. Having found only books on—how to be a great mother, how to cope with postnatal depression, and how to make your toddler a genius—I eventually gave up and went up to the desk. A tall, thin-to-the-point-of-undernourished girl looked up.

"Hello," I said, speaking softly, so the man lining up behind me wouldn't hear. "I'm looking for a book on adoption by John Maclean."

"What? Did you say adoption? You're looking for books on adoption?" she said loudly, as she began to type into her computer.

"Yes," I hissed.

"Name?"

"The Russian Adoption Handbook," I whispered.

"There's a whole section on adoption in the social science and psychology section," she said, and then addressing her colleague on the other side of the room, she roared, "Derek, hey Derek, can you show this woman where we keep the books on adoption."

I squirmed as everyone turned to see who the adopter was. I was bright red and sweating as I followed the obliging Derek and his saggy-assed jeans to the correct section. I found the Maclean book and browsed the other books in the section, which dealt with how to cope when your child wants to meet its birth mother and how to cope with race issues. I decided to stick to the Russian adoption book for the moment. I'd deal with my children's desire to find their birth mothers, when they were eighteen. Besides, they'd be so happy with James and me as parents that they wouldn't have any interest in meeting their biological parents.

When James came home that night, I greeted him—*Dobro pozhalovat*—I exclaimed. He stared at me, nodded and said, "And the same to you too, darling. To what do I owe the pleasure of coming home to my wife wearing a large dead furry animal on her head and speaking Russian?"

"It's all in the name of research James. Isn't the hat great? I bought it today," I said, patting the enormous furry hat perched on my head. "Look, I got one for you too."

"Marvelous. I was hoping you had."

"Come on, sit down, I've loads to tell you," I said, ignoring the sarcasm.

James sat down, and I plonked a large Russian hat on his head. He raised his eyebrows in anticipation

"*Ochin preeyatna,*" I said, beaming at him.

"Sorry, darling," he said, smirking, "One of the two of us doesn't speak Russian, so this could be a long night."

"I'm saying 'pleased to meet you.' I've also learnt *izvineetye*, which means 'excuse me,' and *spasiba*, which means 'thank you.' I've sent off for tapes that will teach us Russian in three months, so we can learn together in the evenings. I reckon we should be fluent by the time we start our adoption course. I also think we should go to Russia on holidays this year."

"Will we go before or after we've mastered the language? I think we should wait until we're fluent. Between the language and our hats we'll blend right in."

"Smart ass."

"Spasiba," said James, getting up and taking off his hat.

"Where are you going? I've loads more to discuss."

"I want to catch the second half of the Man U versus Arsenal game."

"Well tough, this is more important. Besides, you're going to have to start supporting Russian football teams. Anyway, sit down and listen to these statistics: Russia is twice the size of America and has a population of one hundred and forty-five million people—so they must have zillions of orphans. The country is made up of a total mishmash of people. It has Russians and Ukrainians and Moldavians and Tatars and other types of people too. The economy is in a slump, and the average monthly wage is only about fifty euros, and the winters are very very cold."

"That's fascinating, darling, you've given me a real insight into Russia. Can I watch the match now?"

"No you can't. I've rented *Doctor Zhivago,* so we can get a sense of what Russia is like. Come on, you know you want to," I said, squishing the hat back onto his head.

"Oh God, Emma, please not *Doctor* bloody *Zhivago.* I'd rather nail my balls to the mast of a sinking ship. It's about eight hours long. Come on, I've had a long day. I promise never to take my hat off, if you spare me the film."

"There's no need to be so dramatic. We have to do as much research as we can, so shut up and watch the movie," I said, putting the DVD into the player. "Besides, we might pick up some key phrases."

"It's Omar bloody Sharif and Julie Christie, not Gorbachev and Yeltsin."

"I'm aware of that. I just think some of the extras might be speaking Russian in the background and we'll get a feel for pronunciation."

I sobbed through the movie while James fell asleep. Lara, I thought, what a beautiful name. I'd call our daughter Lara and our son Yuri. I woke James up at the end to tell him about the names I'd chosen.

"Is it over? Please tell me it's over?"

"Yes it is, and you slept through ninety percent of it. So what do you think of the names?"

"Lovely, fantastic, whatever you want. Can I please go to bed now?"

"*Da.*"

Two weeks later I came home to find James on the phone. I knew he was talking to his brother Henry, because his accent was much stronger and he was being all "What-ho-ish."

"Don't be silly we'd love you to come over. It'll be great to spend Christmas together. . . . No, Emma won't mind at all. . . . No the kids won't be any trouble. We've two spare bedrooms here so there's plenty of room. . . . Super idea spending the week together with Mother and Father away. . . . Ha ha, yes we should be able to sneak off for a few pints of Guinness and leave the girls to it. . . . Ha ha. Okay, Hen, call me when you've booked your flights."

I stood by the door, praying I had misheard the conversation. James could not be foolish enough or insane enough to have invited his brother, sister-in-law, and their three children for Christmas. He knew how I felt about Imogen the cow and Thomas the brat. The twin girls seemed sweet, but I really didn't fancy having kids in my face for Christmas week. I found it hard being around children. My home was my little haven where I could hide away from children and babies and nosy relations asking me why I wasn't pregnant. I took a deep breath.

"Hi," I said.

"Oh hi, I didn't see you there," said James, looking a little sheepish.

"Who were you on to?"

"Henry."

"Any news?"

"Actually, he was calling about Christmas. You know the way our parents are going on that cruise with the Mason-Joneses this year, well Henry thought it'd be nice for us to spend the day together. So he was calling to ask if they could come and spend Christmas with us."

"And you said?"

"I said yes of course. He's my brother, I'm hardly going to say no."

"So you've invited your bother and his wife and their three children to our house for Christmas without discussing it with me?"

"I'm discussing it with you now."

"No, you're telling me now."

"Well, I think it'll be nice to have Henry and co. around. We see your family all the time, I hardly ever get to spend time with my brother. Besides, it'll be fun having children around at Christmas."

"And when you and Henry are off drinking pints of Guinness, who is going to be entertaining Imogen and the kids?"

"They can entertain themselves. Look, it'll be fine. Don't get all heated up about it."

"I'm not getting heated up," I lied as my temperature rose a few degrees. "But I still find it really hard being around babies, you know that."

"I understand, darling, but you can't avoid children, they're a fact of life and we're on the road to having our own now, so it'll be good practice for us to have kids around," said James, looking very pleased with himself for having come up with that excuse.

"Well, I don't think my mother's going to be too happy about having to feed the cast of *Gandhi* on Christmas day. She finds cooking for her own family a stretch."

"I thought we could have dinner at home this year."

"Excuse me?"

"Imogen's a great cook, so I'm sure she'll be happy to help you, and you're not so bad yourself when you put your mind to it. I can pitch in if needs be."

"It seems that pitching in is your forte. You've just pitched right in and ruined not only my Christmas holidays but you are also now trying to ruin my Christmas dinner. I love Christmas day at my parents' house with the sing-along and the chocolate boxes."

"To be honest, I could live without the sing-along," said James, who always squirmed as we howled out Christmas carols after overeating and drinking.

"Singing is part of the magic of Christmas day. You're just jealous because you never had any craic in your house and had to sit around listening to the queen's message."

"I'll have you know that the queen's annual address to the nation was one of the many highlights of Christmas day in our house."

"Along with Santa not turning up, famine in Africa—"

"Smart ass."

"Just admit it's more fun in my house."

"Marginally livelier. Anyway, the point is, I don't think it's fair for your mother to have to have Henry, Imogen, and their children inflicted on her for dinner."

"What about them being landed on me for a week. Where's the fair in that?"

"Marry me, marry my family," said James, stealing the phrase I always used whenever he complained about my family—which was very rare.

"Look, you call Mum and ask her. She'd never say no to you. Besides, by Christmas day, we'll all need a change of scene after four days of living in one another's pockets."

James called Mum.

"Hello, Mrs. Burke, James here."

"Oh Helloooooo James," I heard my mother coo on the phone. She loved that James still called her Mrs. Burke. She thought it was very gentlemanly of him.

"I'm sorry to land this on you, but my brother Henry and his wife and three children are coming over for Christmas, and we were going to have dinner here, but Emma said she'd rather go to your house as usual, so I wanted to check how you felt about having five more mouths to feed. I quite understand if it's too much trouble."

"Not at all, James, it'll be a pleasure to have them. We'll be delighted to see them again."

"Thank you, that's very kind of you."

"The more the merrier. We'll have a really good sing-along this year," Mum bellowed down the phone as I stifled a giggle and James buried his head in his hands.

"I look forward to it," said the son-in-law of the year.

chapter EIGHT

A MONTH LATER I was standing on the sidelines of a rugby field with Lucy. We huddled together to keep warm. It was the first match in the European Cup, and Leinster was playing some team from England—I think it might have been Bath. Now that Lucy was living with Donal, she felt obliged to support him. It was great having her with me to cheer them on at matches.

"So what exactly is going on here?" asked Lucy. She had never been to a game. She was an only child, and her father had left her mother when Lucy was five years old and moved to America with his mistress. He was an extremely successful property developer and she was always well provided for financially, but without any males in the house, she never watched sports.

I wasn't exactly a sports broadcaster myself, but I knew a bit about rugby from growing up with Dad and Sean watching the international matches. I had also obviously picked up a bit more info now that I was married to James, though I did tend to switch off when he started describing new tactical moves to me. Know your audience, James!

"The easiest way to describe it is this. Numbers nine to fifteen run around a lot, and pass the ball to one another in a long line across the field. Number ten kicks the ball when they have penalties. He's definitely a key player—James was very grumpy last year when he was injured. Numbers one to eight spend most of the time in the muck with ten other players lying on top of them. The only time you really notice them is during the lineups when the number two throws the ball in and they all leap up to catch it. That's really where Donal comes in, he's brilliant at jumping up and catching the ball, and then they all pile on top of him and he gets squished into the mud again."

"So what you're saying is—number six is a crap position because you spend the whole time facedown at the bottom of a pileup," said Lucy, looking a bit disappointed that Donal's position wasn't a bit more glamorous.

"Well, James says it's a key position, but personally I think number fifteen has the best spot, he just jogs around at the back and catches the odd ball when it's hoofed down his end of the field. Donal's position is more dangerous. You have to be tough and strong, which is why he's so good at it," I said, trying to build Donal up. "Look, they're doing a lineup. Watch Donal jump."

Lucy peered down the field and watched as Donal jumped up and caught the ball.

"Hey, he didn't jump, the other guy lifted him up. Isn't that cheating?" asked Lucy.

"No, they do that all the time, it seems to be okay."

"I hope he doesn't get injured again. You should see the scars on his body, he's a wreck. He reckons he's only got two more years left. He says he's pretty old to still be playing."

"How old is he?"

"Thirty-two," mumbled Lucy.

"What? Toy boy! I never knew he was younger than you. I always presumed he was the same age as James," I said, laughing.

"There's only thirty months in the difference. It's not exactly cradle snatching."

"Ivana Trump—eat your heart out. So anyway, how's living with the younger man going? Has he peed on you yet?"

"Very funny. Thankfully we've come to an understanding on that one."

"How did you manage that?"

"Simple. I bought a lock for the door, which he never uses, but I do. So I can now bathe in peace. I must say, living together takes a while to get used to. Dealing with smelly jocks and socks and toenails is a bit gross," she said, squirming at the thought.

"Tell me about it. And you get lumped with their mad families. James has taken it upon himself to invite Henry, Imogen, and the three kids over to stay with us for Christmas."

"Oh God, for how long?"

"A week. Speaking of relations, you never told me how you got on with Annie when she was home from boarding school."

"I didn't tell you because I don't even want to admit to myself what a total nightmare it was. I've been trying to convince myself it wasn't that bad."

"Oh no, Lucy. What happened?"

Lucy said that she had stayed at work late on the Friday night, so Annie and Donal could have some time together. She had checked with Donal to see what Annie's favorite foods were and had duly stocked the fridge full of them. When she arrived home, Donal and Annie were watching MTV and discussing Justin Timberlake's assets. Annie said he was the most divine creature she had ever seen, and Donal said he thought he was a mangy-looking bloke with eyes that were far too small for his head.

"I have to agree with Annie," said Lucy, trying to get off on the right foot. "Justin is a fine thing."

Donal got up to kiss her, while Annie made sick noises.

"Oh God, you're not going to start making out, are you?" she said grumpily.

"No, although I can't say I'm not tempted," said Donal, winking at Lucy. "I'm going to go and book the cinema tickets and let you girls chat."

"So," said Lucy, "how's school?"

"Fine," said the grumpy teenager.

"Great. Uhm, I was wondering if you'd like to do up your bedroom. It'd be a kind of housewarming present from me. If you pick the colors and fabrics, I can organize for it to be finished for the next time you come home. I was thinking we could go into town tomorrow and have a look around so you can see what you like."

"Do you really think I want to spend my free weekend going around bedroom shops with a forty-year-old woman? I always spend the day with Donal on our own."

"Okay, well it was just an idea. Don't worry, I won't interfere with your time with Donal. Now, would you like lasagna? I picked some up on the way home in a great delicatessen beside my office. Donal said it's your favorite."

"I only like the lasagna Mary used to make for me. She was an amazing cook, she'd never buy ready-made food from a shop."

"Mary who?" asked Lucy, beginning to lose patience.

"Donal's girlfriend. She was amazing, I loved her. They were nearly married until you came along," Annie snapped.

What the hell is going on? thought Lucy. She had met Mary six months ago at a dog racing meet that Donal had taken her to.

Mary had been really rude to Lucy and very flirty with Donal, but he had made out that he'd dated her only briefly. Had he been lying? If she was living in the house making lasagna for Annie, she must have been more than a casual fling. Before she could think of anything to say, Donal strolled back in.

"Okay, we're booked in for the nine-thirty show. I've put the lasagna in the oven."

"Actually, Donal, can you help me in the kitchen for a minute?" asked Lucy.

He followed her in and looked around.

"What do you need me to do?"

"How long did you go out with Mary the cordon bleu chef for?"

"Jesus, where did that come from? I thought you wanted me to chop tomatoes."

"How long?"

"I dunno, a few months."

"A few meaning two or a few meaning twenty?"

"Eight, maybe ten, I can't remember."

"Were you serious about her?"

"Serious enough to shag her," said Donal, grinning.

"Donal!"

"No, I wasn't serious about her."

"How come she was hanging out here making lasagna for Annie if it was such a casual relationship?"

"She stayed over the odd time and liked to cook. What's all this about? Is it really about her cooking?"

"Not really." Lucy sighed. "It's about Annie not liking me very much and thinking Mary was wonderful. I'm going to let the two of you go to the cinema alone. She likes to have you to herself and I don't mind."

"Hold on a minute, you're coming to the cinema and that's the end of it. As for Mary, Annie never seemed all that keen on her before, maybe she was just talking about her cooking," said Donal. Kissing Lucy, he added, "Annie's going to love you—as much as I do. She just needs to get to know you better."

Lucy smiled. Sod it, she thought, as long as Donal loves me, the rest doesn't matter. Annie will come around; she's just at a difficult age.

During dinner, Annie behaved politely and was almost nice to Lucy. So when Donal went to get the popcorn at the cinema and Annie turned on her, Lucy was shocked.

"I wouldn't get too comfortable if I were you. Painting the walls cream and trying to lick up to me isn't going to work. Donal doesn't want to get married and have children. He told me himself before you came back. He doesn't like having someone around nagging him all the time. So don't bother spending any more money painting the house because it's a waste of time. You won't last till Christmas."

Lucy wanted to slap her—but restrained herself. For once in her life she had met a guy she really loved. Someone she was completely herself with, and now this little brat was trying to ruin it.

"It's awful, Emma," said Lucy, half laughing and half crying. "I keep having to remind myself that this poor child lost her parents in a horrible car crash and is obviously affected very badly by it, but right there and then in the cinema, I really wanted to hit her. I'm an adult, I should know better. I should be more sympathetic and not take it personally, but I do. I can't help it."

"Little cow," I said, furious at Annie for upsetting Lucy. "She's just trying to wind you up. She's obviously terrified of losing Donal and thinks if he marries you and has kids she'll get left out."

"Yeah, but she seemed to be fine about him going out with Mary."

"Mary, Shmary. I bet she only said that to wind you up. You know Donal loves you. You just need to find a way to deal with his baggage. Maybe you could suggest a truce. Just say 'look, Annie, we both live here now so let's try to get on.' Or something like that."

"I'll have to sort it out soon. She's coming for two weeks at Christmas. I never thought I'd say it, but I'll be glad to go home to my mother's house for Christmas day. At least I'll have one day off."

"I'd invite you to mine if it wasn't going to be equally awful. God, look at the two of us—lumped with our other halves' dodgy families."

"Yap yap yap," said Donal coming up behind us. "Well, what did you think of my try?" he asked Lucy

"Fantastic. An amazing feat of athleticism," she said, smiling.

"It's a pity that I didn't actually score a try," he said, laughing.

"Did you win?" I asked, looking around for James.

"We did, and I wanted to come over and thank you both personally for your great support. It was your voices that I heard soaring above the others all afternoon cheering us on."

"Well, we were talking about you if that counts for anything," said Lucy, "And Emma taught me the rudiments of rugby."

"Did she really?" said James walking over. "I'm dying to hear this."

"She explained it very well. Numbers one to eight are muck eaters and numbers nine to fifteen are the fairies that run around not getting dirty. Number ten is the main man who kicks all the balls, and Donal is important because when his head is out of the muck, he jumps up and catches the ball in the lineups."

The two men cracked up.

"Wonderful summary of the game, darling," said James when he finally stopped laughing. "I couldn't have put it better myself."

"You see," I said, beaming at him, "and you think I don't listen."

chapter NINE

A FEW WEEKS LATER, James and I were out Christmas shopping. We had bought presents for everyone except Thomas and the twins. James went off to the sports shop to get Thomas a mini rugby ball while I went to get the twins little outfits. As I browsed around the shop, looking at the adorable baby clothes, I suddenly realized that I was the only person in the shop without a child. Everyone else had kids with them. They were playing Christmas carols in the background, and the mother beside me began to sing the song to her little baby in the pram—she positively radiated with love. I turned around to focus on the clothes and picked up a tiny pink cord dress with white embroidered flowers on the collar and cuffs. I stared at the dress, and then it hit me, like a kick in the stomach. That all-too-familiar empty feeling was back—I began to cry.

I had been feeling fine. I had been feeling quite positive about things. I had been focusing all my energies on the adoption and how wonderful it was going to be, but suddenly I felt utterly miserable. Why the hell couldn't we have our own child? It would be so much easier. We wouldn't have to go through this torturous waiting period and then embark on a long and arduous assessment process, where everything in our lives would be scrutinized and opened up for examination by strangers. It was so unfair—why did we have to endure being put on trial for parenthood? Why was it so bloody hard? I threw down the dress and hurried out of the shop. I wanted to shout at the mothers and fathers walking around with their children. I wanted to tell them how lucky they were and ask them if they had any idea how hard it was on this side of the fence—looking in. Thankfully I saw James walking toward me before I had the chance to attack some poor unsuspecting family.

"James," I said, sobbing as I reached him.

"I know," he said, handing me a tissue.

"It's just so . . ."

" . . . bloody unfair," he said, reading my mind. "I know, darling, the sports shop was full of proud fathers buying presents for their sons. Come on, let's get the hell out of here."

"But I haven't bought anything." I sniffed, feeling very weak-willed as I looked at James's rugby ball. At least he hadn't bolted out of the shop empty-handed.

"Sod it, we need a drink. We'll give the twins money."

"Have I told you lately how wonderful you are," I said, giving him a watery smile.

"*Spasiba,*" he said, hugging me.

The following month, James and I were standing in the airport arrivals lounge waiting for Henry and Imogen. I was feeling a bit grumpy, having spent the last three days rearranging the bedrooms—one of them stored all my makeup paraphernalia and portfolios. Everything had been shoved under beds and into already overstuffed wardrobes. It was Christmas for goodness' sake— I wanted to lie on the couch and watch old movies while polishing off boxes of candy by a roaring log fire. Instead, I had been charging about with dusters and Hoovers and spraying everything with Flash multipurpose—even the smell of it made the place feel cleaner. I must admit, though, the house had been in need of a good scrub. Some of the things lurking under the bed had been there since we first moved in. Next year I was getting a cleaning lady.

As I was thinking about the logistics of finding a cleaner, I heard a bloodcurdling scream. I looked up to see Thomas violently pulling a little girl's hair while Henry tried to extract him before the girl's father slapped him.

"Bad Thomas. You musn't do that," said Henry, yanking a clump of hair from Thomas's fist and handing it to the girl's father. "I'm terribly sorry, sir. Is she all right?"

"Just about, no thanks to your son here," said the fuming father, pulling out a handkerchief to dry his daughter's tears.

James rushed over to help Henry and steer them away, before the father noticed the bald patch on the right side of his daughter's head. As I watched, trying not to laugh, I heard the all-too-familiar bark of the lovely Imogen, coming from behind the most enormous pile of suitcases I've ever seen.

"Henry, leave Thomas alone," she snapped, moving around to pick up her wailing son. "Poor likkle Thom Thom. Was that nasty man mean to you? Don't worry, Mummy's here now."

I stared at her in shock. Imogen—who I had seen a year ago at the twins' christening carrying at least forty extra pounds—was a stick insect. She was skin and bones. I was furious. The only thing that had got me through the christening had been the fact that Imogen was fat. I know it's bitchy and horrible, but I was childless, pumped full of hormone-inducing drugs, and utterly miserable. At least I had consoled myself I was thinner than her. And now, here she was, looking like she hadn't had a good meal in twelve months.

"Hi, Imogen, you look great," I said, leaning over awkwardly to kiss her.

"Thanks. Here, take Sophie for me," she said, thrusting my goddaughter into my arms and running after Thomas.

I looked down at the soft blond wisps of hair on Sophie's head and smelled her lovely baby smell. She stared up at me, her round face and big blue eyes taking me in as she smiled, displaying her first tooth. My heart skipped a beat. She was so beautiful. I wanted desperately for her to be mine. For a few seconds I considered legging it up the stairs to the departure lounge and hopping on a flight to Cuba—where I would dye my hair, change my name, and bring Sophie up as my own. I'd call her Carmen or . . .

"Emma," said James, tugging my arm, "what are you doing? Come on we're all waiting for you."

I decided not to tell him about my kidnapping plans. Switching the lovely Sophie onto my other hip, I followed him out. Henry, James, the twins, and the three enormous suitcases went in James's jeep. Imogen, Thomas, and I went in my car. Thomas sat behind me and kicked the back of my seat repeatedly.

"Thomas sweetheart," I said, gritting my teeth. "Would you mind not kicking the chair, it's hurting my back? Thanks."

"Noooo," said the brat, sticking his tongue out at me as he tried to dislocate several vertebrae with his mini-hiking boots.

"Thomas, be a good boy now. Stop that," I said, getting a little hot under the collar.

"Oh leave him be, Emma, he's only having a little fun, aren't you, Thom Thom? You're just tiredy-wiredy after that long flight."

"So how are things?" I asked as her son kicked me again and I struggled to—(a) not crash the car and (b) keep myself from turning around and walloping him.

"Hectic. Three children under the age of four is hard work. People who don't have children have no idea how difficult it is. You're on the go all day, you never get a minute to yourself. All the baby weight just fell off me. I didn't even try to lose it—running after my three little angels just keeps me fit. And how are things with you? James looks wonderful as always," she said, pointedly not telling me I looked well.

"Fine, thanks."

"Henry tells me you're thinking of adopting."

She said it as if *adopting* was a dirty word.

"We're not thinking about it, we are going to adopt. We're just waiting to hear from the Adoption Board when the course starts," I said.

"Oh, I see," said Imogen, sounding horrified. "Isn't it rather like wearing someone else's clothes?"

"What do you mean," I said, blood boiling to the surface.

"The child is never going to be really yours is it? It already has parents. It's just not the same thing as having your own children. Why don't you try fertility treatments? I'm sure James would love to have a little boy of his own like Thomas."

"I've had treatments, Imogen," I said, gripping the steering wheel and willing myself to stay calm. "I spent all of last year having treatments, and nothing worked. That's why we're adopting."

"But you only tried IVF once. That's hardly really trying. A friend of mine from the pony club had her baby after six attempts."

"No offense, but unless you've had fertility treatments, you've no idea how awful they are."

"It can't be that bad."

"It is."

"Ha, try childbirth Emma. Try having a cesarean—that's real pain."

"I would like nothing better than to have a cesarean. If I was even lucky enough to get pregnant I would never complain about childbirth. But the thing is, Imogen, I can't get pregnant, so I'm going to adopt and I really don't appreciate you telling me I'm not trying hard enough."

"Oh dear Thom Thom, Auntie Emma is very touchy-wouchy today. Isn't she?"

"OUT," roared Thomas. "I want out, Mummy," he said, squirming to loosen his seat belt, kicking me in the process.

"We're nearly there, darling, just a few more minutes."

"NOW Mummy. I want out NOW," he screamed, throwing a fit with his legs.

"THOMAS," I bellowed, reaching back to grab his legs. "If you kick me once more, I will smack you black and blue."

Thomas, shocked at having a voice raised to him, probably for the first time in his life, was stunned into silence. His mother, however, was not.

"Mean nasty Auntie Emma, shouting at little Thomas like a lunatic. Will I smack her for you? Yes, I think I will," she said, belting me on the arm. "We'd better stay out of her way, darling, Auntie Emma's in a very bad mood."

When we got home, Henry and Imogen went upstairs to unpack and put the children to bed. I took the opportunity to call Lucy. I knew if I told James what had happened in the car that he'd just tell me I was exaggerating and I must have misunderstood what Imogen was saying—which would only have wound me up even further.

"Hello?"

"Hi, it's me"

"A friendly voice," said Lucy, sounding like I felt.

"Uh-oh, that doesn't sound too good. How's it going?"

"Annie is being a complete nightmare. When Donal's around she is nice as pie to me and the minute he leaves the room she turns into a little psycho. She keeps telling me I'm going to get dumped. Happy bloody Christmas. How are you? Have they arrived?"

"Yes, and I've already had a fight with Imogen—she told me I haven't tried hard enough to get pregnant. God she's a cow, and as for that little shit of a son of hers, he must have six-six-six written on his scalp. I'm going to check later, you should probably check Annie's head too," I said, laughing despite myself. "Don't let that little wench get you down. Remember—Donal loves you."

"Thanks and don't you mind that bitch of a sister-in-law of yours. How dare she—"

"Jesus Christ!"

"What?"

"Oh you little bastard," I hissed as I stared down at Thomas, who was covered from head to toe in foundation and lipstick. "Gotta go, Lucy, emergency," I said, hanging up.

I took a deep breath and grabbed Thomas, marching him back to the spare room, where Henry was desperately trying to do some damage control. He was on his hands and knees, screwing the caps back onto bottles and trying to rub the lipstick marks off the walls and carpet. My makeup bags were strewn all over the room. In a few minutes, Thomas had managed to do a huge amount of damage.

Henry looked up. "Oh God, Emma, what can I say. I'm so sorry. We've barely been here an hour and already managed to cause havoc. I insist on replacing everything, just let me know where to buy it and I'll get it for you tomorrow. Thomas—apologize to Auntie Emma."

"Will not. Hate nasty Auntie Emma. She said I am bastod."

"Bold," I said loudly. "I said he was bold. Sorry, Henry, I just got a fright when I saw him covered in my makeup."

"Not at all, Emma, he was bold. Thomas, you're very bold. This is Auntie Emma's work and you have messed it all up. Apologize at once."

"Nooooo," said Thomas, stamping his foot.

"Right, excuse me, Emma, this calls for some action," said Henry, smacking his son on the bottom.

"HENRY!" shouted Imogen, who appeared out of nowhere just at the wrong moment. "We don't smack our children."

"We bloody well do when they are being insolent. Excuse us, Emma," said Henry, taking his wife and son with him into the other spare bedroom and closing the door.

I could hear them arguing as I tried to clean up the mess. The carpet was covered in foundation and eye shadow. Half-open lipsticks lay smudged on the floor. I reckon the little brat had done about five-hundred euros' worth of damage. I took the rest of my products out from under the bed and stashed them away in the wardrobe in my bedroom, locking them in safely. If this is what happened after an hour—how the hell was I going to put up with them for a week?

chapter TEN

FOUR DAYS—one broken phone, two broken picture frames, three broken plates, and a broken teapot—later it was Christmas day. I almost jogged to my parents' house. I have never been so glad to see my family in my life. Anything to get away from Thomas's destructive prowess and Imogen's constant bitching. When Sean answered the door I threw myself at him.

"Hey sis, Happy Christmas! That bad huh?" he whispered in my ear.

"Worse," I groaned.

"Hello everyone and welcome to the Addams Family Christmas dinner," said Sean, shaking hands, kissing babies, and taking coats. We all trooped into the living room, where Dad and Babs were sprawled in front of a roaring log fire watching *It's a Wonderful Life*. Well, Dad was trying to watch it as Babs groaned about how boring it was. They greeted the visitors and I left them to it and went to help Sean get drinks.

"So, how's it going?" I asked

"Okay."

"Have they asked you about Shadee yet?"

"Nope."

"How long are you staying?"

"I'm going back tomorrow."

"What? But that's not even forty-eight hours."

"I know, but I don't want to get into an argument with them about my relationship, so the quicker I leave, the less chance we have of coming to blows over it. Besides, I miss her."

"Come on, you haven't even been here a day."

"What can I say? I guess I'm in love," he said quietly

"Oh, Sean, that's great," I said, hugging him.

It was great, but I wasn't sure how thrilled my parents were going to be—or her parents for that matter. I'd have to find one of those Learning about Iranian Culture and Religion courses in the New Year and book us all in. Basing our knowledge of the country on a film starring Sally Field wasn't exactly well informed. I'd look up the internet when I got home and order some books on Amazon. It was going to be a busy year—what with learning all about Russia and now having to take on Iran. The Minister for Foreign Affairs had better watch out.

"Actually," said Sean, glowing with happiness, "she moved in a few weeks ago, and it's just brilliant."

What? Moved in, already? Thankfully I managed to look happy about it and asked him how Shadee's parents had reacted to the news.

"They don't know yet either," he admitted. "They'll probably go mental when they find out. We agreed to go home for Christmas and tell our respective families ourselves."

"When are you going to tell Mum and Dad?"

"Well, I couldn't face it last night, and I'm obviously not going to announce it today and I'm leaving first thing tomorrow so . . . I was kind of hoping you'd do it for me," said Sean, grinning at me.

"Do what for her?" asked Babs, barging in before I got a chance to tell Sean exactly what I thought of this bright idea.

"Nothing," we said in unison.

"Fine, keep your stupid secret," said the ever grumpy youngest sibling. "Emma, Mum wants you in the kitchen, she needs help."

"So go and help her," I said

"No—she said she wants *you* to help her."

I went in to find my mother looking very harassed, ramming the stuffing up the turkey's backside with a vim and vigor that made me wince. Thank God the bird was long dead.

"Hi, what's up?"

"Your bloody auntie Doreen just called to wish us a Happy Christmas and to say—wasn't it well for us having all the family with us while she was alone, with her three children living in America. So I had to invite her for dinner. She's on her way over— with her rosary beads and the Bible no doubt. Lord, what'll James's family think? I hope she doesn't try to convert them all."

I laughed at the thought of Doreen trying to convert Imogen. My father's sister Doreen claimed to have seen an apparition of the Virgin Mary fifteen years ago in a field in the West of Ireland and had since become a pilgrimage junkie and extreme bead swinger. She was always trying to convert James to the Catholic faith, which we all found highly amusing, although James found it a bit trying at times. Doreen's strongest characteristic was her tenacity.

"Don't worry, Mum, we'll ply her with drink. She'll be fine."

"Anyway enough about that, what's going on with Sean and that girl? Are they still dating?"

"Yes."

"Is it serious?"

"Yes."

"How serious?"

"Pretty serious," I said, deciding not to tell her about the cohabitation just yet. Judging by the way she was cramming the stuffing up that bird, she was in no mood for surprises.

My mother chose to ignore this piece of information. It was a trick she had—if she heard something she didn't like, she disregarded it completely.

"I've organized for young Maureen Doherty to come over tomorrow for a drink with her mother and father, and Sean tells me he's off to London first thing in the morning. He must be working very hard. Only a two-day holiday? It's scandalous. You should see Maureen, she's skin and bones from the Weight Watchers. Like a supermodel she is. She'd be perfect for Sean. Maybe I could get them to come over tonight instead?" Mum said, her mind working overtime.

"No," I said firmly. "There are quite enough people here already today. Sean will be fine. Just leave him be. Stop trying to set him up."

Mum was always worrying about Sean not settling down. Three and a half years ago when he turned thirty, she had decided that as he was obviously incapable of finding himself a nice girl to get hitched to, she'd help him out. Thus began a series of extremely embarrassing setups. Sean would arrive home for a weekend to see his mates and his family. He'd be sitting down to watch a football match with Dad, when all of a sudden Mum would throw the door open and say "You'll never guess who was passing by." Inevitably it was one of her bridge cronies with one of their unmarried daughters, hoping for a union. No doubt Mum had told them Sean was the catch of Dublin—one of the top ten lawyers in the city of London I had heard her boast, and a talented athlete to boot. Sean and I always giggled about that—the only sport Sean had done since gym class in school was to switch the remote control from one hand to the other. As for top ten lawyer—he was doing extremely well, and we were very proud of him, but it was a gross exaggeration, to say the least. Anyway, Mum would drag Sean into the kitchen to have a cup of coffee and then she and her friend would suddenly disappear into the garden to see some incredible plant that had just, that minute, sprouted, leaving the mortified daughter and Sean staring at each other across the table. As they desperately tried to make small talk, their mothers kept a keen eye on the proceedings through the kitchen window. So far Mum had subjected Sean to five girls and had no success.

"Jesus that child's a handful," said Dad coming into the kitchen for some peace and quiet as Thomas bellowed outside. "Is he always that noisy?"

"He's usually a lot worse. Yesterday he—"

The door flew open, and we all turned around to see Babs carrying Thomas under one arm. She set him down and shut the door.

"Right, you little shit," she said. "If you ever kick me or pull my hair again, I will kick you back. Now say you're sorry."

"NO," roared Thomas, kicking her again.

"Barbara, that's enough," said Mum, coming to Thomas's rescue. "He's only a child."

Thomas looked at Mum and then kicked her in the shins too.

Babs grabbed him by the arms and shook him roughly—this time he was on his own.

"You little brat, don't you ever do that again or I will rip your arms and legs off. Do you hear me?" she hissed.

Thomas nodded, looking terrified.

"Now say you're sorry to me and my mother."

"Orry," he whispered.

"Oh there you are, darling," said Imogen—thankfully having just missed Babs's attempts to rearrange her son's internal organs. "I've been looking for you. Are you all right with these strange new people? Was he being shy?" she asked us.

We all nodded, not trusting ourselves to speak. Babs's mouth was twitching, but she managed to control herself.

"Thom Thom's a very shy little boy, aren't you? Come with Mummy, Doreen wants to meet you. She's Emma's auntie and she has a little grandson just your age."

As soon as she shut the door, we roared laughing.

"The poor child will never be the same again after today, especially once Doreen gets her hands on him," said Dad, dabbing his eyes with a tissue. "I've got to see this."

When we had composed ourselves, we trooped back into the living room where Doreen was telling a very subdued Thomas the story of the birth of Jesus in a manger surrounded by shepherds. She was giving Our Lady pretty much all of the kudos for the whole event.

" . . . and then the wonder that is Mary gave birth to baby Jesus and the son of God was born. If it wasn't for Mary there would be no Jesus . . ."

James and Henry grinned at each other, but Imogen didn't seem to notice. She was just delighted that Doreen was paying Thomas so much attention.

"Watch out, Henry, she'll have the rosary beads out next," said Dad, rolling his eyes. As if on cue, Doreen took out her rosary beads for Thomas to play with while the three men tried not to laugh.

"There's a good little boy, you can keep them if you like," said Doreen, shoving the beads into Thomas's hand.

"Will you have a drink, Doreen?" asked Dad, trying to distract her from her determined efforts to convert Thomas.

"No, Dan, not at all. Nothing for me."

"Ah go on, have a drink for the day that's in it. You have to celebrate the birth of Jesus and all Mary's hard work."

"Well, all right then, just a small one."

Dad poured Doreen an enormous gin and tonic, which she proceeded to knock back. A few minutes later, when she thought no one was looking, she sprinkled Thomas with holy water. He squealed and ran over to his mother. The poor kid was having a bad day—I almost felt sorry for him.

Mum came in, and we sat around to open our presents. Henry gave me a box filled with all the makeup products Thomas had ruined. I hugged him for his thoughtfulness. I gave the twins little matching pink duffel coats that I had bought the day before when I had gone for a walk to get out of the madhouse that had formerly been my home. I was so distracted by the mayhem at home that I didn't have time to feel sorry for myself in the shop. Besides, the coats were so adorable that I really wanted to give them to the girls. James gave Thomas the rugby ball, which he proceeded to kick into the TV, much to Dad's horror—the little monster was obviously recovering. Mum gave Sean a travel voucher for Aer Lingus.

"You've no excuse now. You're to come home more regularly and go out socializing with your pals and meet nice Irish girls," she said.

Sean, ignoring her pointed remark, handed her his present. It was a book—*Modern Iran: Roots and Results of Revolution* by Nikki

R. Keddie. Mum fixed a smile on her face and pushed it under the couch but Doreen caught a glimpse of it and pulled it out.

"Iran? Why are you buying your mother a book on Iran?"

"It's nothing, Doreen, now come on Barbara, open your present," snapped Mum.

"I bought it for her because my girlfriend is from Iran and I want Mum to know more about the country," said Sean, glaring at Mum.

"Iran?" said Doreen, sounding appalled. "Did I see a film about—"

"Yes, Doreen, you did—*Not Without My Daughter*," said Babs, loving the drama. "Sean still hasn't seen his girlfriend's face, she wears one of those mad black capes over her head, and they have to have sex through a hole in the sheet," she added, giggling as she stirred things up.

"Shut up," I said, pinching her. "She doesn't wear a yashmak, and she was born and bred in England."

"Is she Catholic, Sean?"

"No, Doreen, she's Muslim."

"Muslim!" said Doreen blessing herself.

"It's nothing," said Mum. "She's just a pal."

"It's not nothing, Mum, it's serious, and we've just moved in together," said Sean, choosing the worst moment possible to announce his news. A deathly silence ensued.

"Living in sin with a Muslim!" squealed Doreen, grabbing her rosary beads back from Thomas to pray for Sean's lost soul.

"There was a really nice bloke in class with James who was from Iran. He was six foot five, a really good cricketer," said Henry, trying to help Sean out as James shook his head and whispered, "I tried that one already—didn't help much."

"I certainly wouldn't want Thomas marrying a Muslim," said

Imogen, bringing the conversation around to her children as always.

"You'll be lucky if Helen Keller wants to marry him. Only a blind, deaf, and dumb person could put up with that brat," said Babs, subtle as always.

"Thank you, Barbara, very delicately put," said Dad, jumping in before a fight broke out. "Now I think we'll have some carols. O Holy night . . ." he sang, drowning out the whinging Thomas, gurgling twins, praying Doreen, and fuming Imogen.

chapter ELEVEN

WE RANG IN THE NEW YEAR, drinking wine on the couch while watching some dreadful program on the "year that was." We had planned to go out, but after a week of Henry, Imogen, and the kids, we were exhausted.

"This doesn't bode well for when we have our own children," I said, fishing about in the box of candies for the sweet with the strawberry center. "If we are this worn out after a week, what'll we be like when we come back from Russia with a baby of our own, who we have to look after twenty-four/seven."

"It'll be easier with just one, and Thomas can be a bit of a handful."

"Do my ears deceive me? Did you just admit that Thomas is a brat?"

"No, darling, I said 'handful.' I was very careful not to use the word *brat*. It's not as if you need any encouragement to give out about him."

"I know, but he really is awful. What if we get a mini-Russian Thomas? What will we do? We can't send him back, can we?"

"No, we definitely can't do that. Boarding school should sort him out."

"You can't send a toddler to boarding school."

"Okay then, we'll just get Auntie Babs to come over and frighten the life out of him," he said with one eye on the television as they announced the upcoming sports highlights of the year.

"I hope we don't have to wait too much longer."

"Mmmm, me too. Excellent, they're showing the rugby."

"James?"

"Yes."

"I think you'll be a brilliant dad."

"So do I," he said, grinning and turning his attention back to the TV as the BBC played the highlights of England's rugby World Cup victory in Sydney for the zillionth time.

"Yesss, what a game," said James. "If only Barry O'Reilly could kick like Johnnie Wilkinson, we'd really have a chance of winning the cup this year . . ."

"James?"

"Yes."

"Don't you think I'll be a great mother?" I asked, feeling a bit put out that he hadn't said so.

"Go on, Johnnie! What a moment to drop a goal like that. The man's a genius," said James, punching his fist in the air, as if he were seeing it for the first time.

"JAMES!"

"What?"

"Will I bloody well be a good mother or not?"

"Not if you roar at the children like that. However, if you nipped into the kitchen and made me a toasted cheese sandwich—

thereby showing your selflessness, generosity, and culinary skills—I may be persuaded to alter my opinion."

One of my new year's resolutions was to hire a cleaning woman—an excellent resolution to make, if I say so myself. You have to know your strengths and weaknesses in life, and cleaning was not one of my stronger points. My contract to do the makeup on *Afternoon with Amanda* five days a week had been renewed and I had got a raise, so with that and weddings and the odd photo shoot—it was going to be a good year for me financially. I could hire a cleaning woman without feeling guilty about it.

I called Lucy to see if the woman who cleaned her house would work for me.

"Hi, I need to get a cleaning woman."

"About bloody time, everyone should have one."

"I agree—when I discovered a moldy apple under our bed as I was cleaning the house for Henry and Imogen's visit, I realized I need help."

"Emma, that's disgusting," said Lucy, laughing.

"I know, I'm ashamed of myself. So do you think Helena would clean my house?"

"Afraid not. I asked her if she'd do a few extra hours for me now I'm living with Donal, whose hygiene habits leave a lot to be desired, and she said she's too busy. But she did say she had a friend who might help out. Hang on, I'll get Helena's number and you can call her yourself."

"Thanks, you're a star. So, are you free to get together next week for a drink?"

"Love to, but I'm going to the States on business for ten days and then spending a week with Dad. I'll give you a call when I get back."

"Two weeks away from Donal . . . will you miss him?" I asked.

"The tragic thing is—I will. I've turned into one of those sad soppy girls I used to scorn, who can't stand to be away from their man. What's happening to me, I'm pathetic!"

"Aaaah, true love's a beautiful thing."

"I'm hanging up."

I called Helena, who was very nice and said she had a cousin over from Poland who would be interested. Two days later Danika arrived on my doorstep.

"Kello, I am Danika. I am cleaning."

Okay, so her English wasn't fluent, but it was a far sight better than my Polish. We'd manage with lots of sign language and goodwill. I welcomed her in and showed her around, telling her what I'd like her to do. I was a bit embarrassed, because I didn't want to seem like a sergeant major barking out orders, but then again if I came across as a pushover, she'd probably just come every week, watch TV, and spray air freshener around. Something similar had actually happened to Lucy. A few years ago she came home one day and found Sisi, her Filipino cleaner, lying on the couch, talking on the phone to her family in Manila and drinking a beer.

Danika, however, seemed very enthusiastic, and when she was leaving I asked her if it would be okay for her to come on Thursdays.

"Fruesday yah."

"Uhm, no, Thursday," I said, not sure if *Fruesday* was Friday, Tuesday, or Thursday.

"Yah Frensday."

"No, I mean Thursday, you know TH-URS-DAY," I said, trying to articulate as well as I could.

"Yah yah FRU-ES-DAY," Danika said slowly.

I smiled back, admitting defeat, and spent the next week leaving notes and money for her on a daily basis. She came on Friday, which was fine really, as it meant the house was nice and clean for the weekend. And as Oprah says—compromise is key, and let's be honest, if she didn't get it face-to-face, what hope did I have over the phone. Friday was fine.

By the time February came around the Russian tapes were still sitting in the box they had been delivered in before Christmas. I decided it was high time James and I started. I opened the box and began to read about the background of the Russian language: "Russian is written in the Cyrillic alphabet dating from around the ninth century. Although at first glance it appears quite different, a number of letters are written and pronounced as in English (*A, K, M, O,* and *T*). Whereas other letters are written in the Roman alphabet but are pronounced differently, i.e., *Y/y* is pronounced 'oo' as in *food* and *X/x* is pronounced 'ch' as in the Scottish word *loch.*"

I glanced down at some of the key words printed on the leaflet.

Da = Yes
Нет: *Nyet* = No
Как дела?: *Kak dila?* = How are you?

There appeared to be two translations. Why was the Russian translation for "How are you?" first in squiggly, illegible writing and then in letters I could read? If I said "Kak dila" were the Russian people going to understand me, or was that just a translation for plebs who were trying to learn the language but couldn't read the old Roman-type letters. Did the Russians have the first translation too, or was it just for beginners? Did Russian students have an equivalent translation when they learned English, like—*Clothes*: klows = whatever Russian word means "clothes"?

I decided to read on, maybe it would shed some light. "There are three persons and three genders: masculine, feminine, and neutral. There are six cases: nominative, genitive, dative, accusative, instrumental, and prepositional. . . . verbs conjugate according to person, number, tense, voice, and mood."

Bloody hell, how was I ever going to learn this language? I couldn't even speak passable French. Okay, I needed to be realistic. The likelihood of my being fluent in Russian this millennium was slim to none. I'd learn key phrases and worry about learning grammar when little Yuri or Lara was older. I looked down the list of phrases and picked out ones I felt would come in handy.

Я (очень) тебя люблю: Ya (ochin') tibya ljublju = I love you (very much)

Ты очень красивая: Ty ocheen' krasivaya = You are very beautiful – to a woman

Ты очень красивый: Ty ocheen' krasivyi = You are very beautiful – to a man

Я счастлива: Ya schasleeva (f) = I am happy

Я счастлив: Ya schasleev (m) = I am happy

When James came home I got him to sit down and practice with me. He was even worse at languages than I was, so we agreed to keep it simple and learn: How are you? You are very beautiful, I love you very much. Which we hoped was: *Kak dila? Ty ocheen' krasivaya. Ya (ochin') tibya ljublu.* Granted, it was a long way from the fluent speakers we had set out to be, but at least it'd get the point across. Despite the brackets around *ochin,'* we decided to keep it in. We wanted our baby to know that we loved them "very much." Maybe we'd even throw in a second *ochin'* just to make sure they knew how we felt.

During the third week in February, six months after my initial inquiry about the adoption, I received a letter from the wonderful Julie Logan, senior executive officer of the Adoption Board's intercountry adoption section. She was delighted to inform me that due to a number of couples dropping out for various reasons, James and I had obtained a place on the adoption course, beginning March 25. I screamed and tried to call James, but he had his mobile switched off, so I jumped into the car and drove down to the practice field.

James was in the middle of the field, surrounded by numbers one to eight of the team, giving them a lecture on some type of new move, when I came charging across squealing and screeching at the top of my lungs.

"Jaaaaaames, we got it. We're in," I bellowed as James, looking decidedly embarrassed, turned around. I threw myself at him, and in my enthusiasm, knocked him over and landed on top of his chest.

"Ah come on now, get a room," said Donal, laughing.

"Emma!" said James, clambering to his feet. "I'm in the middle of practice. Whatever it is, I'm sure it could have waited."

"No! I had to tell you straightaway. We're in, James, we're in. We've got a place on the next adoption course. We're starting in two weeks," I shouted, half-laughing, half-crying.

"Oh," said James.

"Fantastic news," said Donal as he and the other players patted us on the back and then moved off to give us some privacy.

"So what do you think?" I asked. "You don't seem very excited."

"You just took me by surprise," said James, catching his breath.
"Its great news. A little daunting, but great. Yes, really great," he
said, hugging me as the news sunk in.

"*Ya ochin' ochin' tibya ljublu,*" I said, sniffling into his jumper.

"*Y'o skin, tibia, jubly* to you too."

chapter TWELVE

WHILE LUCY WAS IN NEW YORK she found herself missing Donal—a lot. She couldn't wait to see him when she got home. He had said he'd pick her up from the airport, despite the fact that the flight was landing at 5.30 A.M., as he was dying to see her too. On landing, Lucy scuttled into the airport restroom and changed out of her "traveling tacksuit" into her newly purchased Victoria's Secret underwear, figure-hugging jeans, and tight black top. She put on her makeup, brushed her hair, and examined herself in the mirror. Not bad. She felt her stomach flip when she thought of seeing Donal again.

She waited impatiently for her bags to come off the carousel and just about managed to stop herself from running out the arrivals door. She looked around eagerly to find Donal. She thought she'd spot him straightaway as he was so tall, but she couldn't see him anywhere. She skirted around the crowd, but there was still no

sign of him. Maybe he got stuck in traffic, she thought. Yes that
was probably it—oh well so much for the dramatic exit. She sat
down and called his mobile. It was switched off. Maybe he's in the
underground garage, she thought. Yes that's it.

Twenty minutes and ten attempted calls later, she began to get
worried. Maybe he was in a crash. Oh my God, maybe he was
lying in the middle of the road, dead. It'd be just her bloody luck.
She finally meets the man she loves and his car gets mowed down
by a truck on his way to collect her. Alone again. She tried to calm
down by telling herself not to be so ridiculous. There was probably
some very simple reason that he was late, maybe his car broke
down or maybe he had injured himself in yesterday's match. Yes
that was probably what had happened. He was always getting injured. He had probably sprained his ankle or something—well
then why hadn't he called? If it was a simple excuse, why hadn't he
called to let her know?

Lucy decided to get a taxi home. She'd left several messages
on Donal's phone, and for the moment, there was nothing else
she could really do. As the taxi driver droned on about the shocking price of gas, the long hours, the traffic, the disastrous results
of the Irish soccer team . . . Lucy began to panic again. She had a
horrible feeling something dreadful had happened to Donal. Oh
God, she thought as she arrived at the house, his car wasn't in the
driveway. Her stomach sank, but when she opened the door,
Donal was lying facedown on the couch, snoring loudly, and the
room reeked of stale alcohol. All Lucy's concern and worry
turned to anger.

"YOU BIG, THICK HAIRY SAVAGE. WHERE THE HELL
WERE YOU? I THOUGHT YOU WERE DEAD!"

"What? Who?" said Donal, waking up as Lucy ranted and
raved at him.

" . . . selfish bugger . . . promised you'd pick me up . . . unreliable loser."

"Mercy—please. Stop shouting," he begged as his brain began to catch up. "Lucy, I'm sorry. I went out for one pint last night, I even took the car because I was only having one drink, but it turned into a bit of a session, and I got in so late that I decided there was no point going to bed. So I stayed up and watched TV till it was time to go and collect you. It seemed like a great idea last night. I must have nodded off. Sorry about that. Come here to me, you gorgeous thing, I'm delighted to see you."

"Get away. You stink of booze. Thanks a lot—some welcome home this is," said Lucy, pushing past him and stomping into the bedroom.

"Come on, Lucy, forgive me. I'd all the best intentions, I just got carried away last night with the excitement of you coming home and one thing led to another. What can I say, I'm a disgrace to myself and my family and my country."

"Piss off. I'm too annoyed to talk to you. I'm going to get some sleep," she said, throwing her bag on the floor.

"Hit me. Go on, give me a belt, I deserve it. Let your anger out. Come on, thump me," said Donal, obliging her by bending down.

"I'm not going to hit you. Just go away."

"Come on, hit me. It'll make you feel better, and it'll make me feel better. Come on, go for it," he said, lifting her arm.

"No."

"Go on, just do it will you."

"Okay then," said Lucy, swinging a punch that landed right in the middle of Donal's nose.

"Jesus Christ! I said hit me, not break my bloody nose," said Donal, staggering backward.

"You told me to punch you," said Lucy, feeling guilty as blood began to trickle down Donal's chin.

"Yes, because I thought you were a girl, not Mike feckin Tyson in drag. Jesus, I think you've broken it."

"Sorry, but you shouldn't have wound me up. I'll get some ice."

"Where the hell did you learn to swing a punch like that?" asked Donal, following her into the kitchen.

"They had these self-defense classes at work last year, so I went along," said Lucy, fumbling around in the freezer.

"I pity the poor fecker that ever tries to attack you—he'll end up in traction. Did you ever think about taking anger-management classes? It might be safer for the rest of us."

"Shut up and hold this to your nose."

"I've missed you, Rocky," said Donal, grinning from under the packet of frozen peas pressed to his nose.

"Me too. It's a pity you're injured, you should see the underwear I've got on."

"I'm a quick healer," said Donal, chucking the peas to one side and throwing Lucy over his shoulder as he charged into the bedroom.

When Lucy woke up later that afternoon, she saw Donal examining his nose in the mirror.

"Is it bad?" she asked.

"The good news is that despite your best efforts, you didn't break it. The bad news is that I'm going to look like this for a few days," he said turning around to show her two black eyes.

"Oh shit, Donal, I'm sorry," said Lucy.

"You're forgiven. One look at that underwear and I forgot all about my nose. Besides, I'm well used to being battered about on the rugby field."

Lucy winced as she looked at his swollen eyes. "I have something for you that might make up for the punch. It's a little something I picked up in New York. I think you'll like it."

"More sexy underwear from the amazing Victoria's Secret? That woman should be knighted for her services to the male species."

"No. Hang on," said Lucy, fishing about in her bag. "Here it is." She handed him a parcel.

He opened it. It was a framed picture of Pamela Anderson. It said, *To Donal, good luck in the Cup this year captain. Love Pamela x x.*

Donal looked up, mouth open.

"She was staying in my hotel, and I know what a fan you are, so I told her you were this superstar athlete in Ireland and asked her to sign a picture for me. She was really nice about it," said Lucy, grinning at him.

Donal came over and kissed her.

"This is the best present I've ever been given. Wait'll I show the lads. So come on, tell me, how did she look?"

"I have to admit—stunning."

"Lucy Hogan, you never cease to amaze me," said Donal, shaking his head. "Some guys come home to a girl in an apron, baking apple pies. I come home to Mike Tyson, wielding autographs of *Playboy* centerfolds. Where have you been all my life?"

Donal arrived at practice the next day with two black eyes and his framed photo, which he hung proudly in the locker room. He explained the black eyes by claiming he had fallen over drunk and hit his head—he didn't want anyone to know Lucy had thumped him; he'd never live it down.

When Lucy arrived home from work that evening, she couldn't get through the front door because the chain was on.

"Donal? It's me. Why have you got the chain on?" she shouted.

"Just hold on one second, I'm coming now," said Donal, looking around to make sure everything was in order. He opened the door wearing an apron and covered in flour.

"What are you doing?"

"Cooking you dinner."

"Really?"

"Yes. It's a welcome home dinner and an 'I'm sorry I forgot to collect you' dinner."

Lucy was delighted. Donal had cooked the odd frozen pizza before and occasionally rustled up a toasted ham and cheese sandwich, but he had never cooked her a proper meal.

"Sit down there and put your feet up while I fix you a drink. What'll you have?"

"Glass of wine would be lovely," Lucy said as Donal disappeared into the kitchen. She looked around. The room was very tidy, there were fresh flowers in the vase on the table, and Ella Fitzgerald was playing on the stereo. Donal hated her Ella Fitzgerald CD. My God, thought Lucy, he must be feeling very guilty.

Donal came out with a glass of wine and then scurried back into the kitchen. Lucy lay back and enjoyed the pampering.

"Sit down and have a drink with me," she called to him.

"Not yet, just putting the finishing touches on the dinner. You just relax and enjoy yourself."

Forty minutes and three very large glasses of wine later, Lucy was feeling extremely merry. Donal finally came out of the kitchen minus the apron, carrying two plates laden with food.

"Hey, you made couscous . . . and lamb! My favorites," said Lucy.

"Well, apart from apologizing, I also wanted to say thanks for the signed picture. You'll be delighted to hear that Pamela is now the team's official mascot. I got great kudos from the lads. She has pride of place in the locker room and will be coming to all the away games."

"As will I," said Lucy, slurring her words slightly. "I intend to go to all your matches. It's much better now that I understand how important your position as chief jumper and ball catcher is."

"I couldn't have put it better myself."

"So what did the guys say about your black eyes? Do they think I'm a total psycho?"

"Well, I decided not to tell them that my girlfriend beats the living shit out of me—it wouldn't look too good for either of us. So I told them I fell coming in the other night, drunk, and hit my head on the table."

"My hero," said Lucy, beaming at him. "So when's the next big game?"

"Never mind about that. Eat up, I have your favorite dessert coming," said Donal, wolfing down his food.

"Ooooh, lemon cheesecake."

"That's not your favorite dessert."

"Yes it is."

"No it isn't. Your favorite desert is tiramisu."

"Donal, I think I know what my favorite dessert is, and it's lemon cheesecake. Always has been and always will be. I hate tiramisu."

"What?"

"I've never liked it, so you've obviously got me mixed up with someone else. Maybe your ex-girlfriend the amazing chef Mary liked tiramisu," said Lucy, waving her fork at Donal as she swayed in her chair.

"Bollocks," said Donal, looking panic stricken.

"Look at your face. I'm right amen't I? It was Mary's favorite shagging dessert. I can't believe you don't know that mine's lemon cheesecake!"

Lucy stumbled to her feet. "I hate tirami-sodding-su. Where is it?"

She went into the kitchen and saw the offending dessert sitting innocently on a plate. She picked it up and shook it at Donal.

"I've got a great idea. Why don't we put the nasty tiramisu in a box and send it to Mary. Or we could invite the lovely Mary up to share it with us? Come on, let's give her a buzz," she said, reaching over to grab the phone, but she lost her balance and the tiramisu ended up facedown on the floor. "Oops, well it looks like Mary won't be joining us for dessert after all."

Donal bent down to scoop up the cake.

"What are you doing? Trying to save it for her? Do you want to get back with her? Is that it? You want to dump me because I'm violent and get back with superchef, apron-wearing Mary. Don't you forget that I make an excellent tuna melt, not to mention my—"

"Listen, Rocky, will you do me a favor and belt up for a minute so I can ask you something," he said, fishing a tiramisu-sodden ring from the middle of the mess on the floor.

Lucy stared at him. "Ask me what?"

"Lucy Hogan, will you marry me?"

chapter THIRTEEN

BEFORE WE BEGAN the preparation course we were sent a list of documentation to provide. Along with our wedding and birth certificates, the Adoption Board needed to see: medical reports, consultant consent form (detailing the fertility treatments I had undergone), certificate of earnings, clearance from the police (to say we weren't criminals), photographs, and a postplacement consent form—which said it was okay to come to our home and do the home visits. I sprinted around like a lunatic getting these together, and when it came to the photos—I insisted on having them done professionally. I occasionally worked with a fashion photographer called Matt Carney—he was the best in the business. As a favor, he came to the house to take our photos. James, of course, thought it was ridiculous and couldn't understand why we didn't just go to a photo booth and get a couple of passport photos done.

"James," I said, "it's very simple. Ugly photos of us equal ugly baby."

"Emma!"

"Obviously I don't care what the baby looks like—I'd take Quasimodo at this stage—but if we look our best then hopefully we'll get the pick of the crop."

I realize it sounded awful, but I wanted the best, healthiest, most bouncing baby they had in that orphanage, and if it happened to be attractive too—that would be a bonus.

I woke up at 5 A.M. on March 25. My heart was pounding with excitement and apprehension. This was our big day. We needed to make a good impression. I looked over to see if James was awake. He looked asleep but maybe he was only pretending to be. I leaned over.

"James?" I whispered. "James? Are you awake? James?"

Nothing

I put my hand over his nose to stop his breathing, and he woke up with a start.

"What the hell?"

"Oh hi, you're awake too. Great. I can't sleep I'm overexcited. Will we get up and have an early breakfast? Or go for a walk or something?"

"Emma, it's five o'clock, and as you are well aware I was fast asleep before you tried to suffocate me. I am neither hungry nor in the mood for a predawn stroll in the freezing cold. Just lie back, close your eyes, and keep your hands away from my face."

"Come on, James, you're awake now. Let's chat. Let's talk about what we think today will be like. Do you think the other couples will be like us, or older or younger? What do you think I should wear? I was thinking my black trousers with the boots I got at Christmas, but they might be a bit high for the daytime. I want to look attractive but not sexy or racy. Not too conservative either though—not like a granny. What do you think?"

"I think we should have a fashion show. Why don't you try on all the possibilities now and I'll mark them one to ten."

"Really?"

"NO! Now will you please shut up, I'm exhausted, and you don't want me to fall asleep at the meeting, do you?"

"Fine, I'll leave you alone. But just one thing, do you think the boots are a bit too much?"

Silence.

"James? Do you?"

Silence.

"Just a yes or no"

A pillow landed on my head.

Four hours later I was standing at the door shouting at James to hurry up. I had changed six times, cried when I ripped my tights, roared at James when I discovered the shirt I wanted to wear had a stain on it, and made him put on a blazer and tie—which he only agreed to wear to shut me up. We were miles ahead of schedule. I was so wound up that I wanted to leave plenty of time for unforeseen circumstances—in case we got stuck in traffic or had a flat tire or got car-jacked or something. We arrived for the meeting forty minutes early. James wandered off to get the paper while I sat in the car, trying to breathe slowly in a futile attempt to calm down. I was like a tightly wound spring. I don't think I have ever felt so nervous.

James arrived back, brandishing the *Daily Telegraph* and two coffees.

"James?"

"You look lovely, the boots are perfect, the shirt does match the trousers, we're on time, they will like us, we won't get thrown out of the course, everything will be fine," he said, opening the paper.

"Actually, what I was going to say is—thanks. Thanks for putting up with my psychosis this morning and sorry for being so tetchy."

He put down the paper. "At five A.M. I contemplated divorcing you, at half past eight—killing you, and just when I had decided on my murder weapon you go and disarm me with an apology."

"How were you planning on killing me?"

"Suffocation with a pillow."

"But think how boring life would be if you didn't have me around to pinch your nose in the wee hours."

"Emma, (a) I'm English and (b) I'm a man. English men like a quiet life. We have five of these meetings to attend, and while I love your passion for life, I could do without being woken up for footwear analysis or shouted at because your shirt is dirty. If you ever wake me up at an ungodly hour again, it had better be for sex," said James, trying to suppress a grin.

"Well then you better not suffocate me."

When we walked into the room, we were joined by five other couples. Four of them looked very nervous, but one couple was striding about as if they owned the place. We smiled and nodded and sat down. Two social workers then came in and introduced themselves; Yvonne O'Connor and Dervla Egan. I liked Yvonne instantly. She had a sweet, kind face and looked as if she'd go out of her way to help you. Dervla, on the other hand, was a bit scary. She had that "I've seen it all—don't even go there" expression on her face. I prayed she wouldn't be doing our home visits. She was the type who'd know instantly if you were lying or exaggerating. There'd be no room for slipups with Dervla. She'd nip you into next year if you stepped out of line or made a mistake. I couldn't picture her at Yuri's second birthday party, singing "for he's a jolly good fellow" with Mum and Dad. I decided to focus my attention on Yvonne. If I could get her to like me then maybe she'd ask to be our home visit social worker. It was worth a shot. I smiled at her as she introduced herself and welcomed us all.

After the initial pleasantries, we were paired off with new partners and asked to introduce ourselves to each other for a few minutes and then we would introduce the other person to the group. I was lumped with Mr. Confident, strider of the room—Brendan. Before I had a chance to open my mouth, Brendan jumped in and told me his life story. He was the managing director of DFG Advertising—the most successful advertising company in Ireland. He played golf off six and had recently shot seventy-three in the Western Club. He was here because his wife had problems; his sperm were fine and healthy. Nothing wrong with them at all—he said over and over again.

When we came to introducing each other, I was chosen to go first. Although Brendan had bored me rigid, I decided to be supernice, as I wanted to start on the best of terms with everyone. I was nervous about speaking in front of the group. I took a deep breath and launched.

"This is Brendan, he is very successful and runs the advertising agency GFD. He loves golf and plays to seventy-three and hit six the other day in a top golf club (my mind went blank and I couldn't remember the club). He also plays squash, and he wants to make it very clear that he isn't here because he's shooting blanks."

I could see James trying his best not to crack up; his face was turning purple with the effort. Dervla looked appalled, but Yvonne was smiling. Brendan then got up to introduce me.

"Emma here's a beautician and doesn't have a very good memory," he said. "My ad agency is called DFG, I play off six and shot a round of seventy-three in the Western Club on Saturday."

Before I could defend myself from this slander, Yvonne piped up. "Thank you, Brendan. Now, James, will you introduce Joy to us."

James stood up, looking utterly relaxed and at home and proceeded to introduce Joy in an articulate and calm fashion. I was very proud of him. It soon became clear why Joy and Brendan were married—they were cut from the same cloth.

"Joy recently sold the recruitment agency she founded ten years ago, to focus her energies on the adoption process and devote more time to her many other interests. She plays off twelve and recently shot eighty-two in the Western Club. She is also an accomplished pianist and chef. She speaks fluent French and German. Since applying to adopt a year ago, she has spent over six weeks in Moscow perfecting her Russian, which she now speaks like a native."

As James turned to sit down he winked at me, and we tried not to laugh. Joy and Brendan were a formidable duo. Joy introduced James, getting all her facts correct, and then the other pairs introduced each other and they all seemed very nice and normal. Some had children already, some like us had none. Some were older than us, some were younger. But we all had one thing in common—we all desperately wanted a baby.

Yvonne and Dervla then talked us through the subjects we would be covering over the next five sessions. Every session would last half a day. We would be covering all the angles of the adoption process. Each person was then given a big workbook containing essays and exercises that would help us reflect on issues between sessions and highlight areas that we may need more time to resolve or that we'd like to come back to at the home study stage.

The topics we'd be dealing with were going to include: exploring the adoption family tree; adoption bereavement—the impact of loss and separation; child development and medical matters; identity, difference, and belonging; talking about adoption—telling the adoption story; and the adoption life cycle. They also told us that media watching is key.

"You need to become very aware of everything to do with adoption. If you see anything in the papers about adoption or racism, cut it out and bring it to the next session for discussion. It is vital that you keep your ears and eyes open to all media coverage. The more aware you are of the frustrations and difficulties that go hand in hand with adopting a child from a foreign country, the better chances you have of being accepted. Racism is the scourge of our society. You must be conscious of it—your child may face it on a daily basis," ranted Dervla.

She seemed very wound up about it for someone who was white, Irish, and living in Ireland. It's not as if she'd spent twenty-nine years in captivity with Nelson Mandela and the gang on Robben Island. Yvonne then told us—in a calm and normal fashion—that we were now going to be shown a video called *All about Betty*.

The film turned out to be just about the most depressing thing I have ever seen. We all sat around in shock when it ended. It was basically the story of a baby called Betty who was about sixteen months old. Betty's mother fell ill and her father couldn't cope with looking after her, so he put her in a home. She was only in there for ten days, but in those ten days the fun-loving, outgoing Betty became inward and depressed.

What were they trying to do to us? The children we were going to adopt will have been in homes for months, years even. And this documentary was telling us that in ten days a child completely changed personality! For God's sake, give a prospective parent a break. Was this how they separated the men from the mice? I glanced over at James—he looked a bit stunned. Sod them; they weren't going to scare us that easily. I was not going to let this nasty film frighten me off my path to motherhood. Maybe Betty was just weak and soft, and besides, our little orphans probably never had a happy home to start with, so they had nothing to compare the orphanage to and therefore they wouldn't be all introverted and unhappy. They'd be delighted to see us coming—thrilled that we were going to save them. They'd bounce onto the plane with us to Ireland and a new life. Stuff Betty and her attachment deficit disorder, I wasn't budging.

We were split up into two groups and asked to talk about "How the video made you feel." Brendan was in my group and immediately took on the role of team leader. He told us all that he thought Betty just needed a good dose of love and she'd be grand. Denis disagreed—he felt that the damage could be irreversible. Nonsense, said Brendan, everything can be changed, it just takes the know-how. Carole said she was very disturbed by the video and was wondering if she'd be able to cope with a child that had problems like that. It would break her heart to see such sadness.

"Every problem is really an opportunity in disguise, Carole," said Brendan, using his advertising spiel to try to impress us. "You just need to look into the problem and get to the root of it. Then you seek professional advice and send the child to therapy. It's all about your attitude. If you're going to let a twenty-minute documentary put you off adopting, then maybe this is not for you. You need to be strong and confident in your parenting skills to become an adoptive parent, clearly it's not for everyone."

"Just hold on a minute there," I snapped. "First of all, Carole is entitled to her opinion, and I agree with her that it was extremely distressing to watch. A problem is a problem and not an opportunity, and whoever made up that ridiculous phrase is a gobshite. Second of all, I'm a makeup artist not a beautician, and I have an extremely good memory, I just tend to switch off when I'm being bored to death."

"Everything all right here?"

I swiveled around to see Dervla glaring at me. Damn, me and my big mouth.

chapter FOURTEEN

L UCY, JESS, AND I met up to see the ring Donal had proposed with and to discuss her wedding plans. I was interested to see what Donal had chosen in terms of ring, although the fact that Lucy hadn't exchanged it meant it must be nice. Lucy had grown up looking at her mother's large diamonds and, as a result, had expensive taste in jewelry.

She put out her hand and grinned at us.

"Bloody hell, it's the rock of Gibraltar!" I said, staring at the most enormous solitaire I have ever seen.

"The only advantage of getting hitched when you are an old and wrinkled thirty-five-year-old who has resigned herself to a life on the shelf is that the guy tends to have more cash than he had at twenty-five," laughed Lucy.

"Do you think it's too late for me to upgrade?" asked Jess.

"Your ring?" said Lucy

"Yep. Tony wanted to buy me a bracelet after I had Roy, but I told him to wait until I'd lost the three hundred pounds I put on before buying me anything. Now that I see Lucy's whopper I wouldn't mind upgrading my engagement ring instead of getting a bracelet. Is it mean, though? Am I being really unsentimental about it?"

I looked down at my ring. It was three small diamonds in a row. It had been James's grandmother's ring, and he had handed it to me as if it were the Hope Diamond itself. I was a little disappointed at the size of the diamonds—I'm talking small here, not medium, but I'd never want to change it because of what it meant to him and to me. It was sentimental. I had, I confess, wished his grandmother had opted for larger, sparklier diamonds—but I loved the ring for everything it represented.

Jess looked at me. "Well, Emma, you're stuck with yours because it was his granny's, but d'you think I could change mine without upsetting Tony?"

"I don't know. I think Tony would mind," I said.

"Me too," Lucy agreed.

"Fuck him, he wouldn't even notice. Men are all the same—selfish. It's the mothers that bring up the kids single bloody handedly," snapped Jess.

Lucy and I stared at her. This wasn't like Jess at all. She looked up and seeing our faces, blushed.

"God, listen to me. I'm like a bitter old witch. Sorry guys. I'm spending far too much time at home watching daytime TV or having coffee with my baby-group mums. All they do is give out about their husbands being lazy, selfish, and unhelpful. In the beginning I thought they were really disloyal and negative but it seems to have rubbed off a bit. I think I need to go back to work or do a course or something. If the conversation isn't about bad husbands, au pairs, or nannies, it's about jewelry, designer clothes, and cars. I swear last week we spent two hours talking about jeeps—which was the best one to get blah blah blah. When Tony came home I told him I needed a BMW jeep for the kids. I demanded one."

"What did he say?" I asked.

"He handed me the job section of the paper and said he needed a Ferarri."

We laughed.

"Seriously though, I can see myself turning into one of those dissatisfied women who spend all their time wanting more. They become obsessed with material things, using them as some kind of status symbol because it's the only way they have of being somebody. I need a job."

"Yes you do," said Lucy, "and pronto by the sounds of it, before you go off your rocker."

"Speaking of rocks," I said, "let's talk about this rock and this wedding." It was Lucy's night, and I wanted to make sure we didn't end up talking about Jess's job potential for the rest of the evening. I'd call her tomorrow and discuss it with her then. "Okay, Lucy, when and where?"

"Well—not that I've been thinking about it much or trawling the Internet for wedding venues or buying bridal magazines by the truckload or anything—but I did happen to come across a lovely country manor about an hour's drive from Dublin called Perryside Lodge. It looks gorgeous."

"Oh my God, I did a wedding there last year. It's an amazing location. It'd be perfect," I said.

"And small," said Lucy. "I want a small wedding. Small and intimate. And . . . I want you two to be my witnesses. I'm not having bridesmaids, so don't worry there'll be no hideous bridesmaid dresses. You can wear what you want."

I confess I was put out. I had expected to have a starring role,

not a joint one with Jess. After all I was Lucy's best friend and I had
set her up with Donal. I know it's ridiculous at this age to be huffy
about jobs at weddings, but I couldn't help it. James was the best
man, and I had expected to be the maid of honor. I was the gel in
this threesome. I was the one who was more friendly with both Jess
and Lucy. They rarely met up on their own. I was best friend to
both, specifically Lucy, and I didn't fancy sharing center stage with
Jess. As Lucy talked about the guest list, I told myself to get a grip
and stop being so pathetic. I smiled and nodded enthusiastically.

" . . . so it'll be just sixty people, mostly friends."

"Have you told Annie yet?" asked Jess

"Nope. I asked Donal to wait a while, so I could enjoy it all
before he tells her and she goes ballistic. He agreed straightaway, so
he's obviously nervous about telling her himself. To be honest I'm
just blocking that little problem out at the moment. It's going to be
a nightmare. Anyway, we're thinking of getting hitched end of No-
vember/December time, what d'you reckon?"

"Sounds great. Another bottle?" said Jess, getting up to buy
more wine.

While she was gone, Lucy leant over. "You know you're my maid of
honor. I just didn't want Jess to feel left out. I want you to say a
few words on my behalf. I owe all this to you. If it wasn't for you
pushing me to go on that date with Donal, I'd still be sitting at
home, alone and miserable."

"I'd love to," I said, thrilled. "As for Donal, you made it work
all on your own, and you deserve every bit of happiness that comes
your way. Are you sure you want me to speak? I'm not very good at
public speaking, I told you what a disaster I was at the adoption
meeting."

"Positive. You'll be great. And thanks for being such a brilliant friend," said Lucy, getting a bit weepy.

I hugged her. This was great. James and I could do a double act. Best man and maid of honor speech combined. He could say a few words, then I'd come in with a funny one-liner and so on. We'd have them rolling in the aisles.

Jess came back with the drinks, and we discussed the wedding dress. Lucy didn't want anything flouncy. She wanted cream and streamlined. With her figure she could wear a white sheet and still look good.

"So has your mum met him yet?" asked Jess, grinning.

Lucy's mother was an appalling snob. If ever a woman had delusions of grandeur it was Mrs. Hogan. As an only child whose father had left when she was five, Lucy should have been close to her mother—but she wasn't. Her mother drove her bananas. Mrs. Hogan was desperate for Lucy to marry some polo-playing toff with a summer house in St. Tropez. Due to the substantial alimony she received from Lucy's father, Mrs. Hogan lived in a large house on the outskirts of Dublin and spent most of her time lunching with other like-minded snobs. Lucy had kept Donal a secret from her mother, not even telling her when she moved in with him. So to say that Mrs. Hogan was in for a shock when her only child turned up engaged to an unknown entity was an understatement.

"Yes," said Lucy, cringing at the memory. "It was horrendous."

Lucy told us she had visited her mother to fill her in on the romance after they got engaged. Before asking her anything about Donal, Mrs. Hogan had grabbed Lucy's hand to see the size and quality of the ring and was suitably impressed. Only then did she ask her daughter about her fiancé. Who was he? Who were his parents? What did he do for a living?

"You can imagine how that went. I told her his name was

Donal Brady and he was a professional athlete. She, of course, living in lala land, thought I meant he was a polo player. When I told her he was a rugby player and his parents were Mr. and Mrs. Brady from Ballydrum, she nearly passed out."

"Ballydrum?" whispered Mrs. Hogan. "What is that? A village?"

"It's a town outside Limerick."

"I'm sorry, Lucy, this has got to be a joke. Over my dead body are you marrying a small-town boy who plays rugby for a living."

"Mum, I'm marrying Donal whether you like it or not. So you better take that look off your face and start being happy for me," said Lucy, as firmly as she could, trying not to shout. She didn't want her mother thinking there was any room for change. She needed to stress that this was a done deal.

"There's no need to raise your voice, it's very unladylike. What do you mean by 'professional rugby player'? What does he do exactly?" she said, wrinkling up her nose.

"He plays rugby. He's the captain of the Leinster team. He's really good. The team are really well thought of."

"If he's so good, why isn't he playing for the Irish team?"

"Because there's a younger guy who is just a bit better than him that plays the same position."

"How much does he earn?"

"I've no idea."

"How does he plan to support you? He can't play rugby forever."

"He'll probably become a coach or maybe get into sports broadcasting."

"It all sounds a bit vague, Lucy. Is he handsome at least?"

"He's really tall and has a brilliant personality and I think he's very attractive."

"What does his father do? Is he a rugby player too?"

"He owns a shop."

"What kind of shop?"

"A sweet shop."

"Is there something you're not telling me? Are you pregnant? Is that it? Tell me the truth."

"No, I am not. Look, Mum, I'm in love with a guy who thinks I'm fantastic too."

"Does he realize who you are?"

"Who am I?"

"Gerald Hogan's daughter and heiress to a substantial fortune. Mark my words, it's your money he's interested in. This boy's career is almost over and suddenly he wants to get married."

"Is it really so hard to believe that a man wants to marry me because of me?"

"Lucy, you're beautiful and successful. You come from a highly regarded family, and you must realize you're quite a catch. Don't settle for second best."

"If I'm such a catch, then how come it took me thirty-five years to find the guy I want to marry? As for our highly regarded family—really, Mum, look in the mirror. I come from a broken home where my mother still lives in the past and my father lives with his girlfriend on a different continent. I'm the lucky one— Donal comes from a normal, stable, and loving family."

"You deserve more. I want more for you, Lucy, I always have."

"No, Mum, you want more for yourself. I've found what I was looking for, and I'm going home to be with him. I'd like you to come up for dinner on Friday to meet him, but only if you promise to be nice. Think about it and call me."

Lucy finished telling the story and shook her head.

"So what happened when they met?" I asked.

"Well, Mum arrived, dressed from head to toe in Chanel, dripping in diamonds, fur coat—the lot. Donal answered the door, 'Lucy, your twin sister is here.'"

"Oh God, he didn't!" said Jess and I in unison.

"Oh yes, he did," said Lucy, rolling her eyes.

Mrs. Hogan glared at Donal.

"Aren't you a bit old for that nonsense?"

"Come on in, Mrs. Hogan, you're very welcome. Can I take your coat?" said Donal, trying a less cheesy approach.

"So you're Donal, the rugby player," she said loftily. "And you imagine you're going to marry my daughter? I gather you're from some town near Limerick."

Donal was, for once, speechless. He could see that no matter what he did, he wasn't going to change this woman's preconceived opinion of him—she clearly thought he was pond scum.

"Yes, Ballydrum. Will you have a drink?"

"A dry white wine—if you have such a thing."

"I think I might have an old bottle of Blue Nun out back," said Donal, hamming it up.

"I have one or two questions I'd like answers to. How do you expect to support my daughter when your rugby career ends?"

"Oh that's all sorted out. I'm going to stay at home and mind the kids while Lucy goes to work. I'm a big fan of daytime television," said Donal as he left to find Lucy, who was hiding in the kitchen.

"Well? How's it going?" she asked.

"I think she'd rather I die a horrible death than marry you."

" . . . and that's pretty much how the evening went. Mum needling Donal, and Donal playing it up. So I think it's safe to say we won't be going on family holidays together," said Lucy, shrugging.

"Are you okay about it?" I asked.

"Let's face it; Mum wasn't going to approve of anyone I married—unless it was Prince Charles. She'll get over it, and when she gets to know him, she'll like him. It's just going to take a while, and Donal doesn't make the best first impression either."

"What about your dad, what did he say?"

"Dad thinks it's brilliant. He can't believe I'm marrying a rugby player. Donal is the son he always dreamed of having. They've been on the phone a couple of times already, analyzing matches. They're best of buddies, so at least he's happy. And I'm happy, so what the hell . . . Mum'll come around eventually."

"A toast," I said, raising my glass. "To Lucy's six-foot-four boy toy from Ballydrum."

chapter FIFTEEN

THREE WEEKS AFTER our first adoption meeting, we were back for session two. I had cut out several articles about adoption and racism I'd seen in magazines and newspapers. I was determined to impress Dervla and Yvonne with my diligence. I wanted us to be the number one couple in the class so that there was no chance of us getting turned down.

When everyone had arrived and settled down, Dervla asked us if we had seen anything in the media that we'd like to discuss. Before I had the chance to say yes, Brendan shot out of his chair and said he'd like to share some of his findings with the class. With the help of Joy and his laptop computer, he gave us a PowerPoint presentation on the relevant articles that had featured in the news. He had pie charts comparing and contrasting television media coverage with radio and print media. He had bar charts that demonstrated the different demographics being targeted by the various media forms. Relevant headlines flashed before us as Joy handed

out summaries of their findings in personalized color-coded fold-
ers. Dervla looked impressed, while the rest of us sank back in our
chairs, stuffing our newspaper cuttings into our pockets, feeling deflated. Brendan and Joy were a formidable team.

We were then shown a video—this time it was about race and
culture. Black and Asian children who had been adopted by white
couples spoke about their experiences. They explained that although as a child you may not be aware of how different you are,
as an adult, things can become very complicated. Your sense of belonging is taken away, and you feel different everywhere—both in
the place where you were brought up and in the place you came
from originally. They spoke about adoption bereavement—being
taken from your birth parents, your country, and your culture and
thrown into a new society.

When the video ended, Yvonne and Dervla asked us to think
about loss in our own lives. They asked us to do up a loss chart of
all the loved ones who had passed away or of the loss we already
felt because we weren't able to have children or any bereavement we
had felt strongly in our youth.

"Don't worry about your loss seeming insignificant. Everyone
has different levels of experience. Just be honest and put down
what you feel," said Yvonne, smiling at us as we stared blankly at
her. "Okay, start writing whatever comes into your head. It can be
any kind of loss at all."

I chewed the end of my pen and concentrated. All my grandparents died before I was born except my Granny Burke. But she
had suffered from Alzheimer's and died when I was four. My only
memory of her is going to visit her in the home she was in with
Dad. She kept saying "Hello, my name's Gretta" over and over
again. At four this seemed hilarious instead of sad. So in terms of
people, I hadn't really lost anyone close to me. But Garfield kept

springing to mind. I know he was just a cat, but I had loved him, and he'd been around for most of my youth. We got him when I was six, and he got smushed by a truck when I was seventeen and just beginning to lose interest in him. I had been upset when he died. I remember the night very well. Garfield got run over, and despite my grief, I bravely carried on and went to Rory Lawlor's party, where I smoked pot for the first time. It was a great night, I thought I was mad—a regular sex, drugs, and rock'n'roll chick. The other loss I remembered feeling was the day of my first Holy Communion. I was seven, and Mum had pulled out all the stops with my dress. It was snow white with puff sleeves and a big hoop skirt. I had gloves and a bag to match. I felt like a movie star. As I was coming down the stairs and Dad was whistling at me while he took photos, I slipped and hit my mouth off the banisters, knocking out my two front teeth. I ended up arriving at my Holy Communion—late, with bloodstains all over my dress and no front teeth. Now I realize it may seem a bit lame in light of what I had just been watching on the video, but I couldn't think of anything else, so I scribbled those two down.

Never, in my wildest dreams, did I think we would then be swapping "loss charts" and reading each other's out. Dervla collected them, and then one by one chose someone to read another person's chart. Carole's losses were read out first by Denis. Carole had had a shocker—she had lost her mother when she was twelve. Then, on the eve of her twenty-first birthday, her best friend suffered a brain tumor and died. She had also endured three miscarriages.

Jesus Christ, I had to get my loss chart out of there. I began to sweat. I couldn't let anyone see mine. They were ridiculous. I thought it was only for ourselves. Oh God, how was I going to get out of this one? I'd faint. I'd pretend to have a dizzy spell and then hopefully that would distract them. Just as I began to swoon,

Dervla called Gary up to read my chart and everyone turned to smile at me and give nods of encouragement. Shit!

Gary began to read: "Emma has two losses here. The first is when Garfield was run over by a truck and she had to go and scrape his flattened body off the road." Gary's lips were beginning to twitch. I turned purple. "The second is when she lost her two front teeth the day of her first . . . ha ha . . . her first Holy . . . ha ha . . . Communion," he said, shaking with laughter as everyone else joined in.

I wanted to die.

"Well done, darling," whispered James, "you've really put us ahead of the bunch now."

Dervla was not amused. "This is not a subject to be taken lightly," she fumed.

"I wasn't making fun, honestly, I just couldn't think of any-thing—I'm really sorry. I guess I've been very lucky on the loss front, nobody has died on me yet, and I haven't had any miscar-riages. I just have crappy old eggs," I said, fighting back tears. God I'd really blown it this time.

"It's okay, Emma. It can be a difficult exercise. Don't worry, everyone has different levels of loss," said Yvonne, patting me on the arm. "Now, who's next?"

The next hour was the longest of my life. I couldn't wait to get out of the place. I was so humiliated. As we were leaving, Brendan said, "Good luck, Emma, I hope no more tragedies strike you. Be careful not to break a nail or something," he said, laughing as he squeezed his fat ass into his sports car.

"Oh God, James, how bad was it?"

"To be honest, darling, I think you actually outdid yourself today. I particularly enjoyed the toothless Holy Communion."

"I saw everyone scribbling away and I panicked. The only

thing I could think of was Garfield and my teeth. I'm so embarrassed."

"Not your finest hour perhaps, although it did give us all a good laugh."

"Well I don't think putting down losing the semifinal of last year's Rugby Cup was much better," I grumbled at him.

"Did you see the guys' faces? They all agreed that that was a very big loss. The match, teamed with my grandfather—who was like a third parent to me—dying when I was ten, was relevant to the exercise. Scraping your cat's body off the road was just a little off the mark."

"Stop, please. I feel bad enough as it is. Do you think I blew it? Do they all think I'm shallow and ridiculous and not fit to be a mother? Should I go back in and explain that I panicked? Oh God, James, what have I done?" I said, beginning to hyperventilate.

"Emma, hey. It's all right. It wasn't that bad. They thought it was funny and sweet. Of course they're not going to reject us because your family didn't die in a car crash when you were two. Some people have more losses than others. You were just honest about it. Don't worry, it'll be fine."

When we got home I took out the list of questions we had been given to answer for the next session. I wanted to make myself feel better by doing something positive, so I decided to tackle the questions then and there. I read the introduction:

> *Here are fifty questions you might consider about the country and culture you are thinking of adopting from. . . . When you have answered the following fifty questions, you may consider yourself to be well beyond the beginner stage. . . . There will be questions that you cannot answer . . . as a comparison,*

consider how you would find out the answers if they were
questions about Ireland.

Right. I was going to answer every one of these questions before the next session, if it killed me. I'd prove my dedication to the
adoption process by tracking down all the information. I'd fly to
Moscow if I had to. Watch out, Brendan and Joy, your time in the
limelight is coming to an end.

> *Question 1. How many people who are prominent in the af-*
> *fairs (politics, athletics, religion, the arts, etc.) of the country*
> *you are interested in can you name?*

President Putin, Olga Korbut the gymnast, although she was a
bit old at this stage, Rudolf Nureyev, except I think he might have
died. . . . I'd come back to that one. I could look up people on the
Internet. I decided to read all the questions and highlight the difficult ones. Question 2. . . .

I looked down at the page. I had highlighted forty-eight questions.
They included:

> *If, as a customer, you touch or handle merchandise for sale,*
> *will the storekeeper think you are knowledgeable, inconsider-*
> *ate, within your rights, completely outside your rights?*
> *Other?*

Come on! How the hell am I supposed to know? I'd have to go
to Moscow and go around mauling things in shops to find that
out. And what if it *was* considered outside your rights? Would I get

arrested? Whisked off by the KGB and sent to Siberia to shovel snow for twenty years?

If you are invited to dinner, should you arrive early? On time? Late? If late, how late?

So now I had to go to Russia, make friends, hope someone would invite me over for dinner, and then wait in a bush to see what time the other guests arrived at?

If you are invited to a party, who would you expect to find among the other guests?

Were the Adoption Board people obsessed with dinner party behavior? How the hell would I know who to expect?—other normal people? Lunatics? Mafia? What?

Who has the right of way in traffic—vehicles, animals, or pedestrians?

If I meet a cow on the road, am I supposed to let it overtake me? What kinds of questions were these?

I went to find James. He had slouched off when he saw me taking out the questionnaire. I found him lying on the couch, watching rugby.

"What're you watching?"

"Gloucester. We're playing them next week. It's a tape of their last game. Bloody good side too. The scrum half has the best pair of hands in the game. Look at that pass—textbook stuff. Tough team to meet for a place in the quarter finals, I'd have preferred to meet Ulster."

"Don't worry, you'll win. That guy may have good hands, but he's got terrible balance. Why does he keep falling over when he gets the ball?"

"It's the dive pass, darling," said James. "It's the more traditional style of . . . Never mind. What's up?"

"Okay, well I've been looking over the questions they gave us and they're absolutely impossible—one of them even asks if we've read sacred religious Russian writings! So, we're going to have to go to Russia for two weeks, before the next session."

"Hang on. Let me see them."

He read them and looked up. "Well, you're right about them being impossible for us to answer. But with the big game coming up the week after next, I somehow don't see a two-week holiday in Moscow as a runner."

"But, James, we have to make up for my fiasco. I'll go on my own."

"You're not going to Russia on your own."

"I know, maybe Danika can help. Poland is up there beside Russia isn't it? She's bound to know about Russian culture."

"Actually, darling, I think you'll find Poland borders Lithuania, the Ukraine, and Belarus, not Russia. Not to mention the fact that assuming a Polish person knows all about Russian culture is like assuming a French person is up on all aspects of German life," said James, getting all technical and precise on me, which really got up my nose.

"For all you know, Danika may have spent all her summer holidays in Russia, just like half of Germany spend their summers in France."

"A camping holiday in Provence does not make a German tourist an expert on French cultural behavior."

"How about, instead of shooting down all my suggestions in

flames and giving me geography lessons, you actually tried to do something helpful like suggesting a solution," I snapped.

"Doesn't Sean work with a guy who is Russian? Didn't he bring caviar over last year that he got from a colleague?"

"James Hamilton, you're a genius," I said, forgiving him instantly. "He does have a Russian friend. I'll call Sean now and fax him over the questions. Maybe the guy will know someone from his old village who has a baby they don't want and then we won't have to go through the adoption process. We can just hop on a plane and pick the baby up."

"Why don't you ask him for his help with the questions first? You can ask him to kidnap his neighbor's child for us when you get to know him better."

chapter SIXTEEN

SEAN'S FRIEND VLAD was a great help. He filled in all the blanks and agreed that some of the questions on the list were very odd. I managed to refrain from asking him to nip home to Russia and abduct one of his neighbor's babies, much to Sean's relief. After talking to Vlad, I asked my brother how things were going with Shadee, and he said everything was great, so good in fact that he was planning to bring her home in a couple of weeks to meet the family.

The next morning as I was transcribing Vlad's answers into my workbook, Mum called.

"Well—have you heard the latest?"

"What?"

"Sean's bringing that girl home to meet us."

"Her name's Shadee, and yes I had heard."

"Why's he bringing her home? It must be serious. Is it? Is it serious?"

"I dunno. I suppose it is."

"What are we going to do?"

"About what?"

"About the girl."

"Be nice."

"I'll be polite, but I'm not going to pretend I'm happy with the relationship."

"Okay, but promise me you won't bring up *Not Without My Daughter*. Have you read that book Sean gave you on Iran?"

"No."

"Well, now's the time to do it. We should all be more informed. When you've finished, give it to me."

"They're not staying here of course."

"Oh?"

"Staying in a hotel, your brother announces. Want their own space, so they do. Our house obviously isn't good enough for her."

"Mum—that was probably Sean's idea."

"Pffff. Well, I'm having a family dinner for them on Saturday night—I won't have her telling her parents that we weren't welcoming to her. Make sure yourself and James are free. I better go—I haven't time to be chitchatting if I'm to read that encyclopedia of Iran Sean gave me. I might get your father to read it and give me a summary."

"Good idea—get him to do bullet points for me too. Bye."

Babs called over a few days later.

"Hi. I'm starving," she said, pushing past me into the kitchen where she stuck her nose in the fridge. "Have you anything decent to eat?"

"Make yourself at home."

"Thanks, I will," she said as she made herself a sandwich.

"Feel free to bring your own food next time you come."

"So you heard about Shadee?" asked Babs as she stuffed her face.

"Yep."

"Mum's doing my head in. She's been cleaning the house since Sean called her to say they were coming. You'd swear it was a state visit from the queen. I wouldn't mind, but they're not even staying at the house. She barged in at seven yesterday morning and started ranting at me to tidy up my room . . . she wasn't going to have the Iranian people thinking Irish people were slobs . . . she wanted this house to be gleaming . . . and on and on. She has Dad tormented with that stupid book Sean gave her. She keeps following him around, asking him if they're all mad, like in the movie."

"God, poor old Shadee. Five minutes' interrogation from Mum and she'll be swimming back to London."

"She won't get far with the big black sheet weighing her down," said Babs, grinning at me.

When we had finished laughing about Shadee's swim to freedom in a yashmak, Babs asked me how the adoption was going.

"It's a lot harder than I imagined. You get homework and have to analyze your feelings all the time."

"Feelings about being barren?"

"Not really—but thanks for bringing that up! More your feelings about how you think your child will cope with racism and abandonment and a new environment and stuff."

"Do they show you any videos of the orphanages? I saw one where the kids were lying on the cold, wet floors covered in sores and wearing dirty rags and there was this social worker–type woman who was picking them up and hugging them. I dunno how she did it—they were filthy."

"Jesus, Babs."

"What?"

"For God's sake, the children can't help it. They just need to be rescued and loved. Besides, apparently the orphanages have improved a lot."

"Fine, but if I was you, I'd bring a big bottle of disinfectant and some lice shampoo when you go to pick up your baby."

I have to admit she had a point. I was secretly worried about how I'd feel if our little child was covered in open wounds and nits when we went to meet them. I know they say it's different when it's your own child—but it still made me squirm to think about it. I felt evil for even allowing such negative thoughts to enter my head, but I couldn't get the image of oozing puss out of my mind. I wasn't even good with blood. The sight of it made me feel ill—so God knows how bad I'd be with sores.

"We'll be fine," I said, sounding more confident than I felt. "James is well used to blood and gore on the rugby field."

"It's not James I'm worried about," said Babs, smirking.

"I'll be fine too."

"May I remind you of the eczema incident?"

Damn Babs and her elephant memory. The summer I was sixteen, our cousin Deirdre came to stay for a few weeks. Her parents were getting separated, and Mum had told my Auntie Pam to send Deirdre up for a visit to try and distract her. Deirdre was given my room and I shared with Babs—who even at the tender age of four was really annoying. Cousin Deirdre suffered from eczema, and when she got stressed—the eczema got worse. She was clearly very fraught about her parents' divorce—for the three weeks she stayed, her skin peeled off in daily layers. After she left I moved back into my room. While I was helping Mum strip the sheets off the bed, bits of flaky skin fluttered to the ground. I freaked. Mum said not to worry, she'd boil-wash the sheets and they'd be as good as new. I said that not only could she burn the sheets but she could burn the mattress as well because there was no way in hell I was going to sleep on it after Deirdre of the snaky skin had. I was told not to be so ridiculous, but I dug my heels in and no flipping of the mattress, or new sheets, would induce me to sleep in that bed. I had nightmares about dead skin sticking to me. Eventually after two weeks of finding me asleep on the floor, Mum relented and bought me a new mattress.

"That was nineteen years ago, things have changed. I've grown up, and besides, it's different when it's a baby."

"Yeah right," snorted Babs. "Anyway, can you do me a quick makeover? I've got a date tonight."

"New guy?"

"No." She sighed. "I'm recycling an old one out of pure boredom."

"Finding a job might help fill your days. It's what normal people do."

"Actually, I'm starting an acting course next week, so I will be working."

Acting! As if she needed any encouragement to be more dramatic.

A couple of days before Sean and Shadee were due to arrive, I dropped by to see how things were going with the Iranian research. I was hoping Dad would have a quick summary for me so that I wouldn't appear like a complete philistine when I was talking to Shadee. Mum opened the door, looking extremely fraught.

"What's up?" I said, genuinely worried by her pale demeanor.

"I'm at my wits' end," she sniffed, trying not to cry. "I decided to show this girl that we are an open-minded family, so I was going to cook an Iranian meal. I asked Barbara to look on the computer and find me the most popular Iranian dish. This is what she found," said Mum, handing me the printout.

I looked down. It was the recipe for a dish called *maghz*. The main ingredient was lamb brains. The instructions noted: "Wash the brains carefully in cold water and then remove the skin and veins . . ." I looked up. Mum was nodding her head.

"Brains! Sheep's brains. That's what they eat there every day apparently. No wonder they're all lunatics. You get mad cow's disease from eating animal brains. She'll poison Sean with her cooking and then drag him back to Iran. She has him under a mad-cow disease spell."

"Mum, calm down. Let me check this out on the Internet for you. I'll be back down in five minutes."

I had a funny feeling that Babs was winding her up. I checked out Iranian recipes on the Web and found that although *maghz* was an Iranian dish, it was not the most popular and there were plenty others to choose from. I printed out the recipe for *khoresht baamieh*.

"Stewing lamb or beef, potatoes, onions, lime juice . . . ," read Mum, looking ten years younger as she realized she wouldn't have to perform a lobotomy on a sheep for dinner.

Dad strolled in, looking very pleased with himself. He handed us both a sheet of paper with ten numbered points under the heading:

Info on Iran—Based on Facts, Not on a Hollywood Film.

1. Area: 1.64 million sq. km.
2. Population: 68.27 million
3. People: Persian (Farsi) (65%), Azari (25%), Arab (4%), Lors (2%), Turkmen (2%), Kurdish, Armenian, Jewish
4. Language: Persian (Farsi), Kurdish
5. Religion: Shi'ite Muslim (89%), Sunni Muslim (10%), Zoroastrian, Jewish, Christian, Baha'i (1%)
6. Government: Islamic Republic
7. Head of State: Spiritual Leader (Rahbar) Ayatollah Sayyed Ali Khamenei
8. Iranian cuisine is heavily based on rice, bread, fresh vegetables, herbs, and fruit. Meat, usually lamb or mutton minced or cut into small chunks, is used to add flavor but is rarely the dominant ingredient, except in kebabs.
9. The national drink of Iran is *chay* (tea), always served scalding hot, black, and strong.
10. Alcohol is strictly forbidden to Islamic Iranians, though it is permitted for religious purposes, such as communion wine in churches, and to non-Muslims with special permission.

Footnote: I'm all for having an Iranian meal, but I'll need something stronger than that old chay to wash it down with.

Mum and I laughed.

"Thank you, Dan, that's very helpful, and the bit about the boiling hot tea is good to know, although how they can drink it without burning their mouths is beyond me. I'll put some milk out so we can have some ourselves."

"And wine," said Dad. "Lots of wine."

"It says alcohol is strictly forbidden in point nine Dad," I said, waving the list under his nose.

"For Islamic Iranians, Emma—not lapsed Irish Catholics."

James and I arrived late on Saturday for dinner. Leinster had beaten Gloucester in a tight match with a last-minute penalty. James was thrilled and got a bit carried away with the momentum. I eventually dragged him out of the clubhouse, four pints and two hours of postmatch analysis later, and sprinted over to Mum and Dad's.

We arrived just before Sean and Shadee, James swaying a little and reeking of booze—I forced a few extra strong mints into his mouth and perched him in the corner of the couch beside Dad, who was seething at having missed the match, due to Mum's insistence that he cut the grass and rake up the leaves for the visitor. Babs handed James the list of Iranian numbered points, while I went to make him a strong cup of coffee. When the doorbell rang, I jumped up to answer as the others all tried to look nonchalant.

"Hi, sis," said Sean, looking very nervous. "Shadee, this is Emma. She'll be your ally tonight. Make sure you sit between her and James."

Shadee smiled. "It's great to meet you, Emma."

She was petite and pretty with beautiful almond eyes. She was wearing black trousers and a lacey black top. She had a really warm smile. I liked her immediately.

Babs bounded up behind me, "Hi I'm Babs, let me take your coat, yashmak, burka, whatever . . ."

"This is Babs—the shit stirrer," said Sean to Shadee, who was laughing good-naturedly.

They came in, and Sean introduced her to Mum and Dad.

"Wel-come to Ire-land," said Mum, slowly articulating each word.

"Thanks, I'm delighted to be here."

"How did you find the jour-ney," said our newly appointed speech therapist.

"For God's sake, Mum, she's not mentally challenged. She speaks better English than you," said Babs, rolling her eyes.

"I'm only trying to make the girl feel welcome," hissed Mum. "Would you like a nice cup of *chay?* I know it's your people's favorite drink," she asked, nodding knowingly.

"Well, I—"

"She'll have a glass of white wine thanks," said Sean.

"Wine?" said Mum, looking confused. "But they don't drink alcohol. It's strictly forbidden to them."

"Who exactly are 'they'?" snapped Sean.

"Islamic Iranians."

"*Chay* would be fine thanks," said Shadee, trying to diffuse the situation.

"If the girl wants a glass of wine, give it to her," said Dad.

"But I thought you were Muslim?" said Mum.

"My parents are, but I'm not a practicing one. I'm a lapsed one, I'm afraid."

"I'm lapsed myself," said Dad, handing her a goldfish bowl–size glass of wine. "Here you go, get that into you."

Things improved after that. Everyone relaxed—even Mum. Shadee was polite, interesting, intelligent, and utterly charming. Mum, keen to share her recently acquired knowledge on Iran, said that Ireland must feel small to someone from a country with a population of 68.27 million people living in 1.64 million square kilometers. I could see James's shoulders beginning to shake. I looked down and tried not to laugh.

Shadee said that Ireland was a wonderful country that pro-
duced incredible people—she smiled at Sean at that point—and
added that she always thought it would be a lovely place to live.
She was pressing all the right buttons—Mum was delighted.

"And tell me, Shady," said Mum, going into diplomatic over-
drive, "are you one of the eighty-nine percent of shite Muslims or a
ten percent sunny one?"

chapter SEVENTEEN

D URING OUR NEXT ADOPTION SESSION, we discussed all of the possibilities of diseases that a child cared for in an orphanage might have. James and I looked at each other in shock as the list got longer. Brendan kept crashing on about FAS—which turned out to be fetal alcohol syndrome. Apparently in Russia, with its high rate of alcoholism, FAS is a risk and is almost impossible to detect before the child is two years old. Brendan had a list of ways to check if a child had FAS: small upturned nose, low nasal bridge, speech disorders, and clumsiness. He had similar checks for pneumonia, cleft palates, cerebral palsy, HIV, scabies, rickets. . . . Brendan rabbited on with his depressing symptoms and fact findings.

Before the rest of us grabbed our coats and ran for the hills, Yvonne stepped in and gave us some of her own facts and figures. "Yes, it's true that your child could have any number of problems. Children who have been institutionalized are not going to be completely normal. They will have been affected, and that's just something that you have to face. Over fifty percent of institutionalized children in Eastern Europe are born underweight. Some are premature births and some because their mothers drink while pregnant. Orphanages tend to be understaffed, so the children suffer from lack of stimulation, and this delays normal development. Children lose one month of linear growth for every three months they spend in care. But with the right treatment, love, and medical assistance, they will grow and they will thrive."

Thank God for Yvonne. The group breathed an audible sigh of relief. We understood it wasn't going to be a walk in the park. We knew we'd have to work hard with our babies to make up for their crappy start in life, but we didn't need to listen to Brendan giving us a list of the worst-case scenarios. Just when we began to feel a little less despondent, Dervla slapped on a video of sick children in orphanages around the world. Some of the babies were in a terrible state. The women all reached for tissues while the men looked everywhere but at the television screen. It was harrowing stuff. As I watched in horror, I kept thinking about what Babs had said about the eczema incident. Would I be a disaster? By the time the video was over, we were all completely drained.

James and I drove home in silence. Well, we drove down the road in silence and then I asked him what he was thinking.

"Honestly?"

"Yes." I wanted to know if he was having second thoughts.

"That the whole adoption process is an almighty pain in the backside. That I wish we could have had a child of our own and not have to go to these meetings and watch videos of sick children and listen to buffoons like Brendan listing all the problems we may have to face," said James angrily.

"I know. It's not fair." I sighed, looking out the window. "People who have babies naturally don't have the worst-case scenarios thrown at them constantly. You don't go up to a pregnant woman and say—'do you know your child could have leukemia or be autistic or suffer from some disease you've never even heard of.' All they get is praise and 'congratulations' and 'well dones' and 'isn't it so excitings.' God I wish I could've got pregnant the normal way. It's like a constant uphill battle. I'm sick and tired of it all. When did having children get so complicated?"

James looked over at me, "Hey, where's my optimist?"

"She's been battered to death by the evil spirits on the Adoption Board and big, fat, annoying Brendan and his stupid charts."

"At least we're over halfway through the group sessions," said James, in a lame attempt to cheer me up.

"And then we begin the home visits," I grumbled. "Six one-to-one sessions with a social worker, and I bet, knowing our luck, we'll get Dervla."

"Why don't we go away for the weekend? Go to some plush hotel and relax?"

"We can't, we're going to Sally's birthday party on Saturday."

"Pardon?"

"We have to go, James. We never see Jess and Tony's kids or any other children for that matter. We really need to hang out with some toddlers and get our feet wet. Besides, the social worker is bound to ask Jess and Tony if we're good with their kids, and they shouldn't have to lie."

"Somebody shoot me now," groaned James as he swung the car into the driveway.

* * *

We arrived at Jess and Tony's on Saturday afternoon, laden with gifts for Sally. What I had neglected in quality time, I was determined to make up for in material goods.

"Hello, Sally," I beamed.

She looked at me blankly.

"You remember me? Mummy's friend Emma."

Sally shook her head.

"Of course you do," I said, determined to jog her memory. "I went shopping with you and your mummy a little while ago."

Truth be told, it was actually a year and a half ago, but Jess had understood that I didn't want to be around children while I was having my fertility treatment. I found it too difficult. I was too emotional and volatile. Still, it was pretty sad that Jess's daughter didn't even recognize me. I had been very negligent and selfish. I needed to spend a lot more time with Sally and little Roy. I'd call over every week or so and play with them. Quality time was what was needed here. God forbid that Dervla would ask Sally what she thought of Mummy and Daddy's friends Emma and James—only to be met with a blank stare. It would be a disaster, and I certainly didn't need any more black marks on my evaluation form.

I decided not to torment Sally any longer and opted for bribery. I handed over the present. She ripped it open—like mother like daughter, Jess had always loved presents—and squealed with joy. It was Las Vegas Barbie with ten different outfits. I thought it was pretty cool myself. She'll remember me now, I thought smugly.

"Thank you, Mummy's friend," said Sally, reaching up to kiss me. I hugged her. She smelled of apple shampoo. My heart ached. I was ready to be a mother. I wanted a child so badly it hurt physically. I looked up at James. He nodded sadly.

Jess came over at the sounds of her daughter's squeals. "Oh,

Emma, it's perfect. Las Vegas Barbie is the coolest present going for four-year-olds. Thanks," said Jess.

"She's beautiful, Jess. She's a really gorgeous little girl, and you're a brilliant mother. Sorry I don't tell you that enough and sorry for not seeing more of her and Roy," I said, getting a little choked up.

"Hey, you're always telling me I'm a great mum and you've been an amazing friend. You're constantly having to listen to me bitching about my weight, or lack of sleep, or lack of life. I don't know what I'd have done without your support over the last few years. I know it's been really hard for you, but you're going to be a fantastic mum, I can't wait for you to get your baby."

"Jess, I need your help with the music," said Tony as Sally pulled on his leg, shouting to have her Britney CD played. "Oh and Emma, you better watch out, your husband is being chatted up by a very cute young thing called Molly."

I looked over at James, who was deep in discussion with a little girl in a cowboy outfit. They appeared to be discussing sports. I wandered over and sat down to listen in.

"Do you own Liverpool?" asked Molly.

"The football team?"

"Yeah."

"No. I wish I did though."

"My daddy told me you were the team's teacher."

"Oh, I see. I'm actually Leinster's teacher."

"What enster?"

"It's a rugby team."

"What's rugby? Is it the same as soccer?"

"Well, its kind of the same, but you can pick up the ball and run with it in rugby."

"Why?"

"So you can score tries."

"What's tries?"

"It's like a goal in soccer."

"Is there a goalie?"

"No."

"Who stops the ball going into the net?"

"There actually aren't any nets, there are just goal posts."

"Why?"

"Because you have to run over the line with the ball and touch the ground with it, so you don't need a net," said James.

"My daddy says you're an inconsister teacher. Up and down he says." Molly demonstrated this by waving her arms up and down.

"Did he really? Which one's your daddy?" asked James.

"That's my daddy," said Molly, pointing to Tony's partner Gordon Woods.

"Okay, Molly, you go and tell your daddy that I said he should stick to what he knows," said James, laughing as Molly ran over to tell her father.

The rest of the afternoon passed pleasantly enough until I got stuck with Sonia and Maura from Jess's baby group. They both had their children with them, and Sonia was hugely pregnant again. If I was a betting person, I'd have put odds on that she was going to pop at the birthday party. After exchanging the usual pleasantries— weather, cost of groceries, traffic, if and when we'd been on holidays lately, the ages and progress of their children—they asked me if I'd had any children.

"Since we met last year?" I asked.

"God, is it a year ago already? Time flies when you're a mummy," said Sonia.

"No. None."

"Would you like to have children?" asked Maura.

"Uhm." I paused. I could lie and say that I had no desire for children at all. I could say that I hadn't got around to trying yet, or I could just be honest and stop feeling embarrassed and awkward because I couldn't get pregnant. "Yes, I do want children. I want them very much. In fact James and I have just started the adoption process. We're in the middle of our course."

It felt good to be open about wanting children. I felt relieved.

"Trouble down below, was it?" asked Sonia, pointing to my crotch.

I stared at her in shock.

"My sister-in-law had problems in that area. She ended up taking so many fertility hormones that she almost grew a mustache," she said, laughing as Maura joined in.

I took deep breaths and counted to ten. There was no point in losing my temper. They didn't mean to be bitches I reminded myself, they just had no idea what it was like, because every time their husbands winked at them—they got pregnant.

"Isn't adopting a bit of a worry? It's a bit like wearing someone else's clothes, isn't it? I mean, you don't know who the parents are. They could be drug addicts or murderers, and it could be in the genes, you just never know do you," said Maura.

"No, I don't see it like that at all actually. I think it's a wonderful way to have a family. I can't wait to go to Russia to get my baby," I said, plastering a smile on my face.

"I think it's very brave of you," said Sonia, rubbing her big, pregnant stomach affectionately. "I could never do it, but good for you."

"What does your husband think?" asked Maura.

"About what?"

"Having to adopt. I know Stephen wouldn't like it. He wouldn't be open to bringing up someone else's child."

"James doesn't mind at all. In fact, he's delighted about it."

"Really?"

"Yes."

"You're very lucky. He must be very understanding and supportive of you."

"Supportive of what?" asked Lucy, who had just arrived with Donal, who had made a beeline for James.

"The girls here are telling me how lucky I am to have a husband who doesn't mind adopting. They feel it's a bit like wearing someone else's cast-off clothes and could think of nothing worse. They think I'm very brave."

"Lucky and Brave. Wow!" said Lucy. "I think you have it all wrong. Adopting has its advantages you know. For starters, you don't end up looking like a big whale," she said, staring pointedly at Sonia. "Nor do you have to pee every four minutes. You don't have to deal with constant hormonal changes or have your vagina ripped to shreds at childbirth. You don't have to worry about losing all the weight you piled on while you were pregnant, and best of all, your husband wants to have sex with you before, during, and after the baby. Personally, I think you two are the brave ones."

I love Lucy.

chapter EIGHTEEN

OVER THE NEXT FEW WEEKS I saw very little of James. His draconian training regime kept him at the club. He was determined to get to the semifinals again this year and was facing the cup favorites—Biarritz in the next game. He was like a man possessed—if he wasn't at the club, he was at home watching replays of all the Biarritz matches that season. He kept scribbling down messages and reminders on Post-its. They were everywhere: *La Pierre—weak on the high balls. Bring the game to them. Break their rhythm—mix up the plays.* I even found one stuck to the fridge—*Winning is a mind-set, attitude is everything.* I stuck a picture of Cameron Diaz beside it with a note saying—*Being thin is about discipline—say no to chocolate.*

Three days before the big game we attended our fourth adoption session. James was like a cat on a hot tin roof. He couldn't sit still and kept looking at his watch and sighing as the minutes turned into hours. He was flying to France that afternoon with the team. I was flying out with Lucy the next day. James had to be at the airport at two o'clock and our meeting wasn't due to finish until half past one. Half an hour to get to the airport was cutting it very close, and he was getting decidedly agitated. I nudged him.

"Stop it," I whispered.

"What?"

"Stop looking at your watch, you're supposed to be listening."

"I can't help it; my mind's on other things."

"Well, try harder. We need to make a good impression."

"Thinking about the game?" asked Gary, who was sitting directly behind us.

"Yes," said James, grinning. "It's a bit all-consuming."

"They're a good team all right, but I think you've the advantage. Leinster has a bigger pack, that'll swing it for you. How's O'Brien's ankle?"

"Better. He's fit to play, which I can tell you is a relief. We—"

" . . . it is vital that you choose the right moment to tell your child that he or she is adopted," said Dervla, raising her voice and glaring at James and Gary. "I'd like you to break up into groups and discuss how and when you should tell your child they're adopted. What words will you use? How will you approach it? How will you cope if your child reacts badly to the news?"

As usual, I was put in Brendan's group. As usual, he took over, appointed himself group leader, and began to shove his views down our throats.

"My research tells me that it's really only when the child reaches eight years of age that they begin to become more aware of being adopted and go through a grieving process. They want to know why they were abandoned by their birth parents and start looking for answers. The way to deal with it is to be very direct. Just say 'your mother left you in an orphanage where you would've remained for the rest of your life if we hadn't come along and saved you.'"

Hold on a minute. That didn't sound very sensitive to me. Carole looked a bit taken aback too.

"What about saying something like—'your poor mother was very young when she had you and she couldn't really cope, so we were chosen to look after you, and since the day we met you, you've brought nothing but happiness to our lives,'" said Carole.

"That's lovely," I said, smiling at her.

"You're not dealing with the problem," said Brendan. "The child needs to understand that if it wasn't for you he would still be in the orphanage."

"That's not dealing with the problem, that's nursing your own ego," I snapped. "The child isn't supposed to feel that their mother dumped them in the orphanage because she couldn't be bothered with them. It'll only make their abandonment issues worse. At least if they think she loved them but just couldn't manage to raise them because she was too young, or had no money, or was sick or something—they won't feel so rejected. You coming along and saving their lives isn't what we're talking about here—we're supposed to be focusing on the child's feelings, not ours."

Brendan glared at me. "I hardly think someone who cites losing a tooth as a traumatic experience is qualified to lecture me on how to handle my child."

Before I could tell him that a jerk like him shouldn't be inflicted on a child, Yvonne announced that we were now going to watch a video—yet another one—that would give us some insight into the effect that telling your child they are adopted can have. James rolled his eyes and slumped down beside me.

The video was about a man in his late twenties who was adopted but never knew. It was only when he was getting a visa to go to Australia, and saw a copy of his birth certificate, that he dis-covered he was adopted. When he confronted his parents they told him not only that was he adopted, but also that his twin brother, who was also adopted, wasn't his twin or his brother, or even the same age as him. Needless to say, the man was extremely distressed and had to go to therapy to recover from the shock. He never made it to Australia.

I have to admit, I found the video a bit hard to swallow. I mean, come on, who in their right minds would bring up two chil-dren who were not related in any way and not the same age—as twins! When the postvideo discussion started up and we were asked to analyze how we felt about the video, James jumped up.

"Tremendous viewing. I think we all learned a lot from it. Very insightful. A great way to end today's session. Thank you," he said, reaching to put on his coat.

"But, James, it was ridiculous. The parents should never have—"

I stopped as James stood on my toe and glared at me.

"We can discuss this at home," he said, shaking his watch in my face. It was twenty-five past one.

"Ludicrous," said Brendan. "The whole thing was a farce. The parents are clearly stupid, and the man should have just gone to Australia and cleared his head over there. No one with an ounce of intelligence would behave that way."

"Maybe they just never found the right time to tell him and then it was too late," suggested Carole.

"Pretending the brother was his twin was a bit off, though, you have to admit," said Gary.

James at this point was bright red in the face. I think I actually spotted steam coming out of his ears. If he didn't get out of there soon, he'd explode.

"I suppose that was a bit silly," admitted Carole.

"They should never have been allowed to adopt—they are obviously not intelligent enough," snorted Brendan.

"Well, now let's look at it from all the angles," said Yvonne.

"NO," shouted James. "Let's not do that. Let's go home, think it over, and talk about it next week. I think that'd be much better all-round. Can we please not spend any more precious time bickering about this ridiculous video and just wrap this meeting up."

Everyone stared at him. James was normally so polite and calm, and now he was standing there stamping his foot like a child, demanding to be let out of school on time.

"Sorry," I said, trying to smooth it over. "James has a flight to catch, and he's just a bit nervous about missing it."

"We did stress in the first meeting that you should allow for overtime," said Dervla.

"Maybe you *should* think it over at home and tell us your thoughts next week," said Yvonne, our resident peacemaker. "Now don't forget that next week is our last session and we'll be having lunch afterward, so you all need to bring in food from the country that you have chosen to adopt from. I hope you won't be rushing off next week, James?"

"Not only will I not be dashing off, but I will cook a Russian feast for you all," said the old James as he sprinted out the door.

The next day, Lucy and I arrive in Biarritz in time for dinner. James and Donal were so preoccupied by the game that they just barely noticed that we'd arrived. After an early meal, James ordered everyone to bed at ten. Lucy and I stayed up drinking wine, and she filled me in on Annie's reaction to their engagement.

When Annie arrived from boarding school for the night, Lucy hid in the bedroom to give Donal a chance to break the news to her gently and alone. Annie got a bit upset at first, but he kept telling her that she would always be his priority and he'd never abandon her and that this was her home and that wouldn't change.

"But what if you have kids? Then what? You won't have time for me anymore."

"Jesus, Annie, we're not even married yet, we won't be having kids for a while. You don't have to worry about that."

"I don't want a new mum."

"Lucy's not going to be a new mum, she'll be more like a big sister or a friend."

"I don't need a new friend."

"Look, Annie, give me a break here. I promise you nothing will change. I've finally met a woman I want to marry, so please be happy for me, will you? Lucy's mad about you, sure she even wants you to be her bridesmaid," he announced, grasping at straws.

Lucy bit her lip. Bloody hell what did he go and say that for?

"Promise nothing will change?"

"I swear to you."

"Okay then. Congratulations, I'm glad you're happy," she said, throwing her arms around Donal for a bear hug.

"LUCY," hollered Donal. "You can come out now, she's happy for us."

Lucy was mortified. She didn't want Annie to think she had been listening at the door like some sort of spy. It was humiliating. She threw her clothes off and grabbed her bathrobe.

"Sorry, were you calling me?" she asked, pretending to have just got out of the shower.

"Yes," said Donal, looking very pleased with himself. "Annie's got something to say to you."

"Congratulations Lucy, and thanks for asking me to be your bridesmaid."

Lucy knew she was being insincere, but she played along for Donal's sake.

"Thank you. We'll get you something really nice to wear, you can choose it yourself."

"Well, I'll leave you two ladies to discuss dresses while I make a quick call."

"But as soon as Donal left the room," said Lucy, sighing as she glugged down her wine, "Annie attacked me and told me that she hated me and would rather die than be my bridesmaid. She said she wouldn't let me steal Donal from her and there would be no wedding."

"Little cow. What did you say?"

"I tried to explain that I wasn't stealing Donal. I said that I loved Donal and wanted to make him happy and that I totally respected her relationship with him and I wouldn't dream of interfering with it. But it made no difference; she just can't bear to share him with anyone."

"What did Donal say when you told him?"

"I didn't tell him."

"Why?"

"No point. He was delighted because he thought it was all sorted out, and in fairness there's nothing he can do about it. Hopefully when we get married she'll chill out. I dunno though, Emma, she's a handful."

"Thank God for boarding school. Look, in two years time she'll go off to college and you'll hardly ever see her. Besides, at fifteen your hormones are all over the place. She'll mellow."

"Any tips from your course on how to bring up children who hate you?"

"Well I can tell you how to detect diseases, how and when to tell her she's adopted, how to deal with racism, how to talk to her in pidgin Russian, and tell her how to behave if she gets invited for dinner in Moscow. Apart from that I'm useless."

Lucy asked the bartender for another bottle of red wine for two desperate, clueless about-to-become mothers.

By the time I got to bed, I was a bit unsteady on my feet. After knocking over the bedside lamp and stubbing my toe on the side of the bed, I eventually fell over, landing on top of James.

"For goodness' sake, Emma, I am trying to get some sleep here."

"Sorry," I giggled, trying to extricate myself from the bedsheet. "Too much red wine."

"I can see that."

"Oh, relax. Are you being stuffy-wuffy? Is Jamesy-wamsey being stuffy-wuffy?" I giggled, squeezing his cheeks.

"No he is not. Now get into bed and shut up."

"Does Jamesy's little sausage roll want to come out to play?" I said, snorting at my own joke.

"Emma!"

"Come on, you know you want to," I said, lying on top of him.

"Get off me, you lunatic," said James, pushing me aside.

"Come on, it'll be good for you. It'll distract you, and you always sleep well after sex," I said, tugging at his boxer shorts.

"Tempting though the thought of having sex with you right now is, as you breathe red wine and garlic fumes all over me, I think I can live without it. Now go to sleep," he said, shoving me aside.

I rolled off the bed and fell onto the floor.

"Ouch. No need to be so aggressive. Most guys would be delighted if their wives came home and begged them for sex."

"Darling, if Jennifer Lopez was standing naked in front of me right now, I'd say no. I'm too tense about the game. Now if you'll excuse us, my sausage roll, or rather my hot dog and I, are going to try and get some sleep. I suggest you do the same."

I woke up the next day feeling very groggy. James was striding about the room muttering to himself. He looked very tired and very nervous. I kissed him and wished him luck. "Don't worry, James, whatever happens I'm really proud of you. Go Leinster."

He didn't even smile. The man was a wreck.

Biarritz came out guns blazing. By halftime they were up ten points.

"Shit," said Lucy. "How bad is ten points?"

"Not good," said the die-hard Leinster supporter beside us. "Not good at all. That coach had better come up with some new tactics. They're killing us up front and we've the bigger pack."

"Pack of what?"

"The pack is number one to eight. When they all huddle together they're called the pack," I explained.

"So would you say Donal Brady's having a good game?" Lucy asked our new friend.

"Brutal. That's three line-outs in a row he's lost. He's too old."

"He is not too old, and he's doing his best, don't knock him. I'm sure he'll jump higher after half time," said Lucy.

"And I can assure you that the coach has plenty of other tactics to choose from, our house is a treasure trove of tactical options," I said defensively.

"Birds," snorted the die-hard fan.

Thankfully, James did come up with some new plays—namely not to let the other team have the ball at all. And Donal did jump higher in the second half—a lot higher, and he scored the winning try with a great break from the line-out.

"Did you see that? Did you see him?" shouted Lucy. "Too old, my ass."

chapter NINETEEN

A S JAMES HAD SO EAGERLY VOLUNTEERED himself to cook a Russian meal, I decided to let him do the work. My contribution was a bottle of Russian vodka. I busied myself with researching our family trees. We each had to do a detailed family tree, noting who died of what, when, and where. I was a bit hazy about the exact causes of my grandparents' deaths, so I called Mum.

"Hi."

"Hello, love, how are you?"

"Fine, thanks. I need to ask you a few questions for the course."

"No."

"What?"

"No, I do not regret smacking you on the bottom when you misbehaved. I think children today would be a lot better behaved if they got a few smacks on the tush. All this mumbo jumbo about reasoning with them is poppycock. If a child is roaring in the middle of a supermarket because you won't buy it candy that'll rot its teeth—you're hardly going to start up a debate. A quick smack will sort it out for you. I'm sure the social workers say it's the wrong thing to do, but I stand by it. Besides, it never did you any harm."

"Right, okay. Well thanks for that, but actually I need to ask you about the family medical history."

"Oh."

"What did Granny and Grandad die of?"

"My poor mother—God rest her soul—died of kidney failure and my father died of a heart attack."

"What about Dad's parents?"

"His mother died of Alzheimer's and his father died of lung cancer."

"Okay, thanks," I said, scribbling down the details.

"How's it all going anyway?"

"All right, it's tough going. They seem to be intent on freaking us out by showing us videos of horrible orphanages and children who've been adopted and have had really big problems coming to terms with it."

"Those bloody social workers are a scourge on society. Interfering in decent people's lives and claiming that everyone's a child molester."

My mother had no time for social workers. She had a friend who had a friend whose sister's cousin had been accused of abusing her daughter because she had gone to school with bruises on her legs. The parents had been investigated and put through hell until it was established that the daughter had got the bruises while playing hockey. Ever since then, Mum had been anti all social workers. It was a good thing your family couldn't be your adoption referees, there was no way I'd want Mum let loose on them.

" . . . it's just plain ridiculous. Any child would be blessed to end up in a nice home with two good parents."

"Do you think I'll be a good mother?" I asked, fishing for compliments.

"I think you're going to get a shock," said Mum.

"What d'you mean?"

"Having children isn't easy. It's a full-time job. You won't have any time for yourself. Your life as you know it will be turned upside down."

"God, I'm so sick of people saying that. All I keep hearing is how when you have children your life changes so much and it's so hard and you never get time alone, blah blah blah. I'm ready for change. I'm so ready it's a joke. Not having kids is bloody hard work too. My life as I knew it hasn't been the same since I started trying to have children. I've been in limbo hell for nearly three years. Believe me I am ready for the next stage. It's so patronizing to be told how hard it is all the time. I don't go around telling people what a nightmare it is to be infertile," I fumed.

"Lord, I hope you haven't been ranting like that in front of the social workers. They'll be sending you to anger-management classes instead of adoption ones. You need to calm down. It's not good for you to be so stressed."

"I know, it just really gets to me sometimes," I grumbled.

"How's James after his big win?" asked Mum, changing the subject.

"He was thrilled for about a day and now he's totally uptight about the semifinal against Ulster. It's like living with someone with ADD. I can't have a proper conversation with him, because he can't concentrate on anything for more than five minutes. He keeps jumping up and making notes or drawing diagrams of new moves."

"Well, I hope you're being supportive. His career is very important to him. Are you cooking him nice meals when he comes in and listening to him? You need to mind your man, Emma. There are plenty of young blondes out there only dying to run off with him."

"Fantastic. Thanks, Mum. I knew I could count on you to make me feel better. One the one hand you tell me that I need to relax, and then in the same breath you tell me that my husband's going to leave me—in the middle of the adoption process—for a young blonde. Well, I better go and get the cookbooks out so I can make James something really special tonight to try and keep him from leaving me."

When James came home that night, I greeted him at the front door wielding a saucepan in one hand and Jamie Oliver's cookbook in the other.

"If you want to run off with a young one then just sod off and go. I haven't time to be cooking you feasts, I have to learn Russian, finish my family tree, fill out my workbook, hold down my job . . ."

James came over and gently removed the saucepan and cookbook. "I take it you've been talking to your mother?"

"Yes, and she told me that I'm far too stressed out and that I should be nicer to you so you won't run off with a young blonde."

"Did she have any particular blonde in mind?"

"She wasn't specific."

"Pity, now I'll have to eye them all up."

"Not funny."

"Doesn't your mother know I'm a sucker for redheads?"

"It doesn't appear to have registered. Sit down, I need to know what your grandparents died of."

"From affairs to death—never a dull moment. As far as I know, my mother's mother died of breast cancer, and her father died of a stroke. My father's mother was run down by a car and died of internal injuries, and my grandfather died three months later of a broken heart."

"Oh, that's so sad. D'you think if I died you'd die of a broken heart?"

"Not if I had a young blonde to cheer me up."

On the eve of our final adoption group session, I called James to remind him that he had promised to cook for everyone. I even offered to go and get the ingredients on my way home from work, but he assured me that it was all under control. When I got home he was glued to the TV, analyzing with Donal Ulster's previous win.

"Howrya," said Donal, waving at me from the couch.

"Hi, Donal, How's things?"

"Good. You?"

"Fine thanks. By the way did you get the referee form from the adoption people yet?"

"Sure. I filled that out ages ago. Did I not tell you?"

"What?"

"The form—I sent it back to the adoption people a few weeks back."

"But you didn't show it to me. I specifically asked you to show it to me before you sent it back," I said, panic rising in my throat.

"I know, but it said on the form that I wasn't to show it to you because you might influence my comments. So I jotted down a few things and stuck it in the post."

"Did Lucy see it?"

"No."

I tried to remain calm.

"What did you say?"

"Ah, I just said that you were a good pair and that although you fought a fair bit, you always seemed to make up and that you liked to go out and have a few drinks but you weren't alcoholics. I said you hated your nephew, but I was sure you liked children in general—although I'd never actually seen you interacting with any . . ."

Just as I was about to lie down on the floor and wail, I heard a snort from James.

"You bastard," I said, hitting Donal as he roared laughing. "I do not need to be wound up. I nearly had a heart attack."

"Don't worry, Emma. I have the form, but I won't fill it out until you tell me exactly what you want me to say. You can come over and dictate the answers to me."

"I need a drink. Beer?" I asked.

"I'll have one, but Donal won't."

"How come?" I asked.

"No alcohol allowed until after the game," said James, in his serious coach voice.

"He's a slave driver," groaned Donal. "I'll have a cup of tea please. Normal tea though, not that green muck you have Lucy drinking."

"By the way, James, what are you cooking for tomorrow?" I asked.

"It's a surprise."

Later that evening, after Donal had gone, I found James in the kitchen making sandwiches—lots of them.

"What are you doing?"

"Lunch for tomorrow," he said, grinning at me.

"You can't make sandwiches," I said horrified. "You promised you'd bring Russian food. James we have to make a good impression."

"This *is* Russian food," he said, waving a page at me. "I looked up on the Internet to find a recipe and I came across this one."

I looked at the page. It was from the www.ruscuisine.com website. The recipe was called: sandwich with red caviar. The ingredients consisted of—bread, butter, red caviar, and greens. The instructions noted that the bread should be finely sliced with the crusts removed. It should then be buttered, and the red caviar placed on top and decorated with greens.

"You sneak!" I said, shaking my head. "I thought you were going to do something proper like chicken Kiev. I hope the others aren't hungry. These wouldn't fill a mouse."

"Russian food is Russian food, whether it's to Dervla's taste or not is not my concern."

We arrived at the last session with our bottle of vodka and our small plate of fancy sandwiches. Brendan and Joy arrived wheeling a heated hostess tray. The smells wafting from it made our mouths water. Why oh why were they not adopting from Vietnam or China or somewhere else. They were showing us up. Brendan and Joy sat beside their moveable oven, smiling smugly as the rest of us put our plates on the table. When Yvonne walked in, she asked what the lovely smell was. Brendan was up like a shot.

"As you are, I'm sure, aware—beef stroganoff originates from Russia. The name of this dish comes from the Russian Count Grigory Stroganove. Born in 1770, he died in 1857 . . ."

And more's the pity you didn't croak with him, I thought as Brendan waffled on.

"The count was one of the richest noblemen in Russia and enjoyed gourmet food. He hired the best chefs available, and one of these invented an original dish that the count loved. The dish was christened stroganoff—after the count, not the cook."

While Brendan rabbited on, Joy served us plates of steaming hot—and I have to admit—delicious beef stroganoff. But the lecture wasn't over. The class nerd had brought wine. I hid my bottle of Stoli vodka under my chair.

"I'd like you all to taste this wonderful wine from Georgia— 'Old Tbilisi' Alazani," he announced in an exaggerated Russian accent.

"Is it just me, or is he a class-A wanker," grumbled James under his breath.

"The wines from Russia and the former Soviet states tend to be sweeter than European wines. The name Alazani comes from one of the major river systems of Georgia, which borders Georgia with Azerbaijan. The climate is slightly warmer than the rest of the Georgian wine-growing regions and gives rise to much sweeter grapes than those found elsewhere. *Za vas!*" said Brendan, raising his glass.

I didn't know what it meant. I was supposed to be learning Russian and I didn't even know what a simple Russian toast meant. They had gone to so much trouble with their food and wine. We had made a few sandwiches and bought a bottle of vodka—total time allocated to research and assembly, about twenty minutes. James and I were pathetic. We had really been shown up. We were obviously not dedicated enough. I felt completely deflated. Brendan and Joy were going to get the best baby in the orphanage, and we'd be left with a dud. The one that no one wanted. The one with all the diseases that we wouldn't be able to recognize, because we hadn't done enough research. Then we'd make a mess of telling the child they were adopted and they'd piss off back to Russia, find their birth mother, and never contact us again. I sipped my wine and sighed.

"Well done, Brendan and Joy," said Dervla, beaming at them. So the old witch was capable of smiling, I thought bitterly. "Now what has everyone else brought in?"

Much to my relief, the others weren't as well prepared as the golden couple. Gary and his wife had bought a couple of bottles of Tiger beer and Chinese take-out. Carole and her husband had made Vietnamese spring rolls, and the other couple had brought green tea and chocolate chopsticks. The red caviar sandwiches were absolutely revolting and were largely left untouched, but the vodka went down well, and everyone ended up getting quite merry. Emboldened by alcohol, I decided to approach Yvonne and ask if she was going to be our home study social worker.

"I'm sorry, Emma, I can't tell you who's going to be assigned to you. You'll have to wait until it's been finalized."

"Well, could you give me a clue?" I begged. "It would be so great if it was you. Is there anything I can do to get you to choose us?"

"No," said Yvonne, smiling at me. "Don't worry, all the social workers are equally nice."

Yeah right. Dervla was a real sweetie. I decided to press on and ask Yvonne the other question that had been eating away at me. My mouth, egged on by booze, ran away with me.

"Okay, I understand that you can't say. But can I ask you something else? It's about the second session we did. The thing is that I'm a bit worried about having made a fool of myself when we did the loss charts, and I just wanted to ask if I really messed up our chances. Have we been black marked? And if so, what can I do to make it better? Please tell me I haven't blown it. I really want a baby. Honestly, I know I'm not fluent in Russian and stuff, but I'm trying to learn the basics, and I've been reading all about the history of the country and I know I haven't had anything really bad happen to me like my parents dying in a horrible plane crash, but I have been really sad over the past few years with not being able to get pregnant and I know that sometimes I get a bit carried away, but I'm actually a very responsible individual. Honestly I'm very calm and together. As normal a person as you could hope to meet."

Yvonne put her hand on my shoulder. "Don't worry, Emma, you and James are—"

"Yvonne, I think we'd better hand out the home study information leaflets now," said Dervla, interrupting a crucial conversation at exactly the wrong time. What had Yvonne meant? Don't worry you're doing well. Don't worry it's not as bad as you think. Don't worry you can make up for it if you do everything perfectly in the home study. Don't worry what?!

Bloody Dervla. What on earth was I going to do if we got her as our home study social worker?

chapter TWENTY

LUCY AND DONAL were getting on famously. They were madly in love, and Donal was even pretending to be interested in the wedding plans.

"I'm thinking tiger lilies mixed with white roses," said Lucy, looking for approval.

"Oh I do love those tiger lilies," said Donal, clapping his hands together.

"Smart ass. What about your suit. We need to get you fitted out properly."

"I'll wear the suit I have."

"It's brown"

"What's wrong with brown?"

"Donal, that suit is about a hundred years old, and you will not be wearing it to our wedding. I'll book you an appointment with a decent tailor. Now, readings for the church."

"What about them?"

"Do you have any preferences on what ones you'd like?"

"Short ones."

"Okay. Photographs and/or video?"

"Neither. I don't want some poncy bloke chasing me around with a camera saying 'cheese' every five minutes."

"Well, tough because I want nice photos of my wedding."

"Okay, but don't get one of those creative types who'll have us swinging from trees. By the way did you get Annie's dress sorted out?"

Lucy winced. She had been avoiding Annie like the plague. She was supposed to call her at school and arrange a day to go shopping for dresses, but she was dreading it. She knew Annie would just upset her and wind her up, and she really didn't want to get into an argument with her. Lucy was afraid she might snap this time.

"No, I must give her a call about it."

"I'm about to call her now, so I'll put her on to you afterward and you can make arrangements."

Shit, thought Lucy, she really wasn't in the mood for the moody teenager. Donal called Annie and chatted to her for about ten minutes. Then he told her Lucy wanted a word, and he left the room so they could discuss their girly stuff in private.

Lucy took a deep breath. "Hi, Annie, how are you?"

"Fine. What do you want?"

"I wanted to arrange for you to take an afternoon off school so we could go shopping for your bridesmaid dress. When would be best for you?"

"Never."

"Okay, Annie, give me a break here. I'd really like you to be involved in the wedding. I'll buy you any dress you like, the choice is yours."

"I don't want your charity. There isn't going to be a wedding, you're not going to steal Donal away from me. I hate you, and I'd rather die than be your stupid bridesmaid."

Lucy counted to ten. "Look, Donal wants you to be involved, okay? I really don't care what you do, but for his sake can you please work with me on this?"

"Fuck off. I don't want anything to do with you. You don't love Donal. You're just a sad old cow who wants to get married before her vagina shrivels up."

"That's not true, and you know it. I do love Donal," said Lucy, beginning to get upset.

"No, you don't. Mary loved Donal, and she was nice and kind. The only person you care about is yourself. You'll make him miserable because you are a selfish ugly old bitch. I hope you die of cancer."

"Now listen here, you little brat. I've had enough of your insults. I've let you get away with murder. I am going to marry Donal whether you like it or not. So you better get used to the idea. And from now on you will treat me with respect, and if you don't I promise you I will make your life hell. Do you understand me? You're a spoilt little girl who needs a good slap and I'll be happy to oblige. You—"

Donal grabbed the phone. "Annie, it's Donal."

Lucy could hear Annie beginning to bawl down the other end of the phone. She was screaming, "She hates me. She said she's going to make my life hell. . . ."

Lucy left the room and sat on the edge of the bed. She was shaking. How much had Donal heard? Oh God, why had she lost her temper? Why did she rise to the bait? Annie was a teenager for God's sake. Shit shit shit.

Donal came in a few minutes later. He was really angry. The

veins on his neck were bulging. "What the hell were you doing? She's a child. A child who's lost everything. How could you speak to her like that? The poor girl is hysterical. What were you thinking?"

Lucy tried to suppress the lump forming in her throat. "Look, I'm sorry, but she was being really nasty and I just lost my temper."

"She's fifteen," shouted Donal. "I heard you telling her you'd make her life hell and give her a few slaps. What type of a person says that to a child. Jesus Lucy."

"I didn't mean it. She was saying some really horrible things to me and I just lost my temper."

"You're supposed to be the adult. The poor girl has had enough shit to deal with in her life without you threatening her. I'm shocked at you."

"She hates me. Okay? The girl hates me, she keeps telling me the wedding won't go ahead and that you don't love me and I don't love you. Every time you leave the room she starts bitching at me. You just never see it. So tonight I snapped. I was trying to be nice to her, but she kept coming back with nasty little comments. I'm sorry but she just wound me up. She's very difficult to deal with."

"No, she isn't. You've just handled it all wrong. She's a messed-up kid who needs attention and reassurance. My sister left her in my care, she's my priority, Lucy. If that's the way you're going to treat her then we have a serious problem here."

"What?"

"I can't have you upsetting her like that. It's not fair to her."

"What are you saying?"

"Call her back and grovel."

"Grovel?"

"Yes. You've really upset her, so you'll need to do some serious groveling."

"What about the things she said to me. Do I get an apology?"

"Grow up."

"Fuck you."

"Well, that's very mature."

"Are you always going to take her side?"

"Yes."

"Well, then, this isn't going to work."

"It would if you tried harder."

"Jesus, Donal, I've bent over backward for her. I can't do it anymore."

"So that's it? That's your answer?"

"Yes."

Donal didn't stop Lucy when she packed her bag, and he didn't say anything when she left. She cried all the way to my house, where she poured out the story. It was awful. She was devastated. I plied her with wine and tissues and she eventually cried herself to sleep. I went in to talk to James, who had made himself scarce when he saw the suitcase and the teary face.

"Oh God, James, it's awful. They've broken up over that stupid little brat."

"What happened?"

I filled him in.

"I have to say, in Donal's defense, Annie's his child. He has to put her first. And Lucy is the adult, she shouldn't have lost her temper."

"But Annie said she wanted her to die of cancer! Come on, James, the girl is like something from *The Omen*."

"Emma!"

"She is, I'm telling you. She's a total brat, and Donal obviously lets her get away with murder. And now she's broken up the best thing that ever happened to him. You'll have to talk to him. Make him see sense."

"I'll have a word at practice. I hope this doesn't put him off his game."

"James!"

"The semifinal is in five days, and I need Donal to be in top condition. He musn't be distracted. If he plays badly we'll lose."

"Well then tell him to get over here and beg Lucy to get back with him."

"I'll have a word."

"Have several—and don't focus on the rugby. Focus on his feelings and what a treasure Lucy is and how lucky he was to meet her and how he needs to get a grip and get down on his knees and beg her to come back."

The next day at practice, Donal was a mess. He looked as if he hadn't slept a wink. He couldn't concentrate. He kept dropping the ball, tripping over himself, and generally playing like a man with two left feet. James was not impressed. He took him aside after practice and tried to talk to him.

"So what's going on? Lucy stayed with us last night. We've no tissues left in the house."

"She upset Annie. I heard Lucy on the phone roaring at her, the poor child is a mess. What can I do? She says she'll kill herself if I marry Lucy. I know it's probably only talk, but she's a screwed-up kid and Lucy shouldn't have been nasty to her."

"Maybe you should come over tonight and talk to Lucy. I'm sure there's a perfectly reasonable explanation. Lucy's a rational person, she wouldn't have done it unless severely provoked. You did only hear one side of the conversation."

"Annie was distraught, James, you should've heard her. The

headmistress called me last night to ask my permission to give her a sedative to calm her down."

"How is she today?"

"Not too good at first, but when I told her Lucy had left, she cheered up."

"What about Lucy?"

"I dunno what to do. Sure I'm mad about Lucy." Donal sighed. He missed Lucy already. "My brain is fried with it all."

"Donal, you need to sort this out. I need you one hundred and ten percent on Saturday. Do whatever's necessary. Just make sure you're focused at practice tomorrow. We've only got two days left to get the moves right."

"I know, sorry about today, I'm all over the place. I'll be grand tomorrow."

"Well, you know where to find Lucy if you need to talk to her. Mind you, you'll have to get by Emma first, so wear padded clothing. She's not happy with you. And whatever you do, don't get drunk."

Donal went home and wandered around the house. What the hell was he going to do? He tried to figure it out, but his head was throbbing. He lay down and tried to sleep, but he just tossed and turned. Finally he did the one thing he knew would help him forget about it all for a while—he went out and got roaring drunk.

Donal stood at the bar being ear-bashed by a Leinster fan who was giving him chapter and verse on how the team should approach the semifinal against Ulster. Thankfully, Donal could only hear half of what the guy was saying because the music was so loud. He ordered another whiskey and downed it in one. His head was spinning, and just as he was contemplating lying down at the bar for a quick snooze, he saw a girl he recognized. She was young, great body, long blonde hair, very good-looking except for her big nose. How did he know her? He racked his brains. She looked up and caught his eye. She smiled and walked over.

"Well well well, if it isn't Donal Brady, pride of Leinster. Shouldn't you be at home getting your beauty sleep for the big match? I don't think James would be too happy to see the state of you."

chapter TWENTY-ONE

I RANG THE BELL. No answer. He was obviously out. Thank God for that. I was so annoyed with him that I'd probably say something I'd regret. Lucy had asked me to pick up a few things for her from Donal's house—work suits, makeup, and stuff. I put the key in the door and walked in. The place was a mess and reeked of booze. I was making my way over to the bedroom when I heard the toilet flush. Shit, he obviously was here. God, I hope he isn't naked in there.

"Hello," I said.

"Emma?" an all-too-familiar voice asked.

"What the . . ."

Babs strutted out of the bathroom wearing Donal's rugby jersey and nothing else. I stared at her. It couldn't be—Jesus Christ it *was* Babs.

"WHAT THE HELL IS GOING ON?" I screamed. "What are you doing here? What are you wearing? Where the hell is Donal?"

"Stop yelling, he's still in bed," said Babs, yawning.

"There had better be a very good explanation for this."

I grabbed her by the arm and marched into the bedroom where Donal was sitting up, looking panic-stricken.

"Well hello there, Donal. How are you? Good night's sleep then? Excellent. I was just wondering if you'd care to explain why my sister is prancing about your house naked, while your fiancée is sitting in my house HEARTBROKEN."

"Hold on now, don't go jumping to conclusions," said Donal, grasping at straws.

"What conclusions? That you and my naked sister played chess all night?"

"Chill out, Emma, I was bored, he was drunk, big deal."

"Chill out? I'm sorry, was I getting hot and bothered? How silly of me—after all, my sister shagging my best friend's fiancé is no big deal. How could you do this, you TRAMP?"

"Tell me we didn't have sex. Please," groaned Donal.

"Thanks a lot," said Babs, sitting on the edge of the bed. "I didn't hear any complaints last night."

"How did this happen?" said Donal, holding his head in his hands.

"I'd imagine your penis had something to do with it," I snapped.

"Emma, you're not going to tell Lucy are you?" asked Donal, looking petrified. "I'm begging you. Don't tell her. This was a huge mistake. I don't even remember coming home last night. I never meant this to happen. Jesus, Emma, I love Lucy."

"Mistake? Charming!" said Babs, throwing a pillow at him.

"No, I didn't mean mistake, you're a lovely girl, a fine-looking girl, and I'm sure loads of fellas are lining up to have sex with you. But it was not a good idea for me to be one of them. I'm in love with someone else, and the fact that you're Emma's sister isn't help-ing matters."

"Well you should have thought of that before you dragged her into bed," I growled.

"Are you going to tell Lucy?" Donal asked again.

"Are you going to apologize for being a dickhead to her about Annie?"

Donal sighed. "I have to put Annie first, Emma. I'm stuck with that. It's not necessarily what I want, but I was left in charge of her and her happiness is my priority."

"Oh wake up and smell the coffee, you idiot," I snapped. "She's a fifteen-year-old brat who's gotten away with murder. She needs a good talking-to. You have no idea the things she said to Lucy. Do you know she told Lucy she hoped she died of cancer? No you don't—because Lucy is too bloody nice to tell you that your precious Annie is a little bitch."

"Did she really say that to her?" asked Babs.

"Excuse me. Was I talking to you?" I hissed.

"Oh, what? You're ignoring me now?"

"Shut up and get dressed, looking at you in that jersey is mak-ing me sick. I swear Babs, you have gone too far this time."

"Ooooh, Emma, you're really scaring me with your big sister routine."

"Why do you always have to be such a pain in the ass? Don't you care about Lucy's feelings? Don't you give a shit about hurting someone you know?"

"Hey, don't blame me. He told me they'd broken up. How was I supposed to know it was only twenty-four hours ago."

I glared at Donal. "What have you got to say for yourself?"

"Nothing. I'm sorry about your sister. It was a really stupid thing to do. So will you tell Lucy?"

"I dunno. I'm going to think about it for a few days. Let you sweat it out. I'll decide after the match."

I waited for Babs to get dressed and dragged her out.

"How could you?"

"I was bored, he was there, it was easy. I'm single, he said he was too."

"So what are you going to do? Shag your way around Ireland until you get a job?"

"I can think of worse ways to spend your twenties."

"Not funny, Babs. Nothing about you is funny today. I don't want to talk to you anymore. I'm too annoyed."

"Fine with me."

I dropped her home, shoved her out of the car, and went for a drive. I parked the car at the seashore and sat back. What on earth was I going to do? I wanted to talk to James about it, but I knew that he needed to stay focused on the game. I'd tell him afterward, now was not a good time. And then there was Lucy. Should I tell her? No, I thought. No point. It was meaningless sex. Besides I was afraid she might hate me too, because Babs was my sister. Mind you, I'd like to let her loose on Babs. She would eat her for breakfast, and Babs could do with a good telling off. What did she call it? A boredom shag? The girl was impossible. She needed to grow up and start behaving like an adult. I thought back to my twenties. I was no angel either, but if I had an older sister, I wouldn't have gone around sleeping with her friends' boyfriends. Some things were just off-limits. And Donal. What did I think about Donal? Well, he was clearly an idiot—with all the girls in Dublin, he goes and sleeps with my sister.

I'd never really thought about what it must be like for Donal to have got stuck bringing up a teenager when his sister died. It had turned his life around. He had had to move back from a successful rugby career in England to look after her. She was, to all intents and purposes, his daughter, so I suppose he did have to put her first. Still, he should never have let Lucy go. He should have talked to her and found a way to work it out. And getting pissed and shagging Babs was totally out of order. Maybe Lucy was better off without him. He did love her though, you could see that. But was that enough? If he was off having sex with young blondes, twenty-four hours after breaking up with her, what did that demonstrate—weak mind, ruled by his penis, drunken fool, two-timer. . . .

James came home that evening fuming. I was in pretty crappy form myself, having had to lie to Lucy about Donal not being there when I called in to pick up her things. She had a work dinner that night, so James and I had the place to ourselves. James threw his backpack on the ground and stomped into the kitchen.

"Good day at the office?"

"What's the point?" he asked the wall. "What is the bloody point in turning up if you're going to perform like that?"

"What happened?"

"Donal turned up late, stinking of alcohol, and played atrociously. I'm thinking of dropping him for the game. He's the captain for God's sake. What kind of example is that to show the lads?"

"Yeah he's an irresponsible jerk all right," I said, enjoying the Donal bashing.

"He's not supposed to be drinking. Okay, I know he's had problems with Lucy, but I told him to put everything out of his mind until after the game on Saturday. If he doesn't play well it affects everyone. God, Emma, you should have seen him today. He dropped everything, missed tackles, and couldn't win a line-out to save his life. Christ at this rate we're going to lose the most important match of my career. And to add insult to injury, Tom Brown from the *Times* was at training today. I dread to think what the papers will say tomorrow."

"Don't worry. You'll be fine. You've done so much work for this match you'll definitely win."

"Research is no bloody good if you can't put it into practice because your captain's gone off the rails. Of all the times for them to split up, why did it have to be now? Why couldn't Lucy have argued with Annie some other time."

"Don't you dare blame Lucy for this. It's all Donal's stupid fault. If he wasn't such a shithead none of this would have happened. Poor Lucy is heartbroken while he's out getting pissed and shagging girls."

Shit! What had I just said?

"For goodness' sake, Emma, the guy went out for a few drinks to drown his sorrows. There's no need to start accusing him of being unfaithful," said James, thankfully assuming I was exaggerating as usual.

"Okay okay. So what would you like for dinner? Do you want a steak?"

"No, I'll just grab some toast," said the deflated coach, sighing.

"Come on, I'll cook you a nice steak. You need to keep your strength up to motivate the lads tomorrow."

We ate in silence. Both of us fuming with Donal—for very different reasons.

I got up early the next day to grab the paper before James got to it. Tom Brown was not kind and not generous.

Leinster's captain and supposed jewel in the crown, Donal Brady, arrived late to training yesterday, looking as if he'd had a night on the tiles. With only two days to go to the match it was sad to see such unprofessional behavior. Coach James Hamilton was clearly furious and gave Brady a rollicking on the sidelines. The team spent the next two hours practicing line-outs, scrimmaging, and some new back-row moves. But it was marred by Brady's inability to catch the ball, tackle any-one, or run more than five yards without stopping to retch. Unless Hamilton comes up with a miracle, it looks—to this sports writer and disappointed Leinster fan—like an easy victory for Ulster tomorrow.

I sat down on the stairs. James was going to go mad. He'd be so disappointed. I could kill Donal. Not only was he ruining my best friend's life but he was now about to ruin my husband's career. I threw the paper in the trash, hiding it under the leftovers of last night's dinner. James came down.

"Where's the paper?"

"Dunno, it never arrived."

"Emma."

"I swear it didn't come."

"It must be savage if you're protecting me from seeing it. Where is it?"

"Don't read it. It's mean, and that stupid old Tom Brown doesn't know what he's talking about."

James opened the trash and fished out the soggy paper. He turned to the sports page and read in silence.

"Look on the bright side, at least now you're the underdogs, so when you win, the victory will be all the more sweet. Like Britain in the Second World War."

James managed a limp smile and glumly went off to take the final practice session. As he left, the postman arrived. Among the mountains of bills there was an official-looking letter. I opened it: it was from the Adoption Board, telling me that Dervla Egan had been appointed as our home study social worker. She'd be in touch to arrange dates and times.

Could this week possibly get any worse?

chapter TWENTY-TWO

PRACTICE ON FRIDAY went marginally better than Thursday—due mostly to Donal's sobriety. But James was still a wreck on Friday night. He paced up and down the bedroom, muttering to himself about career-defining moments and winning is everything. I had moved the Post-it from the fridge up to the bedroom and stuck it on the headboard—*Winning is a mind-set, attitude is everything.* I tried to get him to calm down. I offered him food, drink, sex, songs, baths, massages . . . anything I could think of, but he was too uptight. Eventually, realizing that I wasn't going to get any sleep either, I went downstairs to make myself some tea. I found Lucy in the kitchen, crying over a glass of wine. I sat down and hugged her.

"I'm just so lonely. I can't believe this is happening. I love him, Emma. He's the first guy I've ever met who I feel totally myself with. He made me feel so good about myself. He's always telling me how clever I am and beautiful and sexy and fun. I never thought a guy could make you feel so wonderful. I miss him. I can't believe we've broken up. Is this it? Am I doomed to go back to the shelf? I can't bear it; I just can't bear to go back to being alone again. I know I'll never find someone who'll love me so completely."

I was crying now too. Poor Lucy, it was awful. Damn Donal and his rotten niece and his drunken sex. I sat up listening to Lucy and tried in vain to console her until we both eventually gave in to sleep and went to bed. Thankfully James had fallen into a fitful sleep, so at least I got a few hours of rest.

The next morning I waved a very pale and anxious-looking coach off to war. I told him how proud I was of him and that no matter what happened today he had already proven to everyone how great he was.

Lucy came to the match with me. We met Dad outside the stadium. Babs was standing beside him. I couldn't believe it.

"What the hell are you doing here?" I snapped.

"Supporting James."

"Since when have you ever supported James?"

"Since now."

"Bored at home were you? Nothing to do but sit around on your ass all day causing havoc."

"Ladies, we're at a rugby game, can you please not bicker for the next two hours. Come on, Lucy, you're the only sane one here," said Dad, talking Lucy by the arm and escorting her in.

"You little cow," I hissed.

"Just wanted to check out if Donal is as good on the field as he is in bed."

I grabbed her arm. "Have you no respect for Lucy's feelings?"

"I didn't know she was going to be here. Dad just said he was meeting you." Babs shrugged. "And if I was you, I'd start being nicer to me or she'll suspect something."

"I don't want to hear another word out of you. Do you understand?"

"Relax, I'm not interested in an old fogey like Donal. I heard the scrum half was cute, so I decided to check him out. I'm planning on taking up your suggestion to shag my way through my boredom. I'm starting with rugby teams."

I decided to ignore her—I was wound up enough about the game and sick with nerves for James. We all sat down together. I put Dad and myself in between Lucy and Babs. Lucy got a bit teary when she saw Donal running onto the field, but she held it together.

"What do you think, Dad?" I asked, desperate for him to tell me Leinster was going to sail through.

"It'll be a tight one, love. That Ulster out-half is a dangerous weapon."

"But Leinster will win won't they?"

Come on, Dad, work with me here. Your son-in-law is giving himself a heart attack down there.

"It's hard to say. It'll be close."

"Dad," I whispered. "I need reassurance, not honesty."

"Right love, sorry. I'd say Leinster will walk away with it. That coach they have is a genius."

"Much better," I said, smiling at him. "Keep it up."

Both teams seemed nervous to begin with. Possession lurched from one side to the other. They were six all—two penalties apiece until five minutes before halftime, when Donal passed the ball, which was intercepted by an Ulster player, who then ran the length of the field and scored a try.

"Jesus Christ," said Dad. "What's Donal doing? That was dreadful. He's having a shocking game. I don't know what's wrong with him. That could cost them the match."

I looked down at James, who was deathly pale. The referee's whistle went, and the teams ran into the locker rooms.

"I hope James has some stern words," said Dad. "They're not playing well. Donal's supposed to be their danger man, and he's not in the game at all. Very poor," he said, shaking his head.

Lucy looked surprisingly upbeat. "He looks miserable. He's obviously missing me too," she said, smiling for the first time in days.

My stomach was doing backflips. If they lost this match James was going to be gutted. Come on Leinster, I prayed—please win. They came back out, and for the next fifteen minutes, Donal lost the ball in the Leinster line-out and then missed a crucial tackle for Ulster to score another try. It was awful. I felt sick. Poor James. Dad was muttering under his breath. Then I saw James motion to the referee—he pulled Donal off and put on a young replacement—Peter O'Hare. Donal walked off the field to some booing. The supporters were not happy with his dreadful performance. For the next half an hour we watched as Leinster pulled back with a couple of penalties and a drop goal. With three minutes left, Peter stole an Ulster line-out ball and charged over the line for a try. If the kicker could convert the try, Leinster would win. Ray Phelan placed the ball down and took three steps back and prepared himself for the most important kick of his career. You could hear a pin drop in the stadium. We all held our breath. He ran toward the ball and kicked it. It wobbled and swayed in the wind and then it hit the post . . . but somehow it managed to drop over. The stadium erupted. Leinster was in the final.

I sobbed with relief as Dad hugged me. James looked up and searched the stands to find us. We waved and jumped up and down. He saw me and beamed. I blew him kisses. Even Dad had tears in his eyes. Donal, meanwhile, walked back to the dressing room, head down. He was a broken man. Lucy was delighted. As far as she was concerned it proved he loved her and missed her as much as she did. She was right—except that the guilt of having had sex with my sister was an additional weight on his mind.

We went to the clubhouse where James was carried in, shoulder high. The atmosphere was fantastic.

"God, James I'm so proud of you," I said, hugging him.

"I feel as if I've run a marathon. What a game. Thank God it's over," he said, beaming at me.

I could see Lucy looking around for Donal. I asked James where he was. He said he'd gone straight home. Donal was devastated by his poor performance. Lucy was upset that she'd missed him, but even she was carried along with the carnival atmosphere in the clubhouse. Babs spent the evening chatting up Donal's replacement, Peter—at least, at twenty-four, he was closer to her age group.

Tom Brown's headline the next day screamed—"Leinster Pulls Back from Brink of Defeat." He lavished praise on James and Peter O'Hare, and absolutely trashed Donal. He said it was sad to see such a talented player stoop so low. He couldn't understand how someone who had played so brilliantly in the quarter finals could have performed so badly a few weeks later. His mind was clearly not on the game. He looked dreadful, he was distracted and had almost lost the match with that appalling intercept pass.

James winced as he read it.

"Poor Donal, that's some roasting. I'll give him a buzz and see how he is."

James tried ringing him, but Donal's mobile was switched off. "I'll call over to him later, see how he's doing. I felt really bad having to pull him off, but he was doing more harm than good."

"Don't you blame yourself. It was his fault he got himself into this mess and his fault he played badly. If you hadn't pulled him off, the team would have lost. Stuff him, let him suffer a bit."

"That's a bit harsh, darling. Donal's our best player, he just had an off day."

"A few off days if you ask me," I mumbled.

"Come on, Emma, give him a break. He's feeling bad enough as it is."

"So he bloody well should. Sly dog that he is."

"Sly?"

"Yes."

"What's he done that's so sly."

"Had sex with Babs," I said, taking a sip of my tea, as if I'd just said something incredibly banal.

"WHAT!" said James. "You're putting me on."

"Shhhhh. I don't want Lucy to hear. He had sex with Babs the night he got really drunk."

"Well hats off to him."

"Hats off? For what? Screwing my sister when he's supposed to be grieving over the breakup with my best friend?"

"Ok, timing-wise it wasn't great. But getting a twenty-three-year-old into bed is good going."

"James, you're talking about Babs here. Not some random young one."

"I'd say she gave him a run for his money," said James, laughing. "No wonder he was in such a state that day, he was obviously exhausted."

James called over to Donal later that day to check up on him and to tease him mercilessly about Babs.

"Howrya," said Donal, answering the door.

"Hi. Sorry Babs couldn't make it, she has play group on Sundays."

"Emma told you."

"You dog."

"I don't even remember it. I was out of my mind drunk. I'm sorry if you're offended about it, being Babs and all. She's a great girl, I didn't mean for anything to happen."

"She's an innocent girl, Donal, you really overstepped the mark."

"Jesus James, I'm sorry, I—" Donal, looked up and saw James smirking at him. "You prick. Innocent my ass, she's as wild as they come. God you had me going there."

"So how are you? You shouldn't have left yesterday after the game you know. You got us to the semis."

"Yeah, and then I made a right balls of it. We nearly lost because of me."

"You had an off day. It happens. Especially when you've broken up with your fiancée and shagged a minor."

"Screw you," groaned Donal. "Peter had a good game."

"Yep he did. Sorry I had to take you off. I knew you weren't going to improve. It was just one of those days."

"What about the final? Will you pick him over me?"

"Not if you can sort out your head and get back to form."

"Don't worry, I'll do my best."

"Okay, well I'll leave you to it. See you at practice on Tuesday."

First thing the next morning, Donal arrived on our doorstep bearing an enormous bunch of tiger lilies and asked to speak to Lucy. I made myself scarce and left them to it. An hour later they emerged, beaming, from the living room. Donal left and Lucy asked me to help her pack.

"Oh my God, Lucy, what happened?"

"It's all sorted. Everything's okay," said Lucy.

She told me what had happened: Annie had called Donal the day after the semifinal. She had watched the match on TV and read the reviews in the paper the next day. In one of the postmatch interviews, Ray Phelan had defended Donal, saying that his disastrous performance was due entirely to his recent breakup with his fiancée and had nothing to do with his age or lack of fitness. Donal's mind simply wasn't on the game, said Ray, the poor man was heartbroken. Ray said he hoped that Donal would be able to sort out his private life before the final, because the team really needed him to be on form to win the cup. Annie began to realize how badly affected Donal was by the split and began to feel guilty.

"Apparently she was sobbing on the phone and telling him she was sorry and she had never meant for Donal to suffer and she didn't want him to lose his job," said Lucy. "Then she confessed to being a bitch to me and told him that she had been doing everything she could to make my life miserable. She told him all the horrible things she used to say to me as soon as he left the room and how she kept telling me that Mary was the love of his life. In fairness to Annie, it seems to have been a very thorough confession," Lucy added.

"Donal said that she admitted it wasn't me she hated, it was the thought of him being devoted to someone else. She's terrified of being left out and said that she can't bear to share him with anyone because he's all she has, but she understands now that she's just being selfish and he has a right to be happy in a relationship. So Donal promised her that nothing would change when we got married and reassured her that she'd always be his number-one priority, but that there was room for more than one person in his life and she was wrong to have interfered and been rude to me."

"About bloody time he stuck up for you," I interrupted.

Lucy smiled. "I know. I was particularly pleased to hear that bit. Anyway, it seems that they talked for ages, and Donal said she'd have to apologize to me."

"Beg you to forgive her would be more appropriate," I said.

"Apparently she's also promised to be extra nice to me from now on, to make up for her behavior. Though I'll believe that when I see it," said Lucy. "But the best part is that Donal got down on one knee and said he was sorrier than he could ever say and the last few days of his life were the worst ever and that he never wanted us to be apart again. He said he was sorry for taking Annie's side, but that it was his instinct to protect her. He said he hated himself for hurting me and he'd do everything he could to make it up to me."

"And so he should," I said. "You make sure he pampers you properly for a long time. He has a lot of making up to do."

"Don't worry, I will. You'll also be pleased to hear that Donal thinks I'm very lucky to have a friend like you and that he hopes you'll forgive him too. He obviously knows how loyal you are and that you're annoyed with him because I was upset, which is sweet."

"Isn't it just," I said.

Nice touch Donal, I thought. Don't worry, your secret is safe.

chapter TWENTY-THREE

A FEW DAYS AFTER THE SEMIFINAL VICTORY we were notified that our first home visit would take place the following week—four days before the final. Leinster was playing Edinburgh in the European Cup final, in Twickenham in London. We were all flying over—Mum and Dad, Lucy and Babs—to support them. Sean was going to meet us there, along with James's parents and Henry.

Three days before the home visit I began to scrub the house. Everything had to be perfect. I knew Dervla would be the type to open wardrobes and look under beds, so I got out the plastic gloves and set to. I cleaned every corner and crevice. Any remotely dangerous-looking objects that could harm a child—like my hair straightener, James's squash racket, the vibrator Babs had given me the year before to spice up our sex life, the ironing board, golf clubs, bleach . . . were locked away. I wanted Dervla to be dazzled by our home. I went out and bought cuddly toys and put them on the bed in the spare room. I scattered numerous—how to be a good parent, raise a normal stable child as opposed to a murdering serial killer one, not make a total mess of your baby's future—books around the house.

When Danika came to clean, she was shocked to see how tidy the house was. She looked around her, open-mouthed.

"So clean!" she exclaimed.

"Yes," I said. "Clean for the adoption people."

"Baby is coming?" she asked, looking surprised. I had tried to fill her in about the adoption, but I wasn't sure how much she had actually understood.

"No, not yet. Uhm, the inspector is coming," I said.

"Ah," she said, nodding. "Inspector is coming to see house."

""Yes, exactly, so it has to be very clean. If it is not clean—then no baby."

"No clean, no baby?" she asked, wide-eyed.

"Well no, not exactly, but we have to make the good impression," I said, resorting to pidgin English as I always seemed to do with Danika, which was no help to her language skills at all. "The inspector must think we are good, clean people."

"But baby from Russia," said Danika. "Not clean in Russia."

She had a point; the orphanages were probably not the most hygienic of places. "Yes, but that is why we must be clean in Ireland. So the baby can be happy."

"Clean house, happy inspector, happy baby."

"Yes," I nodded, smiling at her. That pretty much summed up the situation.

On the eve of the visit, James came in late and was putting his key in the door when I opened it.

"Off," I said, pointing to his sneakers. "I won't have you coming in and messing up the place."

James sighed and took off his shoes. He came in, dumped his bag on the floor, and headed for the shower. I picked up his bag and followed him. He took off his clothes, threw them on the floor, and walked into the bathroom. I went in after him.

"What are you doing?" he asked me, none too pleased that I was following him around.

"Don't splash about when you're in there and use this towel," I said, handing him an old towel. "And make sure you wash down any stray pubic hairs when you're finished, and use the old soap not the nice new one. That's just for show. And don't drip when you get out. Dry yourself in there. I don't want wet footprints on the floor."

James pushed me out the door and locked it.

"And no smelly poos," I shouted through the keyhole. "If you need to do one, either control yourself or go down to the pub. No stinking out our loo tonight. And put the wet towel in the dryer when you're finished, I don't want damp-towel smells in the bathroom either. "

The door opened. "Emma! I'm going to have a shower now and I think it would be wise for you to go downstairs because if you keep shouting instructions through the door, I may have to kill you and that would definitely put a dampener on the adoption plans."

"Fine," I said huffily, picking his clothes up off the floor and folding them. "I hope you're not going to be this aggressive tomorrow. You'd swear I was one of those nagging wives, instead of a slave who goes around cleaning up after you."

James seemed to find this very amusing, I could hear him laughing as he closed the door. I went down and made him a sandwich. I didn't want to cook because it would smell up the kitchen and the pots and pans were all neatly stacked away. When James came down, I handed him the sandwich and told him he had to eat it over the sink because I didn't want crumbs on the floor.

"I'm assuming this is a temporary change of character?" he asked, leaning into the sink. "You aren't going to be like this permanently are you? I'm rather fond of the old Emma. The one who's not adverse to crumbs and allows me to use towels that don't skin me alive when I'm trying to dry myself."

"I'm just trying to make sure that everything is perfect for Dervla's visit. I'm a nervous wreck about it. She clearly thinks I'm an idiot with the worst loss chart she's ever seen, so I'm trying to get good marks for my clean, baby-friendly house," I said, picking a tiny crumb off the floor.

James leaned in closer to the sink and took one last bite.

"Now remember, James, we have to agree on everything. I don't want Dervla to think we have any differences of opinion. So if I say something and you don't agree, just bite your tongue and I'll do the same. And don't try to be funny. I'm sorry, but you just aren't funny and it doesn't work. And if I exaggerate something a little bit, just let it go, don't start picking me up on things. If you see me going like this," I said, rubbing my nose, "stop talking. That's going to be my sign for 'shut up.'"

"I presume it works both ways," said James.

"Well, yes I suppose so," I said.

"So when I rub my nose you'll stop talking?"

"Yes and vice versa. Now I want you to wear your gray trousers, not the—"

James began to rub his nose furiously.

* * *

I got up the next morning feeling very groggy, after a restless night. I had nightmares about Dervla coming to the house and finding me naked, knee deep in foul-smelling rubbish. James was up already doing a telephone interview with the *Scottish Tribune.*

" . . . looking forward to it . . . very pleased to have got to the final . . . Edinburgh is a great side, they'll be hard to beat, but I'm confident we'll put in a good performance . . . Donal Brady will be playing . . . one bad game doesn't mean he's past his prime . . . Peter will be on the subs bench . . . yes he's a fine young player . . . my goal this year was to win the cup and that's what I intend to do. . . ."

I hovered around, plumping cushions and rearranging baby books. At nine o'clock he was still on the phone so I tapped my watch and whispered, "It's nine, she's due any minute, hang up."

James ignored me and turned around to continue his interview. I poked him. He pushed my hand away. I poked him again. "James, hang up."

"Sorry Mike could you excuse me a minute," said James, trying to sound jocular as he covered the receiver with is hand and hissed at me. "I'm in the middle of a bloody interview. Will you please stop poking me. When she arrives I'll hang up. Now go away and clean something."

I went into the kitchen and tried to calm down. Five deep breaths later, the doorbell rang. I heard James hang up. He came in and saw me glued to the seat. I was too scared to move.

"Ready, darling?"

"No!" I said, feeling sick. "I'm terrified."

"It'll be fine," he said squeezing my hand. "Come on, we better let the old dragon in."

* * *

We sat down in the kitchen and I offered Dervla tea or coffee. She said no to both.

"Maybe Dervla needs a whiskey to kick-start the proceedings," said James, trying to be funny when I had specifically told him not to be.

Dervla didn't even crack a smile. "A glass of water would be fine thank you."

"One glass of H_2O coming right up," said our resident comedian as I rubbed my nose vigorously.

Once the glass of water had been delivered, and James was sitting down, Dervla explained what the home study would entail and what ground we would be covering over the six sessions. According to old poker face, we'd be going over a lot of the same ground we had covered in the group sessions but in more detail, as well as discussing some new issues. The visits would cover: our lives in general, the stability of our relationship, our motives for adopting, our knowledge and experience of young children, our capacity for the parenting role, our expectations concerning the child, identity and culture, our attitude to the birth parents, the impact of infertility on our lives, our relations and other social networks, our personalities and interests, religion, and attitude to life, and our openness to individual differences. The interviews were to take place every two weeks and would last for two hours. During this time, our references would also be visited.

I was reeling. My God, by the end of these visits, she'd know more about us than anyone else did. I was worried that James would tell her that I'd been a bit of a lunatic on the fertility drugs the year before. I glanced over at him. He was sipping his coffee, and I could tell by his face that he was thinking about the bloody match. He was miles away. I kicked him under the table.

Dervla went on to say that one of the home study sessions

would require us to be interviewed separately. I didn't like the sound of that. I'd have to coach James to make sure we had the same answers to all potential questions. Then Dervla said she'd like to look around the house. As we moved from room to room, she jotted down notes on her pad, which I tried to read but couldn't. She didn't exactly whoop when she saw the spare room with all the cuddly toys and the baby books. She just kept scribbling on her stupid pad and nodding from time to time. Her silence made me nervous so I twittered on about nothing as we walked around the house. I asked her if she had any children of her own.

"No, none"

"Are you married?"

"No, and I'm really not here to talk about myself. We need to keep focused on you and James," she said, turning her back on me to end the conversation.

Hardly bloody surprising she wasn't married I thought, with a personality like that. We went back downstairs, and Dervla asked us to talk about why we wanted to adopt. Before I had a chance to open my mouth, James was off. He told her that after trying for two years to get pregnant and undergoing several different types of fertility treatment, we had decided to adopt a child.

"Emma was getting very down as the treatments continued to fail, and the drugs she was on were making her very moody and upset, so we decided to pack it in and get back to having a normal life and a sex life that wasn't ruled by a thermometer," said James, laughing as I turned purple from embarrassment and rage. What was he doing? She didn't need to know all this. Him and his big mouth. I glared at him.

"How's your sex life now? Would you describe it as healthy?" asked Dervla.

I decided to jump in and do some damage control. "It's great actually. Very healthy thanks. It was fine when we were trying to have a baby too, just a bit regimented I suppose. No big deal."

"How often would you have sex?"

Nosy cow. Why the hell was she so interested in our sex life? What difference did that make to our child?

"We're always at it. At least twice a day," said the court jester as I rubbed my nose.

"Ha ha," I said in a lame pretense that I found my husband amusing. "No, seriously, our sex life is fine," I added, trying desperately to decide what a "healthy" amount of sex was. Should we be hanging from the rafters every night? Or should we be only doing it at the odd time. Too much would look self-indulgent and she might think we'd be too busy having sex to bring up our child. Too little would make it seem as if we weren't attracted to each other and that our marriage might be on the rocks. I opted for middle ground. "We have sex on average three times a week."

On hearing this blatant lie, James began to choke on his coffee as he tried not to laugh. Luckily I was on hand to thump him on the back—which I did with gusto. While James recovered his breath and dodged my thumps, Dervla began to leaf through our file until she came across an all-too-familiar-looking letter.

"I see from your correspondence that you are willing to adopt siblings," she said.

Shit! I had completely forgotten about the letter I'd written to the adoption people shortly after applying, telling them we'd be happy to adopt a whole family of children—I may have even said a whole village, I couldn't remember. Damn, I hadn't mentioned it to James, and now he was sitting there looking stunned.

"Oh yes, that letter I sent. Well, I was probably being a bit hasty," I said, trying to backtrack. "It would be nice to have a ready-made family in one go, but I realize now that it might be difficult to actually manage more than one child at a time, especially if they're sick or damaged in any way. I see now that it would be better for us to focus on one."

"How do you feel about adopting more than one child, James?"

"I think perhaps Emma was being overenthusiastic as she can be at times," said Judas. "I think one child at a time is quite sufficient."

Dervla made notes as I silently cursed myself. James looked at me, eyebrows raised. I mouthed *sorry.*

"Would you like to adopt a boy or a girl or are you open to either?"

"Either," we both said in unison. At least we agreed on something.

"We really don't mind. We just want a healthy little baby," I said.

"The child may not be healthy though, you must be aware of that," said the voice of doom.

"We know about the pitfalls, but we feel that we'll be able to cope. We have a lot of family support, and we'll obviously get any medical expertise that is required," I said, hoping I sounded more confident than I felt. I was terrified of ending up with a baby who was terminally ill or so emotionally scarred that the baby spent all day banging its head off the wall like the little boy in the video they had shown us.

Thankfully, it seemed to be the right answer because Dervla didn't pursue the line of questioning. I felt as if we were on trial. I was afraid to say anything that might upset our chances.

"Do you get the opportunity to spend much time with children?" asked Dervla.

"Yes. My brother, Henry, has three children. Thomas who's

four and twin girls—Sophie and Luisa—who will be two in a couple of months. They spent Christmas with us this year, so we had some good practice. We had great fun, but we were exhausted after they left, weren't we, darling?" said James.

I frowned at him. I didn't want Dervla to think we were worn out after spending one measly week with three children. She'd think we were pathetic.

"Not really, we were more invigorated than tired," I said, attempting to do some damage control. "I was particularly pleased to get to spend quality time with my godchild, Sophie."

"How would you describe your relationship with your nephew and nieces?"

"Very good," I jumped in before James could tell her how much I loathed Thomas. "They are all lovely children, although I must confess I'm particularly attached to Sophie, who I adore. She's beautiful and very placid. She's just perfect," I said wistfully.

"Tell me, Emma, when you were having fertility treatments did you get very depressed?"

"No, not at all. When James said I got a bit down, he just meant that I was a bit fed up about taking the drugs because the side effects were a bit unpleasant. But I certainly wouldn't use the word *depressed*. God no. I'm a very positive upbeat person. There is no history of depression in my family—none at all." I didn't want her thinking we were all suicidal maniacs.

"Okay, well how did the failure to have a child affect your relationship? It's a very stressful time for couples," said Dervla, showing a human side. "Did it cause tension between you?"

"No," I said.

"Not tension," said James. "But it did take over our lives. It was all-encompassing, which was difficult at times."

At this stage I had practically rubbed my nose off, clearly James was going to ignore our code, so I gave up and let him talk.

"But I can honestly say that the experience has made us closer. In a world where people are having children every day, it can be very isolating when you are struggling with it. I admire Emma so much for what she went through. I would say without a doubt that our relationship has strengthened and deepened because of it."

Sometimes you forget how much you love someone. I could feel a lump forming in my throat as James finished speaking. I willed it away. Now was not the time to cry. Even Dervla looked impressed. She actually smiled at him.

"Is that the way you feel too, Emma?" she asked gently.

I nodded. It was exactly the way I felt.

chapter TWENTY-FOUR

JAMES AND THE TEAM flew to London the day after the home visit. The rest of us flew out two days later, on the eve of the match. Dad collected me and we drove out to the airport. I got into the car and sat beside Babs, who I was still furious with.

"This is all very exciting," said Mum, turning around in the front seat. "I can't remember the last time we went away together. How's poor James? Stressed to the max, I suppose."

"He actually seems okay," I said. "He seemed more nervous before the semifinal, which is a bit weird."

"Well you have to understand, this final is the furthest Leinster has ever got, so he's already broken a record," said Dad. "If they win it'll be incredible, but even if they don't, he has achieved an incredible feat in only two years. He's some coach."

"Is Peter going to be playing?" Babs asked, suddenly taking an interest in the team.

I ignored her.

"Hellooo, Emma, I'm talking to you."

"Piss off. I don't know what the hell you're doing coming over for the match."

"My boyfriend, Peter, is on the team."

"Boyfriend!" I snorted. "Since when?"

"Since the semifinal. We've been out every night, he's mad about me."

"Are you talking about Barbara's new boyfriend," said Mum, looking very pleased. "He seems like a lovely young lad. Very talented too. Will he be playing d'you think?"

"No. Donal will," I snapped.

"Yeah, well, if he plays as badly as he did in the semis James'll have to take him off again and Peter will get on," said Babs.

"If Donal hadn't been so riddled with guilt, he wouldn't have played so badly."

"What was he guilty about?" asked Mum.

"He just did something silly," I said.

"He had the best night of his life," said Babs. "That's why he was so distracted."

"What did he do?" asked Mum

"Nothing," I said, glaring at Babs, who was smirking at me.

"Isn't he engaged to your Lucy?" asked Mum.

"Yes he is, Mum, and they are very happy and very in love."

"Ah, that's nice to hear."

Babs made sick noises.

"Even you'll fall in love someday, Barbara," said Mum. "Look at Lucy and Donal."

"I'd love to end up with a guy like Donal. He's so . . . what's the word, Emma?" she said, beaming at me. "Oh yeah, faithful. He's so faithful and loyal."

"Enough," said Dad. "Where is Sean when I need him? I can't

listen to any more of this drivel. Can we please talk about the match?"

"Okay, Dad. Who's going to win?" I asked.

"I think Leinster will do it. Edinburgh has a slight advantage in that their back row is quicker, but I think—"

"Has Lucy got her dress yet?" asked Mum as Dad thumped the steering wheel in frustration.

Lucy was waiting for us when we got to the airport. I was nervous about leaving Babs alone with her, so I glued myself to Lucy's side and ordered Babs to sit at the other end of the plane. Dad rushed into the bar and had a testosterone-filled thirty minutes talking to other Leinster supporters about the game.

We landed and went straight to the hotel. Sean was going to meet us there for a drink. Dad was delighted to be staying in the team hotel. He was getting a lot of kudos from the supporters for being father-in-law to the coach. He was in his element. James and Donal were with Sean in the bar when we arrived. They were drinking orange juices and looking nervous. Dad plonked himself down between them to get the inside track into the planned tactics for the final. When Donal saw Babs strut into the lounge with Lucy, he nearly passed out. He looked at me, panic-stricken, and I tilted my head toward Peter. Relief flooded his face when Babs went and wrapped herself around Peter. Poor old Peter, he was clearly besotted with her. I could see him hanging on her every word. Still, I thought, at least he was keeping her away from Donal.

Every time I tried to talk to James, a supporter would come up and thump him on the back to wish him luck or quiz him on the game plan or proffer advice. His phone rang constantly as everyone he had ever known called to cheer him on. The atmosphere in the hotel bar was fantastic. Word had got out where the team was staying, and supporters arrived in droves. At ten-thirty James ordered the team to bed. They left to the sound of cheers and whoops. I followed James upstairs as Dad, Sean, and the other supporters settled in for a long night of singing and drinking.

Donal and Lucy got the lift up with us, and as we parted to go to our rooms, Donal and James shook hands grimly.

"Sleep well, captain, big day tomorrow."

"You too, coach, and don't worry, the lads are all fired up. We're going to win it for you."

Lucy and I had to look away. Donal and James were not the touchy-feely emotional types. . . . It was a bit like in *Butch Cassidy and the Sundance Kid* when Robert Redford (how good did he look in that movie!) and Paul Newman (likewise) jumped off the cliff together. I suppose the female equivalent was when Thelma and Louise drove over the cliff in the car—except that Donal and James weren't in a life-threatening situation.

When we got to the room, James collapsed on the bed. He looked shattered.

"Are you all right? You look exhausted," I said, snuggling up to him.

"I'm fine, thanks, I just haven't been sleeping much. I'm completely wired. I can't believe we're in the final. The final, Emma. Who would have thought when I took over in the middle of the season last year that we'd make it this far."

"It's amazing, James. I'm really proud of you. You deserve every bit of it, you've worked so hard."

"Yes, but it's been worth it. Look what the boys gave me tonight at dinner," he said, fishing a package out of his pocket. It was a silver stopwatch and on the back was engraved: *To Coach—use this to time our victory lap tomorrow. From the Squad.*

"Oh, it's lovely."

"It really is. I was very pleased to get it. Right, I better work on my speech. I need to really get them going tomorrow before the game. It has to hit the right note," he said, settling down with his notepad.

I knew he'd take ages over it and I wasn't sleepy, so I went back down to the lounge to see Sean. He was sitting with Dad and a crowd of supporters singing "Dublin in the Rare Auld Time." I pulled him away and we sat up at the bar.

"So, how are you?" I asked.

"Great. You?"

"Fine. How's Shadee?"

"Very well. Things are really good."

"Have her parents come 'round to the idea of an Irish boyfriend?"

"I haven't managed to totally convert them yet, but I'm working on it. We had them over for dinner last week, and it went fairly well."

"Define 'fairly.'"

"Put it this way—I managed to persuade them that I am not an alcoholic, that I didn't come over to London to plant bombs, that I think all terrorists should be locked up, that I'm not going out with their daughter to shock my family, that I have never been a priest or wanted to be one, and that I won't force Shadee to convert to Catholicism, worship the pope, or change anything about herself."

"Wow, it must have been a long night."

"It was. They almost made Mum seem reasonable," said Sean, grinning.

I looked up and saw Babs chatting up some young supporter. "She's unbelievable, Peter has only just gone to bed."

"Ah, she's just young and carefree . . . and a vixen."

"She's getting out of control, Sean. She needs to get a job. She has far too much time on her hands," I said, sounding alarmingly like my mother.

"Not for long," said Sean, laughing. "Dad told her yesterday that he's cutting off her allowance as of this month, so she's going to have to start working."

"About bloody time. She's been sitting on her ass since she graduated."

"I'm glad you feel that way because she told me she was going to work for you as your assistant. To quote her, 'slapping makeup on people is easy and pays well, so I'll just hang around with Emma and learn the ropes before going out on my own.'"

"WHAT? Over my dead body is that little cow coming to work with me," I said, raging at the cheek of her to even suggest it.

"What are you talking about?" asked Dad, joining us.

"Babs thinking she's going to work with me."

"I see. Actually, Emma, I think it's a very good idea. She looks up to you, and it'll only be for a few weeks until she's learned what to do. After that she tells me, she's off to Hollywood to make up the film stars."

"I'm sorry Dad but (a) you should have consulted me first and (b) it's my job we're talking about here, and there is no way I am having that lunatic meeting my clients."

"She has promised to behave. As a favor to me will you let her do it for a couple of weeks? She has us driven mad at home," begged Dad, who had never in his life asked me to do anything for him. "Barbara, come over here," he shouted.

"What?" she asked, hands on hips.

"I've told Emma that you want to work with her and that you promised to behave yourself and just stay quietly in the background to observe and learn. She's a bit dubious, and who can blame her. Tell her what you told me."

"Now that Dad's decided to let me starve, I have to get a job. So I've decided to learn how to be a makeup artist, and it seems stupid to waste money on a course when you do it for a living, so I just want to work with you for a few weeks. It's no big deal. It's not like it's rocket science, I'll pick it up in no time. And don't worry, I won't embarrass you or show you up."

Dad was looking at me with pleading eyes. I sighed and nodded.

"Okay, I'll give you three weeks. Thankfully all my clients are women, so at least I won't have to worry about *that* side of things. But if you open your mouth or annoy me in any way—you're out. Do you understand?"

"Yes, sir, sergeant major I do," said Babs, standing to attention.

"What's going on over here?" asked Mum, looking a bit flushed after a few gin and tonics.

"Dad, in his infinite wisdom, has decided to dump Babs on me for a few weeks of work experience."

"You don't really mind, do you pet? It'll be good for the two of you to spend more time together."

"You're really selling it to me now," I huffed.

"Oh, stop being such a drama queen," said Babs.

"Pot . . . kettle . . . black?" said Sean.

"Put a sock in it, Barbara," snapped Dad. "Now, who'd like a drink? Emma what can I get you?"

"Isn't this lovely," said Mum. "The family out together having fun."

I slept very little that night because James seemed intent on playing the match in bed. He kicked and tossed and flung his arms about in his fitful attempts at sleeping. Eventually, at six, we fell into deep, exhausted comas. What seemed like seconds later, we were woken by the phone. Henry and Mr. Hamilton had arrived and were waiting downstairs to see James before the big game. They cheered when they saw James and pointed to the Leinster jerseys they were wearing. James was thrilled. Mr. Hamilton was looking decidedly emotional for a man who normally kept his emotions in check. He kept patting James on the back and saying "terribly proud of you son" and "tremendous achievement to have come so far." Henry practiced the words of "Molly Malone" with me until he was word perfect. The hotel began to fill with supporters, and a sing-along broke out. James went to gather the team, and I wished him all the luck in the world. "And remember, it doesn't matter what happens, just being here is an incredible achievement."

"Fuck that, we're going to win," said James, grinning at me.

We arrived in Twickenham to the sound of the Leinster fans. They had taken over the east side of the stadium. Opposite us sat the Edinburgh supporters—equally loud and boisterous. Mr. Hamilton and Henry sat beside us and looked around. They were clearly impressed by the huge support Leinster had. I sat between Sean and Lucy. I watched James pacing up and down the sidelines, talking to his assistant coach. The teams came out, and the stadium erupted. Emotions were running very high. Edinburgh had been beaten in the final the year before and they were determined to win . . . but so was Leinster.

The match began, and for the first twenty minutes Leinster had most of the possession but did nothing with it. For the rest of the first half, Edinburgh had the majority of the ball, and with two minutes to go, they scored a try. Suddenly the Leinster supporters weren't so buoyant. Seven, nil to Edinburgh at half-time.

The second half began with Edinburgh camped on Leinster's line. But the lads defended well and pushed the Scottish team right back to their own twenty-two. Scrum to Leinster. Sean squeezed my hand. "We have to use this, we have to score here," he said. Donal picked the ball up from the scrum and bolted for the line. As he got within scoring distance, he could see the Edinburgh full-back coming from behind to tackle him. He put his head down, and as he was tackled, he threw himself over the line, landing awkwardly. The Leinster supporters went wild. We jumped up and down roaring and shouting. Donal remained on the ground, his dislocated shoulder drooping to one side. As he was helped off the field by the medics, the Leinster crowd gave him a standing ovation while his fiancée screamed death threats at the player who had tackled him.

Peter O'Hare came on as Donal's replacement, much to Babs's delight. But it was short-lived, as the supporters around us—having figured out from Lucy's screaming that she was Brady's bird—assured us that while Peter was a good player, he was no Donal Brady. You only get one of those every decade, they agreed. Courage and dedication like that were the things of legends. Lucy glowed, and Babs sulked. She wasn't happy being second best. I could see Peter was going to get dumped. I just hoped she'd move on to soccer players next and stay out of my territory. Between her sex fest with the Leinster squad and now coming to work with me, I was beginning to feel claustrophobic, as if I was being stalked.

Seven points all and ten minutes to go. Edinbugh got a penalty, which they converted. Ten point to seven with five minutes to go.

The noise in the stadium was so loud I thought my ears would burst. Three minutes to go and Leinster had a line-out close to the Scottish team's line. Peter jumped in the air and caught the ball. He passed it out quickly. The scrum-half spun it out wide to the winger. He ran, kicked it over the opposition's head, and catching it on the bounce, flung himself down, ball in hand, grinning like a Cheshire cat. Leinster had won.

chapter TWENTY-FIVE

A FTER A WEEK OF CELEBRATIONS, backslapping, framing of articles, and watching reruns of the match over and over again, I managed to get James and the injured Donal to sit down and go through the adoption reference form.

"I've a problem with question four," said Donal.

James and I read:

> Please comment on the applicants' lifestyle in the context of these capacities as they relate to their health, stability/continuity/security of their home life, etc.—these comments should include reference to the applicants' sobriety and any history of substance abuse.

We looked up. "Where's the problem?" I asked.

"It may have escaped your notice, but your husband here has

been drunk as a skunk for the last week, and I'm worried he might be a closet alcoholic. I won't lie to these good people."

"Very funny, I think if anyone here has a drinking problem it's the guy who blacked out and had sex with my baby sister."

"I hope, Emma, that you're not trying to blackmail me here?" said Donal.

"Certainly not, I'm just jogging your memory."

"Okay," he said, moving swiftly along, "question five asks me to comment on your personal qualities—honesty and trustworthiness."

"It's a good thing you're not the applicant. What would we say about you for shagging a minor and forgetting to tell your fiancée," said James, finding himself very entertaining. Donal thumped him weakly, with the arm that wasn't in a sling.

"Okay, come on, no more messing. We need to get this right," I said.

"Sorry darling. Okay, question six. Please comment on the applicants' relationship with their children (if they have any) and members of their extended family," read James.

"You're both very close to your families, so that's an easy one," said Donal.

"Not as close to some members as you though," I said, unable to resist as James roared laughing.

"Am I going to be abused all night?" groaned Donal.

"That's what happens when you stick it where it doesn't belong," I said, grinning at him. "Okay, moving along. Next question. Please comment on the applicants', their children's, and extended family's acceptance, knowledge of, and experience of people from other cultures, both from within Ireland and abroad."

"Well that's easy, my young sister-in-law has excellent carnal knowledge of a bog man from Ballydrum," said James, unable to resist.

"And Emma here has experience of living with an English wastrel, who moved to Ireland to torment the locals," said Donal, trying to keep a straight face.

"Okay, come on now, no more teasing," I said. "The last main question is: 'Please comment on your experience of the applicants' personal qualities related to—the capacity to understand, recognize, and empathize with the needs of another, to seek and access support either on their own behalf or on behalf of others when it is needed.'"

"I know I know, you had the capacity to understand that Lucy didn't need to know about Babs, you don't have to spell it out," said Donal, preempting the answer. "Look, leave it with me tonight and I'll do up a first draft. I can't do it here with you both looking over my shoulder and reminding me of that awful night. I'll give it to you tomorrow to look over, and then we'll finalize it," said Donal, struggling with his coat.

I helped him put it on, and James gave him a lift home. When he arrived back I said we needed to talk about the one-on-one sessions we were going to have at the end of the week with Dervla. I was worried that if our answers were different at all, she'd give us black marks and we'd blow our chances. We needed to practice, so a reluctant James sat down with me to go over our responses.

"She said she'd be asking us about our past and our relationship and all that stuff, so I've written down a few questions. If we both write down our answers separately and then compare them, we'll be able to see if we're saying the same thing," I said, very pleased with my idea.

James groaned. "It's too much hard work. Can't we just answer verbally?"

"No, this is much better because we can compare them exactly. Now come on, start writing."

We scibbled in silence for about ten minutes and then put the sheets of paper side by side. The first question was—How did you meet? James had written: "Emma saw me in a bar, dumped her boyfriend, and then chatted me up."

I had written: "The night I met James I had just broken up with my boyfriend. I saw James at the bar and we started chatting. It was love at first sight. I knew he was the one."

"No you didn't," said James.

"What?"

"You were still going out with that guy when you met me. You dumped him after you were dazzled by my good looks, charm, and wit."

"Five minutes after I met you, I broke up with him. Do you really think it matters if I bend that truth a tiny bit? I was going to dump Ronan that night anyway because he was such a loser and all he did was sit around on his butt all day and sponge off me. But I don't think it looks very good if Dervla thinks I was two-timing, even if it was for only a few minutes. For goodness' sake James, think before you speak."

"Write."

"What?"

"Think before you write. I wrote the answer."

"Now is not the time to start nitpicking," I snapped.

"Fine, let's move on."

Question two was—What attracted you to each other? James had written: "I'm a sucker for redheads, especially sassy ones with a twinkle in their eye and big breasts."

I had written: "I could see he was a really good person. Responsible, kind, considerate, and I knew that he'd be a brilliant father."

"That's it, I give up. If you're not even going to try to be serious what's the point?" I said, having a total sense-of-humor failure.

"We might as well just forget the whole thing and resign ourselves to a life without children."

James pointed to the last questions. I sighed and picked it up. How long have you been together?

He had written: "We went out for two years and then we got married three years ago. They have been the happiest five years of my life. I can't wait to have a family with Emma. I know she'll be an excellent mother, and it is due to her tenacity and dedication to having children that we are here today."

I had written: "Five years."

"Sorry," I said, leaning over to kiss him. "I know I'm a bit wound up. I just don't want to blow our chances."

"Everything will be fine, just be yourself. It doesn't matter if our memories vary slightly. Dervla will be able to see that we have a solid relationship and we would make excellent parents."

"Do you think saying we have sex three times a week was too much?"

"Not if we make it a fact," said James, leading me upstairs.

Donal dropped the finished form off the next day. It was perfect. I felt quite emotional reading it—as did James, although he pretended not to. Donal said that we had a loving and secure marriage and a closeness that he aspired to in his own relationship. He said we were best friends as well as husband and wife. He said that I was a woman of enormous strength of character who faced adversity head-on and was extremely empathetic to my friends. He said James was one of the few true gentlemen left in the world and was a loyal and trustworthy friend with a huge generosity of spirit. He summed up by saying that he believed there were no more suitable or deserving people willing to adopt.

I forgave Donal everything.

When I called Jess—who had a head like a sieve—to check on their reference, she told me that she had filled out the form with Tony and sent it off but that she had forgotten to keep a copy. I was pissed off that she hadn't shown it to me before sending it in, as I had repeatedly asked her to. I wasn't going to bring it up because I was too angry, and besides I didn't want to argue with Jess. It wouldn't look too good if the social worker visited her after we'd had a blazing row.

However, that night when Lucy, Jess, and I met for a drink, Lucy—oblivious to my annoyance with Jess—brought the subject up.

"So were you pleased with Donal's answers?" she asked.

"They were brilliant. He said such nice things about both of us it was lovely."

"Were the answers similar to Jess's?"

"I wouldn't know, Jess didn't show me hers," I said coldly.

"I forgot. I was so anxious to post it back and not miss the deadline that I forgot to show it to Emma, and now she's pissed off."

"I'm not pissed off, I just wish you'd shown it to me like I asked you to. It's really important that the answers hit the right note."

"Our answers were all fine. We raved about the two of you. Relax, it'll be fine, it's not that big a deal."

"It may not be a big deal to you," I said through gritted teeth, "but to me it's the difference between being approved to have a child or never having one. If we get refused we'll never have a family unless we emigrate somewhere else and start this horrendous process all over again, which funnily enough, I don't much fancy."

"Jesus, Emma, it's not as if I said you'd be crap parents. I said you were both fantastic and wonderful. I'm sorry I forgot to show it to you but I do have other things going on in my life. Sally has been sick with chicken pox all week."

"I'm sorry Sally's been sick, but this is my one chance at a family and I asked you three times to show it to me, but you still forgot, and that really bugs me."

"Jesus, Emma, there's always something wrong with you. Do you have any idea what it's like for me? I've spent the last three years creeping around not mentioning my kids because I knew you were trying to get pregnant. I know it's a sensitive issue, but sometimes it'd be nice if you showed an interest. They are the most important thing in *my* life, and I don't see you knocking yourself out to spend time with them or showing any concern for them whatsoever. We've had two years of your infertility and now it's the adoption. I'm sick of walking on eggshells. I filled out your bloody form in between nursing my sick child back to health while Roy acted up because he wasn't getting any of my attention."

"You're unbelievable. You get pregnant without even trying, have two healthy children while I'm stuck in hospital undergoing shitty tests and injecting myself with drugs, none of which works, and then I have to go through the humiliation of having every aspect of my relationship—including my sex life—dissected by some bitch from the Adoption Board who clearly thinks I'm not good enough, and all you can do is moan about Sally's chicken pox. All kids get chicken pox—it's not fucking AIDS. Which, by the way, is one of the many illnesses my adopted child may well have. But I don't have a choice—I have to take what I'm given with no knowledge of what type of sick, fucked-up parents they had. But apparently I should be calling over to you to play with your two children just so I can rub my nose in what I don't have."

"GUYS!" shouted Lucy. "Stop it. Come on, we never argue. Don't start now. Look, Emma, Jess is sorry she forgot, and I know you'd like to have seen the form, but I'm sure she did a great job with the questions."

"I did," grumbled Jess. "I even lied about how amazing you were with my kids. I said you played with them all the time and they adored you."

Shit. I felt awful. I shouldn't have blown up like that. I knew Jess would have written nice things.

"Thanks, Jess. Sorry for snapping, but the home visits are freaking me out. The social worker thinks I'm an idiot, and I'm genuinely terrified of having our application turned down, because if we do, I think I'll have a nervous breakdown," I said, trying not to cry.

"Jesus, don't cry, you'll start me off," said Jess. "It'll be fine, you'll be great parents, any fool can see that."

"Of course it will," said Lucy. "Come on, Emma, chin up. You haven't too much longer to go. We're here to help if we can."

"Thanks guys, sorry I'm such a moany old cow."

"Do they really ask you about your sex life?" asked Jess.

"Yes. I had to tell them how often we have sex," I said, beginning to smile.

"What did you say?" asked Lucy

"Three times a week."

"Do you?" asked Jess, looking a bit worried. "Tony's lucky if he gets a shag a month."

"No, I lied. Once a week is more honest. Once every two weeks is totally honest," I said, laughing.

"Really?" said Lucy.

Jess and I turned to look at her.

"Go on; depress me with your active, just-engaged love life. How often?" said Jess.

"Three times a week, sometimes more," she said, grinning as Jess and I made sick noises.

chapter TWENTY-SIX

THE NEXT DAY Babs came to work with me. I went to pick her up, grudgingly reminding myself that it was only for a couple of weeks. She hopped into the car wearing a virtually nonexistent mini and thigh-high black leather boots.

"You do realize we're going to put makeup on people?"

"Yeah. So?"

"You look like a cross between a hooker and a fly fisherman in that outfit."

"Yeah, well coming from someone who's wearing a polo neck that was fashionable circa nineteen seventy-three, I take that as a compliment."

"Let's get something straight here. I'm only doing this as a favor to Dad. If you piss me off or do anything to annoy or upset my clients, I will kill you. Just stay in the background and say nothing. I realize that will be supremely difficult for someone as gabby as you—but just try. Try very hard."

"Fine, whatever," said Babs, checking her lipstick in the mirror.

When we got to the studio, I introduced Babs to Amanda and told her that she was going to be with me for a few weeks training and I hoped Amanda didn't mind.

"Not at all. It's nice to meet you, Babs, I've heard a lot about you," said Amanda, winking at me.

Amanda knew all about Babs (except the part where she had sex with Donal). I told her regularly about how much of a live wire Babs was. Amanda loved hearing what she was up to—I think Babs reminded her of herself when she was that age. Even at fifty-plus, Amanda was single, fiercely independent, very attractive, prone to affairs with married men, childless by choice, and very direct.

"I like your boots," she said to Babs.

"Thanks. Emma told me I looked like a fisherman in them."

Amanda laughed at this. "So, are you thinking about following your sister's footsteps into makeup?"

"Well, I really want to be an actress, but I reckon I'll do this for a while, earn some cash to pay for a nose job, and then head out to L.A."

"Have you always wanted a nose job?"

"Hello! Have you seen my nose? As my family likes to remind me—I look like Seabiscuit. It's the only thing I need to change. If I can get a good nose job, I'll be flying."

"I know a good surgeon in London. He's pricey but excellent. He did my eyes," said Amanda, showing Babs her eye lift.

Bloody hell, I thought. This was no good at all. Babs was supposed to be learning about real life—hard work and long hours.

But here she was, sitting beside Amanda, chatting about plastic surgeons.

"What do you think I should go for?" Babs asked her new plastic pal.

"I'd go for something like Julia Roberts's nose. It's still slightly pointed but a lovely shape. It'll transform you."

"That's what I reckon, and there'll be no stopping me then."

"Amanda!" I said, blending on some cream blusher. "You're not supposed to encourage her."

Amanda laughed. "There's no harm in making a few adjustments to what God gave us, if he gave us the wrong parts. Babs is right, her nose is too big for her face. When she gets it fixed, she'll feel like a different person. People in this country are far too close-minded about cosmetic surgery. It's a fact of life, why not improve your looks? Why be embarrassed about it?"

"Exactly," said Babs. "Hey! I've just had a brilliant idea. Why don't you do a profile of me on your show? A before-and-after cosmetic surgery piece. I don't care who knows I've had a nose job as long as I get it done. If you pay for me to have one I'll do it live on the show. It'll be like a fly-on-the-wall documentary about plastic surgery. It'd be brilliant."

"That's a fantastic idea," said Amanda, looking excited. "We could follow you through every step. Yes, I like that idea a lot. Let me talk to my producers about it."

"Sorry to blow your five minutes of fame, Babs, but there is no way that you are having a nose job on national television. Do you have any idea what Mum and Dad would say? Have you no shame?"

"I'd go on TV naked, if it meant getting a free operation," said the shameless one.

"Don't worry, Emma, it'll be tastefully done," said Amanda.

"I'll talk to you later, Babs, when I've run it by my team. But I must say it'd make great reality TV."

When Amanda left to go onto the set, I turned to Babs, who was grinning like a Cheshire cat.

"You can wipe that smirk off your face. There is no way in hell you are doing this."

"Look on the bright side, Emma, it means I won't have to follow you around for three weeks annoying you. If they agree to pay for the operation, I won't need to learn about makeup, I can go straight to Hollywood."

Later that day Amanda called me at home to let me know that her producer thought it was a sensational idea, and she wanted me to know that she had spoken to Babs already. Amanda said she hoped I understood that it was too good an opportunity to pass up. She told me not to worry, that they were getting the best surgeon in London and they'd take extra special care of her. According to Amanda, Babs was ecstatic.

As I was trying to digest the news, Mum called.

"WHAT IS GOING ON? YOUR SISTER HAS JUST TOLD ME SOME COCKAMAMY STORY ABOUT THAT HUSSY AMANDA NOLAN OFFERING TO PAY HER TO GO ON TELEVISION AND MAKE A SHOW OF US ALL . . ."

I held the phone away from my ear as she ranted on.

"Mum . . . Mum . . . MUM," I shouted. "Calm down."

"You were supposed to be keeping an eye on her, keeping her out of trouble and teaching her how to make people up. And now she tells me that woman wants to pay her to go on national television to get a nose job! Over my dead body, Emma. Over my dead body. I told her she was out on her ear if I heard any more of this nonsense, and then she says I'm trying to ruin her life. She said it's my fault she has a big nose because if I'd married a man with a small nose she wouldn't have this problem. Her life has been ruined by this nose apparently and her career can't take off until it has been reduced. Did you ever hear such nonsense. The child has gone mad. Here's your father now, he's just had a word with her."

"Jesus that pair will be the end of me" said Dad, sounding weary. "They've been roaring at each other for over an hour now."

"Are you going to try and stop her?"

"To be honest I'm delighted someone else is footing the bill, she had me tormented with talk of that nose job. She's like a broken-down record about it. Inheriting my nose is preventing her from having a career as an actress, and once she has the new nose she'll be in great demand she tells me. Your mother of course is going mad altogether. She says we'll have to emigrate if Barbara goes on television."

"Where do you think you'll be moving to—France? Spain?"

"We might go out to Iran and stay with Shadee's relatives," said Dad, trying not to laugh.

"I'll miss you."

"Oh Lord," said Dad, "here's your mother back."

"Brat. That's what she is—a brat. It's my fault. I should have been stricter with her. I was too lenient. Having a child at forty is not a good idea. You haven't the energy to discipline them. I was worn out from you and Sean. She got away with murder, and look at her now. Mark my words, Emma, when you have children, be firm. Look what happens when you're not," she said, beginning to sniffle. "It's no good trying to put your foot down when they're older, it's too late. What did I do to deserve this—one daughter who won't let nature take its course and is rushing into adoption, a son living in sin with a Muslim, and a young pup who's going on television to have an operation. I tried, Emma, I really tried," she said, blowing her nose.

"Well this daughter needs to rush off to prepare for her hasty adoption, so good-bye," I said, slamming down the phone.

Two days later, James and I were waiting nervously for Dervla to arrive for our one-on-one session. When the doorbell rang, we both jumped up to let her in. She immediately sat us down and explained that there was no need to be nervous and that the important thing was to be honest. She wanted to get a real sense of our personalities from this session, so we were to be natural and say what we really felt, not what we thought she wanted to hear. She asked us who wanted to go first, and I said I did. I had to get it over with, and I was hoping to get a few minutes in between to brief James.

James left us alone in the kitchen, and Dervla took out her notepad. I hadn't been this nervous since taking my finals in college. I was sweating and shaking inside. I knew this was going to be a really important session and I wanted to do my best. Dervla started off by asking me about my childhood. The house we lived in, my earliest memories . . .

"Did you get on well with your parents?"

"Oh yes really well."

"Do you think they were good parents?"

"Brilliant."

"Did you go through a rebellious phase at all as a teenager?"

"No, I didn't. I was quite boring actually," I lied, leaving out the time I dyed my hair black when I was sixteen and ran away from home. I had actually just stayed the night in Jess's house, but it had seemed wild at the time. Nor did I mention the first time I smoked pot and passed out in a bush in Roger Keegan's house in a pool of my own vomit. These were stories I really didn't want Dervla scribbling down in her notebook.

"Didn't you ever stay out late, get drunk, skip school, or do any of those teenage things?" asked Dervla, clearly not convinced by my angelic childhood.

"Uhm, well I suppose I may have had the odd underage drink, but I never got really drunk or passed out or anything, and I did get caught smoking in school once," I said, deciding to confess in case she checked my school records—which knowing Dervla was highly likely—"and I got suspended for a day, but I learned my lesson and never smoked again."

"What about past relationships? Have you had other boyfriends?"

"Oh, just one or two," I said, failing to mention the scores of snogs, gropes, and flings I had had in my twenties.

"Can you tell me about those?"

"Nothing to tell really. I went out with one guy called David for two years," I lied, stretching my six-week fling to a serious, steady, two-year relationship. "He was a medical student, but we grew apart when he went to America. And then there was Ronan, who I was going out with before I met James. He was a successful freelance journalist and writer," I said, pushing the truth to its limits. Ronan had written one article in his life and spent the rest of his time working on the first few chapters of his novel, which was the biggest load of tripe I had ever read. "We broke up shortly before I met James. He was a bit too poetic for me. Not that I don't appreciate poetry and literature, because I do. I love poetry, but we just weren't totally suited, and then I met James and it was love at first sight. I knew the minute I saw him that he was the man for me."

"How would you describe your relationship?"

"Incredibly stable, loving, and nurturing," I said, even impressing myself with the nurturing comment. Way to go, Emma.

"Do you argue?"

"Oh no. Not at all. No. We never raise our voices to each other."

Dervla raised her eyebrows. "Look, Emma, it's all right to admit you fight. All couples argue. It doesn't mean you're bad people. You don't have to hide behind this facade of perfectness. I need you to be open and honest."

Facade? How dare she imply I was lying. I may have been stretching the truth a little, but who was she to accuse me of lying.

"I'm not hiding behind anything. If I seem stiff it's because I'm nervous. This whole process is extremely difficult, you know. It's not easy having your life dissected by a complete stranger," I said, losing my cool for a minute.

"Look, I know it's not easy, and the questions may appear harsh and probing at times, but you must remember that every couple I approve is my responsibility, and if they mistreat a child, then I have that on my conscience. I need to get to know you—the real Emma, so that I can be sure the baby will be properly looked after. If I don't get to know you, how can I approve you? The welfare of children lies in my hands, so I have to be absolutely certain that all the prospective parents I approve will be good parents. There is no room for error."

Typical—just when I wanted to throttle her, she disarms me. I hadn't thought of it from her point of view before. It must be a huge responsibility to approve a couple to adopt. If they turned out to be total psychos it was all your fault. I suddenly felt human toward Dervla. I didn't like her, but I began to understand where she was coming from and why she had to be so thorough.

I nodded. "Okay, I admit we do argue, occasionally, but only over silly things and we always make up almost immediately."

"Did your parents ever strike you in order to discipline you?"

"No. I mean they didn't hit us, my mother slapped us on the bottom the odd time, but only if we were very out of line, and always gently," I said, deciding to omit the episodes where she chased us down around the garden to belt us with her slipper. Honesty in small measures was best.

"I see that your referees Jessica and Tony Hughes have two children. How do you get on with them?"

"Very well. I adore little Sally and Roy. I don't see them every week, but I do spend time with them regularly, and I'm extremely fond of them. Jess is my best friend," I said, temporarily relegating Lucy to second place, "and her children mean the world to me."

Dervla then asked me about my relationship with my siblings, my parents, my colleagues, my in-laws . . . everyone I had ever met. I lurched from being honest to lying a little about my close relationship with Imogen and the fact that Babs would make an excellent auntie. Eventually, after what seemed like ten days, she said we were finished.

I went to get James for his grilling, and as I stood up, I could feel my legs shaking, I was completely drained. I was hugely relieved it was over but worried about James being too honest. I tried to brief him before he went in.

"I told her I got on with everyone and that we saw a lot of Sally and Roy."

"Who?" said James, not helping to ease my tension.

"Jesus, James," I hissed. "Sally and Roy are Jess's kids."

"Okay, okay, I remember now."

"I told her we rarely fight and that I get on famously with Imogen. So don't blow it. Don't be too honest," I said, grabbing his arm as he went to walk out. "Say positive things and don't mention my tendency to lose my temper when stressed. And don't say that—"

"Emma! Let go of my arm. It's okay, it'll be fine. Now breathe and relax. You can debrief me afterward."

I paced up and down the living room like a cat on a hot tin roof. I wanted to tiptoe up to the door to listen in, but I was afraid if Dervla suddenly got up to go to the bathroom and found me lurking outside, that she'd blackball us for good. After what seemed like forever, they appeared out of the kichen, and after Dervla said her good-byes and left, I pounced on James.

"Well? How was it? What did you say? Come on tell me? What did you say when she asked about previous relationships?"

"I said I moved to Ireland because I'd shagged everyone in England and needed new meat."

"James! I am too stressed for jokes."

"Relax. I said I'd gone out with a few girls, but nothing serious until I met you."

"Did she ask about when you were young?"

"Yes."

"And?"

"And I said I had a normal childhood, and while I had enjoyed boarding school, I wouldn't necessarily send my children there."

"Okay good, what else?"

"She asked if I was as keen on adopting as you were, and I admitted I hadn't been totally enthusiastic about it all in the beginning, but that it was a means to an end and I wanted to support you."

"Means to an end? Please tell me you're kidding me? 'Means to an end' sounds like something you've been dragged into. Why the hell didn't you tell her you were mad keen on adopting. Jesus,

James, that could blow our chances. It sounds really unenthusiastic. For God's sake, it sounds like I bullied you into the whole thing."

"No it doesn't, stop being so dramatic. Besides, I was being honest. I wasn't one hundred percent keen on adopting initially, but now I'm all for it."

"But did you say that? Did you make it clear that now you really want to? Did you?"

"God, Emma, I can't remember every little thing I said. I'm sure I did say something to that effect."

"James," I said, getting really angry, "this is really important. Focus. Did you tell her you were really keen to adopt now. Did you?"

"I think so."

"For God's sake that's a vital point. If she thinks you're still not keen, we'll never get approved. Jesus, James, think—what exactly did you say?"

"Christ, Emma, I can't remember the words, but believe it or not I didn't thwart our chances of adopting by revealing my annual trips to Thailand to bugger underage boys senseless," roared James, getting very red in the face.

We heard someone clearing their throat behind us. We swung round. It was Dervla, standing by the front door, which in my haste to debrief James I hadn't closed properly.

"Sorry, I forgot my car keys and the door was open, so . . ."

chapter TWENTY-SEVEN

I LOCKED MYSELF IN THE BATHROOM and cried for an hour after Dervla left. As far as I was concerned that was it. We had blown it. Not only had she heard us shouting at each other, but now she also thought James was a pedophile. Eventually, after much persuasion from an apologetic James, I came out of the bathroom, puffy faced and slitty eyed.

"It's not that bad," he said.

I glared at him—or rather squinted at him through swollen eyes. "She thinks you're a child molester. Somehow, I don't think that pedophiles are top of the list for approval."

"She knows I was joking. Come on, Emma, don't overreact."

"Jesus, James, she gave me this whole speech about how every child was her responsibility and she could only ever approve parents she was one hundred percent sure of. She just saw us having a huge row, and you shouting about fondling young boys. It's not exactly the perfect setup."

"Look, I agree it wasn't ideal for her to see us arguing, but that's all it was—a silly argument. All couples fight, she knows that."

"Yeah, but now she probably thinks you were molested in boarding school by the chaps in upper sixth or whatever it's called and as a result you can't help yourself with little boys. Everyone thinks boys in boarding school spend all their spare time having sex in the showers or shoving soap up their bums."

"First of all, that is a gross exaggeration, not everyone thinks that. Secondly, it wasn't soap, it was ferrets."

"Am I laughing? Do you see my lips twitching? This is serious, James."

"Look, darling, stop getting yourself into a state and calm down. Dervla is perfectly aware that we are a normal, healthy, solid couple who will make great parents, she can see that. One silly argument means nothing. Next time, though, close the door properly."

"Next time, I'll bolt the door along with your big mouth."

The phone rang. Thankfully it was Sean, who was just about the only person I felt like talking to.

"What the hell is going on?" he asked. "I've had Mum on the phone ranting on about Babs having some operation on TV."

"You know Babs. I took her to work, as a favor to Dad, to learn the ropes about makeup, and somehow she managed to wrangle herself a starring role on the show and a free nose job."

"How?"

"Amanda Nolan, the presenter, thinks that a fly-on-the-wall documentary about a young girl having cosmetic surgery would boost ratings. It was Babs's idea and she fell for it hook, line, and sinker. So now our little sister is getting what she always wanted, free of charge."

"God, she'll be unbearable with a nice nose. That schnozz is the only thing that makes her human."

"I know. Now it's off to Hollywood, with her new nose."

"As if she's not bad enough already. No wonder Mum was going nuts. Can we stop it?"

"As if."

"Is it even worth a try?" he asked.

"Does Dolly Parton sleep on her stomach?"

"Yeah, you're right. She'll never give up a new nose. Is it dangerous?"

"No. They're sending her to a top guy in London, and let's face it they're not going to risk anything on TV. She'll be getting the best treatment."

"No more Seabiscuit."

"No more Barbra Streisand."

"No more Barry Manilow."

"It was beautiful while it lasted." I sighed. "The hours of fun we've had, teasing her about that honker."

"All over now."

"Yep."

"Unless they screw it up and make it worse."

"Oh wouldn't that be great."

"Fantastic," agreed Sean.

"Anyway, enough about Babs. How are things with you? How's Shadee?"

"Great, thanks. Still going really well. I'm in shock. It's been a year. My longest relationship ever."

"God, Sean, I can't believe it's been that long. That's great."

"How's the adoption going? Have you started the home visits?"

"Unfortunately yes."

"Uh-oh, that sounds ominous."

"Well, it was all going swimmingly until James and I had a massive scrap just after the social worker, Dervla, left. I was nagging him about what he had said and he got annoyed and roared at me that he said all the right things and not to worry because he hadn't told Dervla he was a closet pedophile—when we realized she was standing behind us. I hadn't closed the front door properly and she had come back in to get her keys."

Sean struggled not to laugh, but it was too much. Once he started he couldn't stop, and I even ended up joining in. It was funny—in a sick, farcical way.

"Sorry, sis, I didn't mean to laugh," said Sean. "What did you say to her?"

"Nothing. We were both so shocked that we just stared at her in silence. She grabbed her keys and bolted out to her car."

"When are you seeing her again?"

"Next week, so we'll have to do some serious groveling."

"Just tell her it's James's twisted English sense of humor. By the way, I need your advice."

"Sure, what's up?"

"Well . . . I'm going to ask Shadee to marry me, and I want to know what kind of ring I should get."

"WHAT! Oh my God, Sean, that's amazing. When did you decide?" I said, realizing that I was genuinely thrilled for him. Although I had only met Shadee once, she seemed like a really lovely person, and it was clear she adored Sean. And whenever he told me stories about her they were always really nice—she always seemed to be putting herself out for him or doing things to make him happy.

"To be honest I've known for ages that she was the one. But considering the disastrous decisions I've made in the past, I had to be sure, so I waited. And now I'm positive. So what do you think? A solitaire or three diamonds in a row? Gold or plat-inum?"

"What does she wear—gold or silver?"

"Gold mostly."

"Well, you can't go wrong with a solitaire on a gold band. Lucy's is stunning."

"Great. I'll do that. Thanks, sis. Needless to say, not a word to anyone. I'll let Mum get over Babs's cosmetic surgery before spring-ing this on her. I don't want to push her over the edge."

"It's a bit late for that, she's certifiable. Good luck with the ring and call me when you've proposed."

"Will do. It won't be for a few weeks, I'm going to wait until her birthday."

"Lucky girl."

"Lucky guy," said Sean, modest as ever.

The one good thing about Babs getting the nose job was that it meant I didn't have her traipsing after me, driving me insane. Amanda's production team was sorting out the details, and they were hoping to tape the whole process in a diary format, with Babs talking into a camera for ten minutes every day, before, during, and after the operation. Amanda said they hoped to be ready to shoot in six to eight weeks.

Time dragged until the next home visit, and as the day ap-proached I got more and more nervous. I had decided that honesty was the best policy and I was just going to say it straight out to Dervla when I saw her.

She arrived, and after offering her a cup of coffee, I opened my mouth, but James jumped in. "Dervla we're a bit embar-rassed about the last session, when you came back for your keys

248 sinead moriarty

and we were having a bit of a tiff. Emma seems to think that you may have taken my joke about Thai boys seriously because apparently everyone assumes English boys in boarding school like having sex with each other. I can assure you we don't. If any of the other boys had come near me I would have given them a right hook."

"Not that James is homophobic," I added, making sure we covered all angles.

Dervla nodded and smiled—she actually smiled! "It's all right James. I didn't have you down as a child molester."

James and I beamed at each other. Dervla had smiled—we were back on track. The meeting went well, we went over old ground in more detail. We discussed our motivation for adopting, our feelings about adoption, our capacity to safeguard a child and promote its development and understand the impact that being an adopted child from overseas has on a child's identity. For the first time since the process began I was totally myself. I felt calm and relaxed. When Dervla left that day I felt really positive about the adoption and our chances of being approved.

While we were progressing with our adoption, Lucy and Donal were planning their wedding.

"You must be joking," said Lucy when she saw the guest list Donal handed her. "There are over seventy people on this. We're having a small wedding. Sixty guests in total. Thirty for you and thirty for me. You'll have to change it."

"Why are we only having sixty people? People will think we've no pals."

"Because big weddings are stupid, especially when the bride

is thirty-five. I want a small, sophisticated wedding, with close friends and family."

"We country folk like big weddings."

"Well then, you should have married Mary and had a big country wedding in a big barn with five hundred relations dancing around haystacks."

"Now that sounds like a wedding to me. There's no way I can only invite thirty people. Sure the team alone plus James and their other halves is thirty, and that's not including the squad."

"Stuff the squad. Just invite James and one or two of the lads you're closest to."

"Jesus, Lucy, I can't not invite the lads. We've played together every day for years. There's no way I can leave them out."

"I'm only inviting two people from work."

"You don't like the people you work with—I do."

"Well then invite James and no on else. Then they won't feel left out."

"I can't."

"Fine, invite the team—not the squad—plus your parents and that'll be thirty-two," said Lucy impatiently.

"And what about my brother? Is he allowed to come, or does he not qualify as a close enough relative? And my cousin Frankie from across the road who was like a sister to me, and her parents and—"

"The team, your parents, and your brother. Cousin Frankie from across the road can sod off, she's not coming."

"I couldn't not invite Frankie, or Joe McGrath."

"Who the hell is Joe McGrath?" said Lucy, losing patience.

"Joe McGrath is the man who gave me my first break. The man who spotted my talent as a young lad running around the fields in Ballydrum," said Donal, eyes misting over. "If it wasn't for Joe I wouldn't be where I am today."

"If Joe McGrath was such a big bloody deal, how come you never mentioned him before?"

"I'm always talking about Joe, you just never listen."

"Yeah right. Sorry, Donal, the wonderful Joe isn't coming. No room at the inn."

"Show me your list," said Donal, grabbing it. "And who the hell is Nora Killeen when she's at home?"

"Nora's my beautician."

"What?"

"I've been going to her for years. We're very close."

"You're inviting some bird who waxes your armpits, and I'm not allowed to invite Joe?" said Donal, in disbelief.

"Nora Killeen discovered me as a young girl running around Dublin with bushy eyebrows. If it wasn't for her I wouldn't be where I am today," said Lucy, smirking.

"You're a riot," said Donal, looking down the list. "Babs!" he exclaimed.

"Well, Emma's been my best friend since we were kids. Her parents were always really nice to me, and I get on really well with Sean too, so I didn't want to leave Babs out. I know she's a bit of a handful, but she's just young and immature."

"No, Lucy. I don't want her at the wedding," said Donal firmly.

"Come on, she's not that bad."

"Yes she is."

"I didn't think you knew her that well," said Lucy, looking puzzled.

"Jesus, I don't, I barely know her at all. I just hear from James that she tends to cause havoc wherever she goes. I don't want her ruining our wedding."

"She'll be grand, we'll stick her beside one of the rugby guys."

"No, Lucy, I really think we should leave her out."

"No, Donal, Emma's my friend and she's been really good to me, especially recently when I had to move in with her," said Lucy pointedly. "I want to invite her whole family. Babs is coming and that's the end of it."

chapter TWENTY-EIGHT

OVER THE NEXT SIX WEEKS we had our final three home sessions, and Dervla chose to visit Donal as our reference. Well she would, wouldn't she. Why choose a nice safe family unit like Jess and Tony to visit when you can visit the bachelor guy who, while engaged to my best friend, slept with my sister. I was a nervous wreck when Donal phoned to say Dervla had made an appointment to call on him. Donal, needless to say, was as confident as ever and told me to relax, that he had it all under control and that charming the pants off women was his forte.

"Believe me, Donal, I'm all too familiar with your charms, just do me a favor and try not to have sex with her."

"I'll try and control myself."

"Just reiterate all the nice things you wrote down in the form and don't be laddish or try to be funny. She doesn't have a sense of humor, and she takes her job very seriously, so no gags. Wear something other than your tracksuit. A suit would be great or just nice trousers and a shirt. Don't offer her alcohol and—"

"Don't fart, belch, pick your nose, scratch your balls, smile too much, frown too much, or breathe loudly. Am I right?"

"Well, now that you mention it, you do scratch your balls a lot, you're always poking around down there, so try and control it."

"James is a saint," said Donal.

"As is Lucy. Oh and Donal, try not to mention your fetish for young blondes," I replied.

"Are you ever going to let that one go?" he groaned.

"Not until after the meeting with Dervla. If it goes well, I might consider forgetting about it."

Before Donal's reference meeting, we had another home visit where we covered our experiences of loss and our family support network. With James's family all living in England, the onus was really on my family to pick up the baton. I said my parents would be a great help and had always been very supportive. Unfortunately the only sibling I had living in Dublin was Babs, so we bent the truth and said she would be a great asset to have around and the fact that she was young and energetic was a bonus. When we talked about loss, I focused on my feelings of grief at not being able to have a child of my own, which were still quite raw, and I think Dervla was relieved that I didn't mention Garfield or my front teeth.

I called Lucy the day of Dervla's visit to Donal.

"Is the house clean?"

"Spotless, I promise," she assured me.

"Did you pick out something respectable for him to wear?"

"Yes, he's wearing a lovely blue shirt I bought him and very conservative navy trousers."

"Did you remind him not to be scratching his balls or cracking jokes?"

"I did."

"Sorry to be a pest, it's just really important that she thinks he's a good referee.""He knows that. Don't worry, he'll be brilliant."

Dervla arrived at exactly four o'clock. Donal answered the door in his smart clothes and welcomed her in. He offered her tea and coffee, but she said a glass of water would be fine. They sat opposite each other, and while Dervla was getting her notepad out, Donal decided to break the ice with a joke.

"What is the difference between God and a social worker? God doesn't pretend to be a social worker."

Dervla looked up at him. Mistaking this for encouragement, Donal continued. "What's the difference between a social worker and a pit bull terrier? At least you can get part of your baby back from the pit bull," he said, roaring laughing.

Unsurprisingly, Dervla was not amused. She cleared her throat. "When you're ready, Mr. Brady, I'd like to start the interview, or do you have any more jokes you'd like to get out of the way first?"

"No, thank you, that's it on the joke front. Please fire ahead," said Donal, silently cursing himself for misjudging the situation. This bird was in no mood for comedy. Shit, he'd have to make up for it by doing a spectacular interview.

"How long have you known James and Emma Hamilton?"

"I've known James seven years and Emma five."

"How would you describe their relationship."

"Excellent. I recently got engaged myself, and I can honestly say that I'd love for Lucy and myself to have as happy a marriage as the two of them."

"You have described James as your best friend. Is that correct?"

"Absolutely. He's going to be the best man at my wedding.

We've worked together every day now for seven years. He's a great fella altogether."

"Does he confide in you?"

"In what way?"

"When they were having problems getting pregnant, did he talk to you about how he felt?"

"Well, he'd say the odd thing, like he'd say Emma was doing gymnastics after sex—handstands and the like—or that things weren't going too well on the baby front, but we don't have a touchy-feely relationship, if that's what you mean."

"That's not what I mean. Did he discuss his feelings and frustrations with you? Did he tell you he was disappointed not to be able to have a child of his own?"

"No, but I knew he was."

"How did you know that?"

"I just did, he wasn't himself for a bit, so I figured that was why."

"Did he discuss the medical side of things with you?"

"You mean did he tell me if he was shooting blanks? No he never said, and I never asked. That's his own business, but I got the impression that it was Emma who was having the problems."

"How so?"

God, this was tough going, thought Donal. She wanted every detail. He was beginning to sweat.

"I just knew from Lucy, who's Emma's best friend, that she was on these drugs that made her a bit mad."

"Do you think Emma was depressed?"

"Ah no, I'm not saying she was depressed, just a bit stressed out maybe."

"Stress can lead to depression. Did James ever tell you Emma was depressed?"

"No. I could see she was a bit down in the dumps the odd time, but she bounced back. She's a great girl, full of life."

"Do they argue much as a couple?"

"No, not really."

"What do you mean by 'not really'?" asked Dervla, pushing Donal to the limit.

"Look it, Dervla, I don't know what I mean by it. The bottom line is that they are a great pair. They're mad about each other and they're lovely people. James is a true gentleman and a fantastic friend, and Emma is a great girl too. Any child—especially one from some hole in Russia—would be lucky to have them as parents."

"That's all very well, Mr. Brady, but it's my responsibility to look after the welfare of each child, and I need to be sure about the Hamiltons. I need to know exactly what kind of parents they would make and what kind of a life the child would have with them."

"I'm guardian to my fifteen-year-old niece, Annie. My sister died five years ago, and left me in charge of her. And the way I see it is this—you sink or swim," said Donal, trying not to show his annoyance. "None of us knows what we're doing as parents. You just get on with it, and sometimes you make mistakes and sometimes you get it right. But there is no perfect parent. If you're a decent person, well then hopefully you'll get more right than wrong and the kid will turn out okay. There are no guarantees; you just give it your best shot. And I can tell you right now, James and Emma will do everything they can to be good parents, so don't be asking me about their innermost feelings, because I don't know what they are. I just know that they're good people and they deserve a break."

Dervla was clearly taken aback. Donal hoped he hadn't blown

it by ramming the point home, but he was fed up with her psycho-analysis. They looked at each other in silence; Dervla jotted down some notes and then got up to leave. Donal wasn't sure if the look on her face was one of shock, dislike, or grudging admiration. He was hoping for the latter, because if he had messed up, he'd never be forgiven.

When Dervla came for the home visit after seeing Donal, I tried to get a reaction from her, but she was giving nothing away. Donal had told us he thought it had gone well, but he hadn't been overly confident, and I was worried that he may have given the wrong impression.

"So how did it go with Donal?" I asked.

"Fine," said my monosyllabic home visitor.

"He's a nice guy. He can seem a bit laddish, but he's really a good person and he's done a great job raising his niece," I added, hoping to pull at her heartstrings—if she had any.

"So it would seem."

"Did he give us a good reference?" I asked, deciding to cut to the chase.

"The meeting went well, Emma, that's all I can say."

Fine, you stupid old cow, I thought, turning around to make a face at the wall. God she could be a cold fish at times. James came in, and we began our penultimate session. We were both relieved they were nearly over. The meetings were very draining, and we were sick of talking about the same things over and over. That day we discussed our capacity to provide an environment where the child's original race, nationality, culture, religion, and language would be valued and promoted.

I told Dervla that we had been learning Russian for a few months now, and while we weren't fluent speakers, we could certainly get by. Then, to demonstrate, I had a one-way conversation with James—where I said every sentence I could think of, and he said *"Spasiba"* and *"Da"* at regular intervals. She didn't exactly stand up and cheer, but at least she could see we were making an effort. We assured Dervla that we were very open to teaching the child about its culture and background. I gave her a brief history of Russia that I had memorized—and believe me, with my memory it was brief—but it covered the main points.

As usual it was a one-sided conversation, with James and I doing all the talking while Dervla took notes. When the two hours were up she made the final appointment to see us in two weeks and told us that we'd be covering our hopes and expectations and how we felt the adoption would affect our lives.

While I was thumbing through *The Russian Adoption Handbook* by John Maclean in an attempt to dazzle Dervla with my research during our final meeting, I stumbled across the part where he says how much a Russian adoption costs.

> *The general rule of thumb is that the adoption should cost between $12,000 and $20,000, not including an additional $4,000 for traveling and staying in Russia.*

WHAT? The adoption people had said that there would be some fees, depending on the country you decided to adopt from and the agencies you used to match you with your baby, but I had never thought it would be that much. It was going to cost us twenty thousand euros to adopt one child. And what about the others? I wanted three. Sixty thousand euros for a family? It was daylight robbery. I had expected to pay a couple of thousand maybe, but my God, that was insane. We'd have to get a bank loan and spend years paying it off.

"James, you're not going to believe this," I said, shaking the book in his face. "This adoption is going to cost us twenty grand."

"Pardon?"

"Twenty grand, it says so here."

James took the book and read it. "Well, perhaps the Russians like to rip the Americans off," he said. "I'm sure they don't charge as much for fellow Europeans. They couldn't. That's outrageous. I'm sure it's just a way of getting back at the Yanks."

"Maybe, I'll check it on the Inernet."

I came back down half an hour later.

"James, we need to go and see the bank manager tomorrow to get a twenty-grand loan. It's true, they do charge that much for all adoptions in Russia. Apparently the Russian adoption agencies are now charging more than ever to match you up with a child, because the demand has skyrocketed."

"But that's ridiculous. It's unethical."

"Since when have the Russians been ethical? Sure aren't they all mad from living in the snow year-round."

"Christ," said James, looking decidedly put out.

"You know the worst part."

"What?"

"We want to adopt three, so it's going to cost us sixty grand."

"Can't you get two for the price of one?"

"I wanted to adopt two, but you said it wasn't a good idea, that we should see how we get on with one."

"Well, maybe I'm changing my mind. Jesus, this adoption thing is just one bloody hurdle after another."

"I know, but it'll be worth it when we get our little baby."

"I hope so, Emma, I really hope so," grumbled James.

I couldn't allow negative thoughts at this late stage. We were nearly there. We couldn't back out now. And what was money when you compared it to the years of joy a child would bring?

When Dervla arrived for our final session neither James nor I was feeling particularly sunny about the adoption. We were still reeling from the cost factor. When Dervla asked us how we felt the adoption would change our lives and to discuss our hopes and expectations, James said, "Well, Dervla, I hope that we get a healthy child, particularly now that I've discovered that it will change our lives by crippling us financially."

Dervla nodded. "I understand that it's hard when you feel that you are essentially buying your child, but I'm afraid that is a fact of life when it comes to most overseas adoptions. There will always be costs involved. Is this changing your minds at all?" she asked, looking at James's glowering face.

"No, I jumped in. We only found out about the costs a few days ago, so we're just coming to terms with it. It's fine, we are still absolutely committed to adopting a child and giving it a happy and healthy home."

"You do realize that despite the costs, your child may not be healthy. In fact they will most likely be underweight and in some cases very undernourished. Children who have been in institutional care will often show delays in language and social skills, behavioral problems, and abnormalities in attachment behavior. . . ."

I looked out the window as Dervla reminded us once again of all the things that could go wrong. I wanted to cry. Were we mad? I wondered. Should I go back to having IVF? This whole adoption process was such a leap of faith. If James was having doubts, maybe we should stop. But we'd come so far and been through so much. Then again, we had no idea what type of child we'd get. If we got approved, we'd be placing our trust in some Russian agency to find us a baby. They didn't know us, they didn't care about us. We were a statistic. I glanced over at James. He nodded slowly and reached out to hold my hand.

"Thank you, Dervla," he said, interrupting her. "We are well versed in all the possible ailments a child may have, but despite this and despite the astronomical cost, we are still committed to this process. Now let's move on shall we."

chapter TWENTY-NINE

IT WAS A FOUR-WEEK WAIT until we found out whether or not we had been approved—or disapproved. I lurched from feeling positive to feeling utterly negative. I tormented James on an hourly basis.

"Do you think we'll get through?"

"Yes, I'm sure we will."

"How can you be sure?"

"Because Dervla can see that we are normal, sane people who will be good parents."

"I don't think we will. She didn't like us, especially me. She thinks I'm an idiot, especially after the day we did the loss charts."

"Emma, we've gone over this a hundred times. Dervla understands that you were nervous and don't really count losing your front teeth as a life-altering incident."

"Does she really though?"

"Yes."

"How do you know? She never said anything."

"Because nobody in their right minds would admit to being traumatized by the loss of a tooth—it was obvious you were just babbling. Dervla could see that."

"Actually, James, I was upset by it. At seven years of age it is a big deal to turn up at your first Holy Communion in a blood-stained dress with no front teeth."

"Fine. Whatever."

"Don't whatever me. I'm the one that whatevers. So what do you think?"

"About what exactly?" said James, getting annoyed.

"Our chances of being approved."

"As I said five minutes ago—I think they are good. Now can we please talk about something else."

"Fine, whatever."

Thankfully, for James, I was flat out with work—averaging three weddings a week plus my regular slot with Amanda—so I could only quiz him on an irregular basis. Amanda's production team had put the final touches in place for Babs's operation, and she was coming into the studio for an interview before she flew to London to begin her preoperation filming. Babs was a natural on TV. Her confidence, total disregard for what anyone else thought of her, and brutal honesty made for excellent viewing. Although Babs was being deadly serious, everyone else thought she was hilarious. She sat on the couch with Amanda and talked about the upcoming operation.

"So, Babs, why are you having this operation?"

"It's very simple. I'd be really good-looking if it wasn't for my stupid nose. My family calls me Seabiscuit—you know, like the racehorse. They think it's really funny. My dad keeps telling me how lucky I am to have inherited his honker. The nose is bad enough on him—but on a girl, especially a skinny girl like me, it's a disaster. When I was a kid, I used to tape my nose every night. I'd wrap the tape around my head to squish my nose down, but it made no difference, and I just ended up with a rash on my face from the glue," said Babs as the audience tried not to laugh. "So you see I've wanted this nose job since I was very young. I've spent the last ten years begging my dad to pay for a new nose, but he kept telling me that I'd grow into it—how the hell are you supposed to grow into a nose?—put on a hundred and fifty pounds and have a sex change? My mother kept telling me not to be so shallow, that beauty was from within. Hello? What a load of crap. If you look like a big fat ugly oaf then you can be sure that you'll feel like one. What looks like shit, feels like shit."

"How do you think having cosmetic surgery will change your life?" asked Amanda, jumping in with a question before Babs cursed again. Live TV can be tricky when your guest is as spontaneous as Babs.

"Simple. It'll make me a star. Once I get my new nose, I won't look like a young Barbra Streisand anymore, I'll look like a young Jennifer Aniston. I'm heading straight out to Hollywood to become an actress."

"What would you say to other young girls who are considering plastic surgery?"

"Go for it. If you need to change something, change it. There's no point sitting around feeling sorry for yourself. Sort it out."

"Are you nervous at all about going under the knife?" Amanda asked.

"Are you mad? I've been waiting to have this done since the

first day I ever looked in the mirror. I can't wait to get to London and have the operation. Bring it on!"

"How does your family feel about you going through with this operation on national television?"

Babs laughed. "My mother's planning on entering the witness protection program because of the shame of it all. But my dad's happy enough because he doesn't have to foot the bill."

I stood to the side of the set and watched as my little sister encouraged the daytime TV viewers to go under the knife. The girl was a law unto herself. I knew Mum would be watching at home, having a seizure. Amanda, on the other hand, was thrilled. Babs was exactly the kind of person she wanted on her show—outspoken, controversial, and blunt. She knew the media would pick up on the story and that the papers would be full of debates about Babs's forthcoming plastic surgery. Amanda's ratings would go through the roof. A controversial guest was every presenter's dream. Amanda did however warn Babs about her cursing—she'd have to be more careful about that.

When I got home, Mum was parked outside the house, in a pair of dark glasses and a scarf. She darted through the front door after me and hissed at me to pull down the blinds.

"Mum, what is going on?" I asked as I turned the light on in the now pitch-dark kitchen.

"What did I do, Emma? What did I do to deserve this? Did you see that sister of yours on the program today? Did you? Did you see her?"

"Yes, Mum, of course I saw her. I work on the show—remember."

"Telling all the young girls in the country to go out and get plastic surgery. I've already had Nuala on about it. Needless to say, I pretended I wasn't home, but she left a long message on the machine. Delighted she is. Gloating."

Nuala was my mother's best friend. They'd been pals since they met in secretarial school at the age of eighteen, and they drove each other insane. Whenever any of us were in trouble, Nuala was the first to call over to offer her condolences—but she was really only coming over to gloat and make herself feel better about her own brood, according to my mother. When Nuala's son, Terry, had come out of the closet and announced he was gay—my mother had been over like a shot, armed with self-help books for parents of gay children. He had spent most of his teenage years wearing mascara and worshiping Liza Minnelli, so it was more of a surprise to everyone that it had taken Terry so long to admit it, than anything else. Anyway, suffice it to say that Mum and Nuala had a love-hate relationship, based on one-up-manship.

"'I just saw Barbara on the television,' says Nuala," recounted my mother, tapping her fingers on the table. "'Isn't it well for her, getting a new nose and heading off to Hollywood. You must be very proud. It's lovely to see the young people today being so open about themselves. But then again, Barbara was always outspoken. She looked well, sure why wouldn't she wear a short little skirt if she has the legs. Anyway, you're probably out celebrating your daughter's new fame. I'll try you again later.' The cheek of her," Mum fumed.

I wasn't sure if she was furious now about Nuala or Babs. Probably both.

"Ringing me up to laugh at me, she was. And who could blame her, with my wild daughter half naked on the television making a show of herself. She may laugh about her poor mother entering the witness protection program, but it won't be so funny when I do disappear and go off to Canada with a false name. You won't all be laughing then."

"Canada?"

"I saw a show on it the other night; it's supposed to be a beautiful country. Anyway, what's all this nonsense about Barbara going to Hollywood? Over my dead body is she going over there, sure those film people are well known to be out of their minds on drugs the whole time. She'll end up a drug addict or in that cult they're all in—the Scientistolgists. They may pretend they're normal but I've read about it—they're just like the Moonies. They brainwash all the famous stars to join the sect and then get them to make big donations . . ."

How we had jumped from the nose job to the Moonies was beyond me, but I decided to jump in before we ended up talking about the possibility of Babs being abducted by aliens.

"Mum, it'll be fine. Babs is all talk. She's not going to go to Hollywood because she has no money, knows no one, and couldn't act her way out of a plastic bag. She'll come back from London with a new nose and continue to sponge off you and Dad until she lands herself a rich guy to look after her."

"She needs a nice boyfriend to calm her down all right. It's a pity the relationship with Peter from James's team didn't work out. Is there anyone else on the team that might be nice for her?" Mum asked innocently as I choked on my tea.

"No."

"There must be someone you could set her up with. I think she needs an older lad. Someone mature who'll steer her in the right direction and get her to behave like an adult, instead of a young hussy. It's a pity Donal's taken, he's a nice responsible fellow."

"Mmmm," I said, not trusting myself to speak.

"Anyway pet, how are things with you. I've been so distracted with that sister of yours I haven't even asked you about the adoption. Any word?"

I shook my head. "No. Nothing yet. It'll be four weeks the day after tomorrow. They said it'd take a month, but I'm really worried that we're going to get turned down. I honestly don't know what I'll do if we are, Mum. I just don't think I could face it. It's our only hope," I said, my eyes welling up.

"Now now," said Mum, patting my arm. "Of course you'll get accepted. Sure they only turn away lunatics and pedophiles, not good honest people like James and yourself. Don't be getting yourself crazy. You're no good to anyone in a state. I have to admit, with all the distractions of the meetings I thought you'd get pregnant naturally while you were doing the course because you wouldn't be thinking about it. Still, never mind, sure a little Russian baby is nearly the same."

"It is the same, Mum," I said sternly. "It's exactly the same as having a baby of our own, as far as we're concerned—it just took a lot longer than a natural pregnancy."

"Well, Emma, it isn't quite the same. The child might want to meet its parents in the future and you'll have to deal with that."

"MUM," I snapped. "Don't even think about telling me what I may or may not have to face. I have spent the last six months having the horrors of all the things that can go wrong with adopting a baby shoved down my throat. I really don't need you sticking your oar in now. If I allow myself to think about all the bad things that could happen, I'll lose my nerve and back out. Adoption is a huge step and we need support from everyone. I only want to hear positive things. Okay?"

"Lord, Emma, I was only saying—"

"Mum, it's bad enough having my sister—who I told the adoption people was an extremely responsible adult who would be a great help to me when I brought the baby home—making a fool of herself on TV. I really don't need you telling me the baby's going to piss off back to Russia as soon as it can walk."

"Well you shouldn't have lied to them about Barbara. I've told you before about lying to people. No good comes of it."

"MUM!"

"But, as I was going to say before you roared at me, I am quite sure that your sister being silly will have no effect on your application, and your social worker would hardly be watching daytime television now would she?"

"Suppose not," I grumbled.

"Right, well I better go and contact the police or MI5 or whoever it is that I need to get in touch with to get my new identity. Maybe I should go to Russia and you could come to visit me with the baby. Your father suggested Afghanistan because of the big blue sheets the women wear over there. He said even Nuala wouldn't be able to track me down. He's a real comedian, I can see where Barbara gets it. Anyway, I'll say a prayer for the adoption. Let me know. And don't take your frustrations out on James. It's bad enough his sister-in-law is making a show of him on television without his wife shouting at him when he comes home. What must he think of us? The English are so much more reserved. Right, well, I'll go then. Bye now."

Three days later, as I was driving down to Wexford to do a wedding party's makeup, my mobile rang. It was James. A letter had arrived from the Adoption Board. We had been accepted. I pulled over and sobbed.

chapter THIRTY

Now that we'd been approved by the Adoption Board and added the twenty thousand euro loan onto our already substantial mortgage—which at least spread the repayments over twenty years—we had to find an agency. According to my research the agency was the most vital part of the process. If you went with some bandit agency you could end up with a very sick child, or else they'd just do a runner with your money and you'd have no child at all. A good agency would not only match you with a baby but also get all your documents translated for you and authorized by the Ministry of Education and Health in Russia, organize a court date for you, and have a facilitator meet you on your arrival in Moscow and guide you through your visit, translating and interpreting for you. Two visits to Russia were required. The first visit is when you go to meet the child you have been matched with, the second is when you go back—once the court date has been set up—to legally adopt your baby and bring him or her home.

I had heard about an agency called Help Is at Hand run by a man named Alexander. He had been mentioned on a number of the websites I had been browsing as the best in the business. The agency was based in Georgia in the United States, so I e-mailed him a list of questions that I had compiled from reference books and Internet adoption chat rooms.

What is the age range of the children available for adoption? How many children did you place last year? What is the breakdown of costs? What is the average time between submitting a dossier and receiving a referral? How long between accepting the referral and our first trip over? How long between the first and second trips? How long will we get to spend with the child on the first trip? Will we have a translator on hand when we get to Russia? Will you be translating all documents into and out of Russian?

I sent them off, and while I was waiting for a response set about compiling all our documents—known as our dossier. The paper trail for adoption was a never-ending nightmare. I looked down at the long list of documents required: copies of our birth and marriage certificates and passports; a statement of income provided by our employers; documents certifying ownership of our home; a letter from the adoption agency giving commitment to provide postplacement supervision and postplacement reports to the Russian authorities; a medical letter from our doctor drafted in the format prescribed by the Russian Ministry of Education and Health, which includes the need for an HIV test; a letter giving power of attorney to the agency; written statements that we will register the adopted child at the consular office of the Russian Federation in Ireland; photographs of us; home study assessment report; Department of Health's certificate of eligibility; police reports for both of us; and a letter confirming that the application complies with both Irish and Russian adoption laws.

I sighed as I put the list down on the table. These adoption people really knew how to ruin a girl's buzz. Just when I thought that things were going to get easier—they were actually becoming even more of a headache. Okay, come on, Emma, I said to myself, chop chop. There is no point sitting around feeling weary, get up off your ass and start sorting out the paperwork.

I spent the next three weeks, galloping around Dublin—with James in tow some of the time—sorting out documents, having HIV tests and stalking Alexander. I was determined to have my dossier completed before going to London with Amanda to film Babs's cosmetic surgery. Alexander e-mailed me with answers to all my questions—including a breakdown of the costs. We decided to go with him, because he had been running his agency for over ten years, he seemed very professional, and because the pictures of the children on his website were very sweet. They all looked very cute and happy. The day before we flew to London, I sent by FedEx our paperwork to the United States with a large check.

James came with us to London, as he was meeting with one or two players he was hoping to persuade to move to Leinster next season. I was glad to have him with me, because Babs was driving me insane. She seemed to be under some illusion that she was a celebrity and insisted on wearing sunglasses in the airport and on the plane. After we had landed and checked into our hotel, we went to meet

Sean and Shadee for dinner. Babs was still wearing the sunglasses when we arrived at the restaurant.

"What's with the dark glasses, Seabiscuit?" Sean asked.

"Enjoy your final tease Sean," said Babs, smirking, "because in two days you won't be able to call me that anymore."

"You can take the nose off the girl, but you can't take the girl off the nose," said Sean, laughing as Babs whipped off her sunglasses to glare at him.

While they bickered, I was staring at the enormous rock on Shadee's finger.

"Wow," I exclaimed, "it's stunning."

Shadee smiled and lifted her hand so I could get a closer look.

"It's gorgeous, Sean," I said. "Congratulations to both of you."

"What? You're engaged?" said our C-list celeb. "Since when? Have you told Mum and Dad? Come on let's call them now, it'll take the heat off me. They'll go mad when they hear this," she said, subtle as always.

"No they won't," snapped Sean. "They'll be fine about it. We've been together for a year, they're hardly going to be surprised."

"Want to bet?" said Babs.

"Have you told your parents?" I asked Shadee.

She nodded and sighed. "Yes. It was difficult, but they are very fond of Sean, and they can see how happy I am, so they're coming around to the idea."

"So will our parents," I said, reassuring her. "They think you're great."

"What are we waiting for? Let's call them now," said Babs.

"Shut up will you," said Sean. "Big nose, big mouth. We're going to wait and see if you survive the operation before pouncing our news on them. If you don't die on the operating table, we'll tell them this weekend."

"Well I think this calls for champagne," said James.

"Absolutely," said Sean, "to celebrate our engagement and your adoption."

"And my new nose," shouted Babs, not wanting to be left out.

"And Babs's new nose. Let's hope they don't make it worse," I said.

"Or that the knife slips and she ends up with a scar down the side of her face," added Sean.

"Fuck off the lot of you. You're just jealous because you're both carrot heads and I'm blonde and gorgeous."

"With a penchant for older rugby players," said James, chuckling into his drink as I kicked him under the table. I hadn't told Sean, because I knew he'd be shocked.

"I can't help it if men find me irresistible, James."

"Who are we talking about here?" asked Sean.

"Me shagging Donal Brady," said Babs.

"WHAT? When? I thought he was engaged to Lucy."

"He was, but he still couldn't keep his hands off me."

"Ignore her. They had broken up and he was out of his head drunk and he bumped into Babs and one thing led to another. He got back with Lucy a few days later. No one knows, so don't say a word," I said, glaring at Babs.

"You really are the limit," said Sean. "Why can't you find someone your own age who isn't attached? What's wrong with you?"

"That's rich, coming from someone who's marrying the first girl that he's ever gone out with that didn't cheat on him."

"It's a far sight better than behaving like a tramp."

"Okay, enough," I said, jumping in. "We're supposed to be celebrating here."

* * *

The next day, Babs, Amanda, and I went to the clinic where the operation was taking place. I did their makeup while the production team set up the cameras. The surgeon—a Dr. Browns-Dent—who had more marbles in his mouth than Prince Charles, arrived to talk Babs through the procedure. I applied some light makeup to his already perfectly tanned face, and we were ready to film.

"With rhinoplasty, complications are infrequent and usually minor," warbled the surgeon.

"What's rhinoplasty?" asked Babs, looking put out. "It sounds like something you do to a rhinoceros, not a human."

"It's a medical term, my dear," said Dr. Browns-Dent patronizingly, talking directly to the camera. "As your procedure is relatively straightforward I would imagine we will have completed the operation within an hour."

"Okay, so what exactly happens?" asked Babs, dying to hear all the gory details. "During surgery the skin of the nose is separated from its supporting framework of bone and cartilage, which is then sculpted into the desired shape. When this has been completed satisfactorily, the skin will be redraped over the new framework."

"Cool!" said Babs as Amanda and I squirmed. "What happens when I wake up? I hope I won't be too puffy and bruised? How long till I can go out?"

"When the surgery is complete, a splint will be applied to help your nose maintain its new shape," said the surgeon, smiling into the camera. Babs was irrelevant to him, the audience was key. He was pitching to all those potential clients in Ireland. "After surgery—particularly during the first twenty-four hours—your face will feel puffy and your nose may feel a little uncomfortable. But don't worry; we can control any discomfort you may experience with pain medication. I recommend a day's rest, and then you can go home. Applying cold compresses to the area will help reduce the swelling. I can assure you that all my patients have been extremely satisfied with the results and amazed by the lack of pain they suffer at my expert hands."

"Great, when can we start?" asked Seabiscuit, chomping at the bit.

"You're scheduled for five o'clock today. I will see you then," he said, giving the audience a dazzling smile as he strode out of the room, head to toe Savile Row.

I was feeling a bit nervous for Babs after hearing the details of what went on during the operation. She, on the other hand, was on a high. She was recording her solo piece for the show.

"Well, it's eleven o'clock now, so I've only got six more hours until I get my new nose. I would recommend this to anyone. My life is about to change dramatically. I'm going to look amazing. I just wish I hadn't waited so long. I'll see you all after the operation."

Later that day, as Babs was waiting for the orderlies to come and wheel her down to the operating room, she suddenly looked very young and vulnerable. She was fidgeting nervously with the hat that was holding her hair back.

"Are you okay?" I asked.

"I'm fine. I've just never had an operation before, so I don't know what to expect," she said with a shrug.

"You know you don't have to go through with this if you don't want to. It's not too late to back out."

"No way. I want to get a new nose."

"The one you have really isn't so bad."

"Yeah right. That's why every guy I've ever gone out with said I'd be gorgeous if it wasn't for my nose."

"Well, it's not as if they stopped lining up."

"Look, Emma, I appreciate the concern, but I'm not doing it for them, I'm doing this for me."

"Okay."

"Thanks though. I'm glad you're here. I'd be a bit freaked out on my own."

Just as Babs and I shared the only *Little House on the Prairie* moment we've ever had, the producers came in to set up the camera to film her being wheeled down to the operating room. The minute the camera was switched on, Babs went from young and scared to confident and smiling. They followed her through the anesthesia and then filmed the hour-long operation. I paced nervously up and down outside in the corridor, waiting for her to come out. I prayed nothing would go wrong. God knows she drove us all mad, but life would be very dull without her. At exactly six o'clock, an immaculate Dr. Browns-Dent came out of the operating room to tell the cameras that the operation had been successful and that Babs was now in recovery. I went in and sat beside her until she woke up.

"How did it go?" she slurred, still groggy from the anesthesia.

"Fine. Everything went really well according to your posh surgeon. How are you feeling?"

"Fan-fucking-tastic. These drugs are great, I feel as if I'm floating."

"Okay, well get some sleep, I'll be here when you wake up."

The next morning we arrived back to film the postoperation section, to find Babs sitting up, staring into a mirror and looking a state. Her eyes and nose were puffy and black and blue. As far as her nose was concerned I could see no difference because of the swelling. She didn't look too pleased.

"I look a state. Do something," she hissed at me.

"What exactly am I supposed to do?"

"Make me look better—it's your bloody job. I can't go on TV looking like this."

"There is nothing I can do about the puffiness, and I can't mask your black eyes. Besides, the surgeon said you were to avoid touching the area at all for a few days."

"Shit," said Babs, looking in the mirror as she tried to pull her hair down over her face. "I look like a bloody panda bear, and my nose is killing me. What does it look like? Can you see it under the swelling?"

"It looks dreadful," I said honestly.

"Well, it may not look great now, but it will be fab. The doctor said so, and I trust him. He does all the celebrity noses," she said, trying to convince herself that the big lump in the middle of her face was not the finished product.

Amanda sat on the side of the bed to do the postop interview.

"I'm here with Babs Burke, who has woken up this morning from last night's surgery to see her new nose for the first time. Can you tell us how you're feeling?"

"Like shit, actually. My head's throbbing, and I've just seen my new nose in the mirror. I look like an English bulldog with two black eyes."

"Well, of course the surgeon did say that there would be swelling for a few days, but he seems pleased with the operation."

"Yeah, well, it's not his nose is it? I can't say what I think until the swelling has gone down. I'll comment then. It better be nice because otherwise I'm going to sue you all."

Amanda looked taken aback. Sometimes controversial guests were more of a headache than a ratings booster.

chapter THIRTY-ONE

A WEEK LATER, the swelling had gone down, and Babs's nose was definitely smaller. But to me it looked odd. I was so used to her face with the big schnozz that this button nose looked out of place. She, however, was delighted and spent all day staring at herself in the mirror.

As Mum recovered from the shame and worry of her youngest daughter being operated on in front of the whole country, Sean picked his moment to tell her about his engagement. He took the coward's way out and told her over the phone, saying he was too tied up at work to come home, but he'd see her at Lucy's wedding in six weeks where Shadee could show her the ring and discuss wedding details then. Mum called me straightaway.

"Your brother just called to tell me he's engaged. I presume you knew about this but decided to say nothing."

"He told me last week, when we were in London, but it wasn't up to me to tell you, Mum. It's his news, not mine."

"I suppose the wedding will be in Iran and we'll all have to be covered from head to toe in black sheets and eat sheep's brains for dinner."

"As far as I know they're thinking of getting married in some little country village in Cornwall, where Shadee used to go on holidays."

"And what's wrong with getting married in a little village in Ireland? Not good enough for them is it?"

"Why don't you call Sean and discuss it with him?"

"What type of ceremony will it be? Muslim I suppose. Oh she may say she's not practicing, but mark my words when push comes to shove, the Muslim in her will come out. They'll make him convert, they're a persuasive lot. He'll be a Muslim, and then my little grandchildren will be Muslims, too. We'll never get to see them because her family won't want us trying to convert them. What did I do to deserve this? Joan Cantrell from the bridge club told me only last week that she saw a documentary on Iran or Iraq—she couldn't remember exactly—but anyway the men treat the women like dirt she said. The girls can't go to school or be educated or anything. I don't want my grandchildren brought up in that kind of world," said Mum, beginning to sniffle.

"For goodness' sake, do you honestly think if they treat women that badly that Shadee will want to go anywhere near the place?" I snapped.

"She's used to it so she'd think it was normal."

"She's a math teacher for God's sake. She went to school and college in England, why the hell would she want to go back to that. Jesus, Mum, listen to yourself."

"Well there's no need to take my head off. You're very grumpy today. What's wrong with you?"

"Let's see now. Could it be because I'm waiting to hear back from the agency about matching us up with a baby? Every time the phone rings I stop breathing because I think it might be Alexander and he's found us a child. But instead I pick up the phone and it's you giving me an earful about Sean's wedding. Not my wedding, not my problem. Call Sean, and do not ring me again unless it is to lend me your support or ask me how things are going in my life. I am sick to death of discussing Babs and Sean with you. Now go and torment someone else."

"Emma!"

"What?"

"Was the ring nice?"

"Stunning. Good-bye."

For the next three weeks I literally ran around in circles. I stood in supermarkets staring at the shelves, with no idea why I had come in or what I wanted to buy. I consulted with bride-to-bes about their wedding makeup, not hearing a word they were saying while I stared at my phone, willing it to ring. I bought baby clothes and then returned them to the shop because I was scared of tempting fate. I walked around with a knot in my chest, and sometimes I felt as if I couldn't breathe. I limited myself to calling Alexander every two days to ask, in my now desperate voice, why he hadn't matched us up yet. He told me to be patient. I refrained from telling him to shove his advice up his ass. Patient—I had been told to be patient when I was trying to get pregnant. I had been told to be patient when I was on the fertility drugs, when we were on the adoption list, when we were taking the course, when we were waiting for the home study approval, and now while we were waiting to be matched. I was sick and tired of being told to be PATIENT.

I couldn't sleep because I was so wound up about the baby, so I decided to paint the smaller spare bedroom—which was going to be the nursery. I thought a neutral green would be nice, but then I decided yellow would be better. Then I thought maybe lilac, but lilac was a bit girly, and we didn't know what sex the baby would be. I went back to the paint store five times. The owner thought I was on some very strange drugs. James spent a lot of time avoiding me and occasionally tried to talk to me and calm me down. One night at four in the morning he woke up to a crash and a shriek. I had been on the step ladder, painting the top half of the wall yellow—I had finally settled on yellow—when I'd lost my balance, possibly due to exhaustion and sleep deprivation. I had fallen down, bringing the paint can with me, and when James opened the door I was lying on the ground covered in yellow paint.

"Are you all right?"

"Do I look all right?"

James pulled me up and helped me out of my paint-sodden clothes. He then led me to the shower, where I tried to scrub the paint out of my hair. When I came out of the shower, he was sitting on the bed with a tray on his lap. He handed me a hot cup of tea and a slice of buttered toast.

"Darling, you have to calm down. You need to get some rest. The painting can wait."

"I can't sleep. I tried but I can't. Every time I close my eyes I see disfigured children or filthy orphanages with babies covered in sores. I'm terrified of being matched with a sick child and not being able to say no, because they've got no one else."

"Emma," said James sternly, "you don't have to worry about that, because I will say no. We agreed not to take on a sick child and we are not going to change our minds on that—no matter what."

"But what if it's the sweetest little girl you ever saw who has

AIDS. We could help her. I just want the waiting to be over, it's killing me."

"Emma, we are not knowingly going to take on a child with AIDS. We're first-time adopters with no real idea what the experience is going to be like. It's our first experience of parenthood, and we need to keep it as straightforward as possible, for the child's sake as much as for ours. I understand that the waiting is frustrating, I'm finding it difficult too, but we just have to keep busy and try to distract ourselves."

"That's what I was trying to do tonight."

"Not at four in the morning. You need to get some sleep. You'll be no use to anyone, least of all a baby, if you're exhausted. Now come on, into bed. The painting can wait until tomorrow," he said, putting down the tray and tucking me in.

"James?"

"Yes."

"Do you think I should have gone with the green?"

"No. The yellow is perfect."

"Would you have liked a yellow bedroom?"

"I would have loved it."

"Really?"

"Yes."

"Then how come your bedroom in your parents' house is blue?"

"Emma."

"Shut up?"

"Yes, please."

With Lucy's wedding looming, I met up with her and Jess for a catch-up and full analysis of dresses, shoes, menus, etc. I arrived looking like I'd been dragged through a bush backward. I hadn't slept properly in three weeks, I felt sick all the time, I was too distracted to care about my appearance, and at thirty-six—it shows.

"Hi," said Lucy, hugging me. "How are you? How's it all going?"

"Okay," I said, attempting a smile. "Still waiting by the phone, still no news."

"You look a bit worn out, are you okay?" asked Jess.

"Not sleeping very well. I'm lucky if I get three hours on the trot." I sighed.

"Well, it's good training for when the baby comes," said Jess.

"Good point," I said, smiling. "I hadn't thought of that. No wonder they say the ideal age to have children physically is sixteen. You don't need eight hours sleep at sixteen. At our age you bloody well do. Look at the state of me. One look at me and the baby will refuse to be matched with us."

"Hey, you look fine. Nothing a day at a spa won't cure," said Lucy. "Which, it so happens, is exactly what I have planned for us a week before the wedding. I don't want any mention of any hen party. If I see one of those wind-up, backflipping penises I'll scream. So I've booked us all a day's pampering at the Blue Lagoon Spa in Wicklow. Facials, massages, reflexology—the works."

"Oh God, Lucy, that sounds amazing," I said, thinking the masseuse would have her work cut out trying to get the knots out of my back. "Now, onto more important things, have you sorted out your dress?"

"Well, you know how I was in New York recently with work?"

"Yes," said Jess and I in unison.

"I popped my head into Vera Wang. Just for a look you understand, and sure while I was there it would have been rude not to try some of the dresses on, so I did. And the fourth one I tried on was it—the perfect dress. So I bought it and it's beautiful, if I say so myself," she said, beaming.

"Wow," I said. "You're going to be stunning."

"How's your mother?" asked Jess.

Lucy rolled her eyes. "Usual nightmare. She's now bought three outfits for the wedding—each more over the top than the next. And then she called me last night to tell me that it still wasn't too late to back out and there were plenty more 'suitable fish in the sea.' When I told her I was going ahead with the wedding, she told me the invitations looked cheap, the wine we've chosen is second class, and we have to change the menu because she doesn't like smoked salmon."

"Oh God, Lucy, I thought mine was bad. What did you say?" I asked.

"Nothing. I just said I'd look into it and I hung up. I'll just avoid her calls and hope she doesn't cause a scene on the day."

"Speaking of weddings, what's Sean planning?" asked Jess.

"If he's any sense he'll go to Las Vegas and get married there without any family or fuss. Between her family and ours, they're never going to win. He's really happy though, and she's a lovely girl."

"How's Babs's nose?" asked Lucy.

"Small. I think it looks weird, but she's delighted with it."

"She was very funny on the show," said Jess.

"Don't tell her that. She's been offered an audition to do some presenting job on some satellite channel in England. I think it's the shopping channel or one of those crappy ones, but needless to say she thinks she's a TV star now. If she gets it, she'll be insufferable. Sean—"

My mobile rang. I dove into my bag to answer it. It was Alexander, he sounded very pleased with himself. I held my breath—he had a match. I burst into tears as the girls joined in and hugged me. Then I raced down to the practice field to find James. I drove like a maniac; my hands were shaking so much I couldn't work the stick shift, so I drove at fifty miles an hour in first gear. James heard the car screeching into the parking lot and looked out his office window. He saw me staggering out of the car, half crying, half laughing. He ran down to meet me.

"What happened?"

I had managed to keep some small semblance of control until I saw James, and then I fell apart completely. I sobbed into his shoulder.

"Alexander called. They've matched us up," I wailed.

"But that's wonderful," said James, wiping my tears.

"It's a little boy, James. He's ten months old and his name is . . . uh uh uh," I sobbed. "His name is Yuri, like in *Doctor Zhivago*. It's fate James. It's fate."

chapter THIRTY-TWO

ALEXANDER SAID he was sending us by FedEx a video and medical summary of Yuri the next morning. I paraded up and down the road two days later, looking for the postman, and when I caught sight of him, strolling along, I charged over to him and started rifling through his bag. The poor man nearly died of fright. Granted he probably thought he was being attacked by a recent lunatic asylum escapee. I had a mad glint in my eye, was wearing yellow-paint-splattered pajamas, and my hair was standing in independent wiry tufts. When Postman Pat eventually managed to explain to me that he didn't deliver the couriered post, I helped him pick up the letters I had flung across the footpath in my eagerness to find my video. As I tried to explain to him that I was normally quite rational, but I was waiting for some very important documents, he just nodded and backed away from me slowly. I went home and sat by the window waiting for the FedEx van.

Alexander had said that Yuri was blond and brown eyed and

very healthy and very beautiful. James was a bit skeptical when I told him and was waiting to make up his own mind when he saw the video.

"Now, Emma," he said to me when I came back from postman stalking. "Don't get too excited until we see the video. This may not be the right match for us."

"Don't be ridiculous, of course it is. His name's Yuri, it's fate."

"Half the boys in the bloody country are probably called Yuri. It's not fate, it's just a coincidence. We need to wait and see the video and medical records before jumping in."

I nodded. There was no point arguing. He could call it a coincidence, but I knew fate when I saw it. Yuri was going to be perfect. I could feel it in my bones. Five long hours and ten bitten nails later, the FedEx van pulled up outside the house. I sprinted out to sign for the package. My hands were trembling as I put it down on the table. James, who was only marginally calmer than I was at this stage, opened it and put the video into the VCR.

"Wait," I shouted as he was about to press Play.

"What?"

"Unless he's really badly damaged or sick I want to keep him."

"Let's wait and see."

"Promise me you'll keep an open mind."

"Fine."

"James?"

"Yes?"

"I love you," I said, gulping back tears.

"I love you too," he said, squeezing my hand as he pressed play.

A very small, pale boy with sandy-colored hair and enormous brown eyes stared at us. He looked very young and very frail. He did nothing for a few seconds and then someone began to talk to him, and he looked up. He frowned and then after a few more seconds, slowly began to smile. A sad smile, but a smile nonetheless, and in that instant I fell in love for the second time in my life. I was afraid to look at James. I knew he was wondering about how small Yuri seemed for a ten-month-old. We sat in silence as we watched Yuri playing with a little furry dog. He seemed a very serious child. Just as the video ended, someone began to play some music, and his ears pricked up as he crawled over to listen, smiling to himself.

We sat in silence. For once I didn't know what to say and I was terrified of what James was going to say. I knew what I wanted, but I had to let James make up his own mind. I couldn't try to sway his decision. Finally, after what seemed like forever, he spoke.

"Yuri Daniel Hamilton. Has a nice ring to it, don't you think?"

"JAMES! Really? Are you sure? Daniel, after my dad? Oh my God, James, we're going to be parents," I squealed as I threw my arms around him.

"Well, we need the pediatrician to look at the video and to review the medical records, but he looks healthy enough to me," said James, looking shaken but very happy. "Christ I need a drink. Come on put your shoes on, we're going to the pub."

The next day we were in Dr. Liz Costello's office and she was reviewing the video. I listened closely as she talked us through the tape.

"Ten fingers and toes . . . head circumference proportional to body . . . responds well when spoken to . . . seems very alert . . . good movement, good muscle mass . . . no signs of discomfort when he crawls . . . good response to music . . ."

After she had looked over the medical records, she told us that as far as she was concerned he seemed like a healthy young boy. He was small for his age, but a lot of children who had been institutionalized were underweight. His senses seemed to be in good working order, and he seemed very alert.

"It's impossible to say for definite from looking at a five-minute video if this child is perfectly healthy. As you know there are risks involved here. But from what I can see, this little boy seems in good health."

We left on a high. Yuri was going to be our son. We were going to be his parents. After three long years, we were going to have a baby. We rang Alexander and told him we were happy to travel to Russia to meet Yuri and then officially accept the referral. He said we needed to book flights to Moscow and he would sort out the transfer details, set up a visit to the children's home, and have a translator waiting to meet us. If everything went according to plan, he would then try to organize a court date for as soon after our visit as possible, but it could take up to a month, he warned us. We should apply for a visa now, he said. It took two weeks to process the visas, so we should aim to be ready to travel in three weeks' time.

I called Mum next and she came straight over to see the video.

"Oh, is that him?" she asked as she stared at the only child on the screen.

"Yes, isn't he beautiful?" I answered dreamily. "I think he looks like James."

Mum looked at me as if I were mad. "He looks nothing like him, but he is a sweet little thing. Very small though? Is he sickly?"

"No. The pediatrician said he's fine."

"Looks very small to me."

"They're all small for their age."

"Seems a sad little fellow."

"Well what do you expect; he's been locked up in an institution for the past eight months after his mother abandoned him.

He's hardly going to be backflipping across the orphanage singing "When Irish Eyes Are Smiling," now is he?"

"I suppose not. Still, the Russians can be a melancholy lot. You wouldn't want a depressed little baby."

"He's not depressed, look he's smiling."

"Ah yes, he looks better when he smiles, less wan."

"Everyone looks better when they smile."

"He's definitely all right? No hidden diseases?"

"Not that we know of, but you can never be one hundred percent sure when you're adopting. You just have to trust your instincts. He's going to be your grandson, so you better be nice about him and you better smother him with love."

"I'll love him more than if he was your own flesh and blood. Sure he's a little angel. I'm just being cautious for you. Oh look, he likes music. Well that's a good sign. He might end up being a famous musician, or a ballet dancer like that Rudolf Nureven."

James walked in at this point. "God, I hope not Mrs. B. I don't want my son prancing about in tights. He's going to be a good old rugby player if I've anything to do with it."

"I don't know about a career in rugby," said Mum, looking at Yuri's tiny little pale face.

"He can be whatever he damn well likes, and if he's gay, who cares," I said.

"Gay!" said Mum and James.

"Well, you were talking about Rudolph Nureyev and he was gay."

"Yuri won't be gay," said James.

"Rudolf was having an affair with Margot Fonteyn, he wasn't gay," said Mum.

"Come on, Mum, he was as gay as Christmas. Everyone knows that."

"He was not. I'm sick of you young ones saying everyone's gay. Anyone with any bit of creativity now is homosexual according to you lot. It's ridiculous. Sure that man had women throwing themselves at him all day long. They used to throw their knickers at him at the ballet. Can you imagine, the ballet crowd throwing knickers. Gay my foot. James you tell her."

"I think actually in this case, Emma's right," said James.

"What? I don't believe it. He couldn't be—"

"Who bloody well cares," I interrupted sharply. I couldn't believe we were having a debate about Rudolf stupid Nureyev and his gayness when we were supposed to be talking about our beautiful son. "The only thing that matters is that our son is beautiful and alert and likes music. And despite what you say, I think he looks like James. He has his eyes."

"We all fancied Rudolf, he couldn't be gay," mumbled Mum as she digested the news that her teenage pinup turned out to favor men.

James and I spent the next few weeks preparing to go to Russia. I took notes from all the adoption websites. They recommended that we bring educational toys with us and a list of medical questions to ask the children's home director when we got there. They said we should hold Yuri and see if he responds well to sound, see what motor skills he does and doesn't have, and check him naked for any signs of abuse or illness. Watch how he interacts with the other children. Is he loving and helpful? Does he seem to accept discipline? Does he show aggression? Does he cry easily? The questions went on and on. I jotted down twenty and went out to buy educational toys for a ten-month-old.

Alexander also told us that we'd be flying to Moscow, then taking a connecting flight to Gelendzhik, near Novorossiysk—two thousand miles south of Moscow. We were going to be staying with a Russian family who lived not far from the orphanage. Alexander told us to bring gifts for the family, gifts for the staff of the children's home, for the translator, doctor, driver, and pretty much everyone we met along the way. He suggested watches, perfume, good quality chocolate bars and sweets, silk scarves, makeup, tights, computer games, glossy magazines, and sweatshirts. He told us not to be surprised if we got little or no reaction to our gifts as the Russian people are not demonstrative with strangers. It didn't mean they weren't happy with the presents, they just mightn't show it.

The advice from other adoptees on the websites said to pack as lightly as possible, but considering it was November, we had to bring warm clothes. I checked the weather in Novorossiysk—it was actually quite mild. Still though, it was Russia, so I decided to pack ski jackets and thermal underwear anyway. Packing medicine was also vital. Antibiotics, aspirin, Pepto-Bismol for upset stomachs, and lots of antibacterial wipes were recommended. We ran around buying far too much and ended up having to leave cuddly toys and several enormous bars of Toblerone behind.

Everyone called to wish us luck, and as the day grew closer we became increasingly nervous. It was the biggest decision we would ever make. We were going to meet our son and hold him and arrange to bring him home. We were nervous wrecks. Even James couldn't sleep, and we stayed up half the night talking about the future and what it would bring.

"Do you think he'll like us?" I asked, nervously twiddling the button on my pajamas.

"I hope so, though I'd say it could take a while for him to get used to us. You mustn't worry if he doesn't take to us straightaway. After all we're complete strangers."

"God, I hope he doesn't take one look at us and crawl in the other direction. Imagine if he did? What would we do?"

"Think positive, darling."

"What if he hates redheads? He may never have seen one before. There probably aren't many redheads in Russia. Do you think I should wear my Russian hat? I don't want to freak him out."

"I think the enormous furry Russian hat would be much more likely to scare the child than your hair. Stop fretting, I have no doubt that he'll fall in love with you at first sight—just like his father did."

The day we were due to leave, Dad came to collect us and bring us to the airport. He rang the doorbell and shouted at us to hurry up. We could hear a commotion outside. Beeping car horns and shouting. When we opened the door, there were three cars. Mum, Dad, and Babs in one, all wearing Russian hats. Lucy and Donal in another car, with GOOD LUCK painted along the side, and Jess, Tony, little Sally, and Roy in the last car, all wearing furry hats and cheering as we came out of the house. I was so moved that I couldn't speak. I hugged Dad and cried into the side of his hat.

"We couldn't let you go without a proper send-off. Everyone wanted to join in. We're all behind you, pet."

"Come on you two, you'll miss your flight," shouted Donal, who had jumped out to help James with our enormous suitcases.

We climbed into the back of the car, where Babs handed us two Russian hats, and while Mum pretended not to cry, Dad drove us to the airport, followed by our best friends.

chapter THIRTY-THREE

As we sat on the plane and Moscow loomed closer, we began to get very anxious. James's nerves manifested themselves in a grumpy outburst about our living arrangements.

"I have to say, I'd much rather stay in a hotel. I'm not sure about this living with a Russian family business," he said.

"I know, but Alexander said there were no decent hotels nearby and that it would be good for us to see how a normal Russian family lives."

"Can't we visit them for an afternoon? I'd really much rather hire a driver and go back to a hotel every night, regardless of the distance. I don't fancy having to speak pidgin Russian after spending the day in an orphanage. We won't have any privacy," grumbled James. "This place Novorofsky or whatever it's called is in the armpit of Russia, so I doubt this family has much money, which means we'll be sleeping on top of each other."

"For goodness' sake, James, it's not bloody New York, there

doesn't happen to be a Hilton Hotel nearby. We'll just have to make the most of it. It's only for a few days, it'll be fine."

"Ludicrous. Why the hell couldn't they match us with a child in an orphanage near Moscow. Two thousand bloody miles outside Moscow is a farce."

"Children's home"

"Pardon?"

"Don't call it an orphanage. They only like to be referred to as children's homes."

"Considering its location in the back arse of Russia, it's probably a barn."

"Fine."

"What?"

"There's no point talking to you, you're determined to be negative about everything."

"I am not."

"James, so far today you've complained about the weight of our cases, the bumpy flight, the size of our seats, the location of the children's home, and our lodging arrangements. Next time we do this—you can bloody well arrange everything and we'll see how well you get on. I've done my best to make this as seamless as possible, so will you please just put a sock in it. I know you're nervous, but so am I, and your constant moaning is not helping matters."

James sighed. "You're right. Sorry, darling. I promise to be positive about everything. Even if our hosts lodge us in an outhouse and serve us pigs' feet I'll be politeness itself."

When we landed in Sheremetyevo-2 (Moscow Airport to us non-Russians, named after the family on whose estate it is located—how loaded are they!) we were surrounded by porters wearing green vests, clamoring to carry our bags. I tried to bargain with them while James stood beside me looking uncomfortable. Eventually I handed over a bunch of euros to the strongest-looking man—I didn't want anyone to put their back out carrying our overweight luggage—and we followed him as he flew through customs where we had our declaration form stamped. In the arrivals area a driver was waiting for us with a sign saying HAMILTON. He didn't speak much English, and so we drove in silence to the domestic airport, which took nearly an hour.

We then boarded a very old and decrepit-looking plane and spent the next two and a half hours flying to Gelendzhik, near Novorossiysk. When we dragged our luggage out—no eager men in green at this airport—our translator, Olga, was waiting for us. She was a very serious young woman who shook our hands solemnly and without batting an eyelid threw both suitcases into the trunk of her car—clearly Olga was an Olympic weight lifter in a former life. We then drove to Novorossiysk, which Olga informed us was the largest trading port in southern Russia. While driving through the city, James nudged me several times and pointed to the hotels we passed along the way.

We eventually pulled up outside a very uninviting, gray apartment block where, Olga announced, our hosts lived. We trundled into the building and headed for the elevator, which was broken— our new home was situated on the eighth floor. As Olga bounced up the steps carrying one bag, James huffed and puffed behind her, dragging his suitcase as if it were the cross of Calvary itself. He cursed under his breath while I got a fit of very badly timed giggles. It was a mixture of nerves, exhaustion, and tension, but once I started I couldn't stop. Every time I looked back at James's red, angry face, I collapsed. He, needless to say, found nothing remotely amusing in our situation, and my laughter just caused him to get more wound up. By the time we reached the eighth floor, I was verging on the hysterical and James was close to murdering me. Our hosts opened the door to a giggling mess and her sweaty, grouchy husband. I managed to control myself as Olga reminded us to take off our shoes before introducing us. When she called James Mr. Hamiloon, I was off again, shoulders shaking. Somewhere between wanting to kill me and gasping for breath, James got the giggles too. Our poor hosts, Mr. and Mrs. Vlavoski, just stared at us in bemusement.

Twenty minutes, a clothes change, and a reality check later, James and I appeared out of our bedroom, bearing gifts and apologizing for our earlier display of hysteria. We asked Olga to explain that we were overtired and emotional. The Vlavoskis' eighteen-year-old daughter, Nikki, had arrived home from work, and she helped break the ice when she hugged me after opening her present of makeup and perfume. Her parents took a little longer to warm to us. They were clearly still in doubt about the state of our mental health.

After a lovely meal of vegetable soup and dumplings filled with potato, James and I fell into bed. We had been given Nikki's room, while she slept on the couch. It was a nice room, but the double bed was very small—it was really a large single, so we spent the night rolling into each other and trying to sleep in the spoon position—which looks very comfortable in the movies, but in reality means that one of you ends up with their nose pressed against the wall. In this case it was me. We got up the next morning after very little sleep and packed our knapsack with all the gifts for Yuri and the staff of the children's home. We had our camera and video recorder with us as well. Olga arrived at nine sharp to collect us. I was a nervous wreck. I tried to eat the pancakes we were given for breakfast, but I just felt sick. James looked a bit green himself. This was it. We were finally going to meet our son.

As Olga explained what we should expect from the day, James and I sat in the back of the car holding hands—well, gripping each other's hands to be precise. The children's home was a two-story building that looked a bit run-down. Inside, the paint was peeling off the walls, and it was cold and dark. We were ushered into a large, drafty reception room that was filled with toys and playpens while a couple of sofas were pushed back against the wall. It wasn't as bad as I had expected. Behind this room was the dormitory, where all the children slept. It was a large room crammed full of little beds and cots. Although it was old-fashioned, it was clean, and you could see the staff did the best they could with what they had. The director of the home showed us around. Speaking via Olga, he told us how delighted he was that we were going to meet Yuri. He assured us that he was a very healthy little boy and as bright as a button. We sat nervously on the couch—neither of us able to speak—as we waited for the children to come in from breakfast. The door burst open and twenty or more children rushed in. I looked around desperately to see Yuri. Where was he? My heart was pounding in my chest, I thought I was going to black out—and then I saw him. He was crawling along the floor in the middle of the bunch, concentrating on getting to the other side without being trampled. I grabbed James's arm.

"There," I said hoarsely, pointing to the tiny little boy in the blue romper suit. James froze.

The director picked Yuri up, spoke gently to him in Russian, and then handed him to me. I held the little boy in my arms, and he stared up at me with his huge brown eyes, frowning at the sight of this unfamiliar face. I smiled and he broke my heart by smiling back. As I stood there crying and smiling, James, snapping out of his trance, came over. I handed Yuri to him, I wanted them to bond.

"Hey there little fellow," he said as he smiled down at his son. "Welcome to our family."

Yuri looked up at James and then reached up and touched his face. His little hand rested on James's cheek, and for the first time I saw my husband cry. I turned away, it was their private moment. I moved across the room and took deep breaths. I wanted to lie down and wail. We had come so far, and it had been such a long, bumpy, and emotional roller coaster that sometimes I had wondered if it was worth it. But now, seeing James holding our beautiful son, I knew it was worth every minute.

We spent most of the day playing with Yuri and watching as he played with the educational toys we had brought. He was as a bright as a button, and he adored the musical mat we lay him on. It played Mozart when he rolled on it. I quizzed the director with my list of questions and got satisfactory answers to most. He had very little information on Yuri's birth mother. He said she was very young and already had three children, so she wasn't able to cope with another. She had dumped Yuri with them and left in a hurry. James and I checked Yuri for signs of bruising or scars of any kind and found none.

We spent the next three days getting to know our son and delighting in every tiny thing he did. We talked of nothing else. Yuri consumed our thoughts and conversations. "Did you see that smile?"; "What about when he danced to the music?"; "The way he put those bricks one on top of the other." We had turned into those people we had always sworn not to—the boring parents who talk of nothing but their child. That was us—Mr. and Mrs. Hamilton-bore.

The fourth day with Yuri was our last. We were going home while Alexander's people organized a court date. They had promised to get the earliest one possible but said that it would be at least two weeks. Saying good-bye to Yuri was the hardest thing we'd ever had to do. I made the director swear over and over again that he would take special care of Yuri until we came back to collect him. I cried all the way home—and I mean all the way.

"What if he has an accident?" I asked James on the flight from Moscow. "What if his mother comes back and swipes him?" "What if he gets really sick and dies?" "What if some Russian couple go to the home and decide they don't want the baby allocated to them, they want Yuri, because he's so beautiful and because they're Russians they get first choice?"

"Emma!" said James, sounding utterly exasperated. "You've been doing the 'what ifs' now for six hours. Please stop. It's all going to be fine. This is the way adoptions work. Nothing is going to happen. Stop tormenting yourself and me. We'll be back in three weeks to pick him up and bring him home, and we'll never let him out of our sight again."

"How am I going to get through the next few weeks?"

"I'm sure Lucy's wedding will be a good source of distraction."

"My God, I'd completely forgotten about it."

chapter THIRTY-FOUR

ONCE WE GOT HOME, the days dragged—they were the longest of my life. We waited impatiently for Alexander to call us with our court date. Meanwhile, I rang the children's home every day to check on Yuri. I knew I was driving the director insane, but I didn't care, it made me feel better to know he was alright. James and I talked of nothing but Yuri and how wonderful he was, how smart and alert and beautiful and good-natured. We made everyone sit through a thirty-minute video of Yuri eating, crawling, lying on his play mat, and sleeping.

A week before the wedding Lucy, Jess, and I went away to the spa for a day of pampering. As we lay back side by side being massaged with wonderful-smelling oils, I asked Jess what it was like.

"What do you mean?"

"I mean, when you have a child, when you give birth, what's it like? What do you feel when you hold the baby for the first time?"

"God, well, it's amazing. By the time you've given birth you're usually pretty exhausted, so half of you is just thrilled it's all over and the baby is okay. But when they hand the baby to you and you hold him for the first time—it's just magical. I honestly don't know how to describe it."

"Like being hit by a bolt of lightning and falling in love at first sight," I said.

"Yeah, that's exactly how it feels, and you forget all the pain when you look at their little face."

"And you think—how can I love something I don't even know, so much. It's really scary."

"Yes, it's so frightening because you know if anything happens to them you'll die," Jess agreed.

"I know, it's exactly the way I feel when I look at Annie," said Lucy, giggling. "Come on, girls, this is supposed to be a fun day, and you're both nearly in tears. Enough of the baby love."

"Sorry, Lucy," I said, smiling at her. "Oh, did I tell you about Yuri when I gave him the little quacking duck?"

"Yes," said Lucy and Jess.

"Did I mention how he lights up when he hears classical music?"

"Yes," they groaned.

"Have you noticed how interesting my conversation has become since I went to Russia?" I said, laughing. "Speaking of Annie—how's she been?" I asked.

"Angelic," said Lucy. "In fact, she was being so nice to me that it was beginning to freak me out a bit. She keeps telling me how thrilled she is that I'm marrying Donal and how wonderful I am and how much she loves her dress. But then yesterday she had a freak attack when she discovered she wasn't sitting beside Donal at the top table, so we had to change the place names around. I was relieved, to be honest, her perfect behavior wasn't fooling me. She's a million times better than she was, but she's still a teenager."

"God, Lucy, this day next week you'll be walking up the aisle. Mrs. Lucy Brady."

"I don't think so. I'll be hanging on to my own name. I'm not burning my bra over the issue, but it's too much hassle to change it at work, so I'll still be Lucy Hogan."

"I couldn't wait to change mine. Burke is a desperate name. Hamilton is a lot better. Yuri Hamilton sounds great doesn't it?"

"Yes," said Lucy and Jess, rolling their eyes.

The next morning Alexander called. Our court date had been fixed. We were going to become Yuri's official parents in exactly two weeks' time. We were flying to Russia two days after Lucy's wedding to spend a few days with Yuri, and then we'd take him to court and have him officially adopted. Alexander told me to be prepared to answer questions from the judge.

"Russians view the woman as the primary caregiver," he said, "so most of the court's attention will be on you. Some questions the judge may ask include—describe your house, how old is the child? Why did you choose this child? Are you aware of his medical record? How will you teach your child about his heritage? Why are you adopting from Russia . . . that kind of thing. But don't worry, Emma, he will probably only ask a couple of simple questions. Just dress smart and keep calm. Also, don't forget to bring clothes and bottles and a portable crib for Yuri."

"Don't worry, I won't," I said, smiling at the thought of the amount of baby gear I had crammed into the nursery.

I rang James and screamed down the phone. The anxious knot

in my stomach was gone. It was okay now, we had a date. Yuri would be ours in two weeks. I called Mum and told her.

"Oh, Emma," she said, getting emotional. "That's wonderful, pet. I've been really worried you know. I thought they might change their minds on you. I was down on my knees praying for you."

"Thanks, Mum. I'm so relieved it's all nearly over. You'll be a granny soon."

"And a little dote he is too. Thank God it's sorted out. You just never know with those Russians. The wall may have come down, but once a Communist, always a Communist."

"Mum, you have to remember that Yuri is Russian, so you can't be criticizing them."

"He's not Russian, he's Irish."

"No, he'll be half Russian, half Irish. I want him to know all about his roots, so no negative comments about Russia please."

"Would you not change the child's name? It'd be easier for him in school. Yuri's a bit foreign sounding. He might get bullied."

"Yuri is a beautiful name, and it's what he will be called for the rest of his life, so get used to it."

"How about a nice Irish name like Seamus."

"Mum."

"Or Donal?"

"Mum."

"Oh I know what'd suit him—Colm. He's a real look of a Colm about him."

"Mother! His name is Yuri. End of discussion. End of conversation. End of subject—never to be raised again. Yuri Daniel Hamilton."

The night before Lucy's wedding, Sean and Shadee arrived, and we went out for a family meal. Mum was very impressed with the ring, and Shadee was saying all the right things. Sean had clearly prepped her for the wedding question onslaught.

"Where do you think you'd like to get married?" asked Mum

"We're looking at a lovely country hotel in Cornwall," said Shadee.

"Oh. Would you not think of getting married here in Ireland?"

"Yeah, in the pissing rain and the freezing cold. Great idea," said Babs.

"Babs may have a smaller nose but her mouth is as big as ever," said Dad, chuckling to himself.

"We know some people who own a very nice hotel outside Dublin that would be suitable," continued Mum in her quest to strong-arm Shadee into getting married in Ireland, where Mum could control the whole event.

"That sounds nice, but—" said Shadee.

"Mum, we're getting married in Cornwall. It's not bloody Tehran. You should be pleased," said Sean.

"Will you have many of the shite Muslims coming over from your country?" asked Mum.

"No, all of my family now lives in the UK. The only relation I have left in Tehran is my uncle Tony, and he is a bit of a black sheep I'm afraid."

"We all have those," said Dad, pointing to Babs as we laughed.

"So, guys, tell me about Yuri," asked Sean, changing the subject.

"Noooo," squealed Babs. "Don't get them started, they'll never shut up. We'll be having a slide show in a minute. Why don't we talk about my new job instead."

"What new job," asked mum suspiciously.

"Let me guess, you're going to have a boob job live on TV," said Sean.

"No, smart ass, I'm going to be presenting on BFL."

"What's BFL?" asked Dad.

"It's Buy for Less—a shopping channel," I said.

"What will you be selling?" asked James, trying not to laugh.

"Harnesses?" said Sean as we roared laughing.

"Saddles?" I said, giggling.

"Riding crops?" said James, joining in.

"Stop, please you're cracking me up," said a humorless Babs. "I'm actually going to be selling carpet-stain remover initially and then I'll probably move on to jewelry."

"I'd say Nicole Kidman's quaking in her boots," said Dad, choking on his drink.

"You'll have an Oscar in no time," said Sean.

"Laugh all you want. Everyone has to start somewhere. I'll be moving to London next month. So Sean I'll be crashing at your place until I get settled."

"Excuse me?" said Sean.

"So anyway," I interrupted. "About Yuri . . ."

While James spent the morning of the wedding with Donal, doing God knows what, Jess and Lucy and I lolled about in our dressing gowns, sipping champagne and taking our time getting ready. I did their makeup and then my own. The hairdresser did our hair. Everything was simple—the way Lucy wanted it. Then Lucy went to put on her dress, and when she came out, Jess and I gasped. She was truly the most beautiful bride I have ever seen. Her long black hair was in stunning contrast to the off-white Vera Wang dress. It fit her like a glove and showed off her fantastic figure. She looked radiant. Jess and I began to get emotional, but Lucy nipped us in the bud.

"No more crying. God, you mothers are emotional wrecks. I don't want you ruining your makeup. Come on now, let's go. I've waited thirty-six and a half years for this, I'll be damned if I'm going to be late."

When Lucy walked up the aisle, Donal came forward to meet her.

"Jesus, could you not have made an effort, today of all days," he said, beaming at her.

"You don't look so bad yourself," she said, smiling up at him. "We should get you out of that tracksuit more often."

"Anytime you want to get me out of my tracksuit is fine with me."

"Donal!" said Lucy. "We're in a church."

The ceremony passed without a hitch and an hour later they were officially married.

When dinner was over, Donal stood up to speak.

"I'm not usually a man who's stuck for words, but when I tried to write down how I felt about Lucy I got tongue-tied. I know—there's a first for everything," he said, smiling. "I suppose it's fair to say that I'm not very good at the romantic talk, so I've decided to leave it to a man I've admired all my life, a man who can really express his emotions. Lucy, these may not be my words, but they sum up exactly how I feel about you. As Christy Moore says—

> Black is the color of my true love's hair,
> Her lips are like some roses fair,
> She's the sweetest smile, and the gentlest hands,
> I love the ground, whereon she stands.
> I love my love and well she knows,
> I love the ground, whereon she goes,

I wish the day, it soon would come,
When she and I could be as one.

There wasn't a dry eye in the house. Lucy stood up and hugged Donal, tears streaming down her face.

"What a sap," snorted Babs. "She's welcome to him."

"And Sean's welcome to you," I said, winking at Sean, who put his head in his hands and groaned.

The first dance was to Lucy's favorite song—"My Heart Will Go On," by Celine Dion. Lucy had impeccable taste in everything, but when it came to music—she was a bit cheesy. James and I shuffled around, trying not to step on each other's toes.

"Happy darling?" he asked, beaming at me.

"Very," I said, smiling back.

"Only two more days and we'll see Yuri again," said the besotted father.

"I know, it's great. By the way, did I mention that I'm pregnant."

"What?" said James, stopping abruptly middance.

The words tumbled out of my mouth. "Last night Jess asked me if I had any spare Tampax. I didn't, but it made me realize that I hadn't had a period in ages. So when I got back to the room I checked my diary. I'm four weeks late. With all the to-ing and fro-ing to Russia, I hadn't even noticed. So when I got up this morning, I drove down to the drugstore and bought a pregnancy test, and I'm pregnant."

"But, we're going to court in a week. What about Yuri?"

"Well, it looks like Yuri's going to have a little sister or brother," I said, grinning at him.

"How do you say—Fuck me!—in Russian?"

The Right Fit

sinead moriarty

A Readers Club Guide

About this Guide

The suggested questions are intended to help your reading group find new and interesting angles and topics for discussion for Sinead Moriarty's *The Right Fit*. We hope that these ideas will enrich your conversation and increase your enjoyment of the book.

Many fine books from Washington Square Press feature Readers Club Guides. For a complete listing, or to read the guides online, visit www.BookClubReader.com.

Questions for the Author

Q: How was writing a sequel different from writing *The Baby Trail*? Was it easier or more difficult, and why?

A: Writing the sequel was in some ways easier because I was familiar with the characters. Emma and James had become very real and dear to me over the first book, and the sequel flowed as they continued their quest for parenthood.

Q: Why did you decide to make Sean's girlfriend of Iranian descent?

A: I thought there was a lot of potential humor with Emma's mother's over-the-top reaction to her beloved son being involved in a relationship with an Iranian girl. I also wanted to show how preconceptions—from both Emma's mother and Shadee's parents—can be so silly and misinformed.

Q: In an article for *Image* magazine, you recount how, in response to your concerns about not getting pregnant right away, your gynecologist informed you that "women should be giving birth at sixteen years of age." How did you respond to the doctor? Do you think your doctor should have told you this?

A: When my gynecologist told me that women are physically primed to give birth at sixteen, I felt like hitting him over the head with my handbag. I was thirty-two and desperate to have a baby. This nugget of information was of no use to me whatsoever and at sixteen I was barely able to look after myself never mind a baby!

Q: An interview in *The Irish Times* reports you saying that joining a creative writing group was "hugely helpful" to writing your first novel. How did it help you? Would you recommend that aspiring writers find a creative writing group?

A: Joining a creative writing group was a turning point for me. It meant that I was getting serious about my writing and was ready to open myself up to criticism. It's very nerve-wracking when you show other people your work for the first time, but it is incredibly useful. The feedback and support I got from the other aspiring writers and my tutor gave me the confidence to finish my book and dare to hope that it might one day be published.

Q: Who are the greatest influences on your writing and why? Whose work would you like your books to be compared to?

A: I've always been a voracious reader; my parents instilled that in all of us when we were growing up. I read everything from historical biographies to the classics to popular fiction. I think you can be influenced by everything you read—no matter how good or bad. I also think that life experiences have a big influence on a writer. I strive to do the best I can with each book, and hope that I will continue to grow as a writer.

Q: **In your books, Emma is Irish and her husband is English. Yet there doesn't seem to be any of the animosity that stereotypically is heard about the Irish and the English. Are the animosities merely hype?**

A: I think that those animosities between the Irish and the English are now—thankfully—a thing of the past. Having lived in London for six years, I experienced nothing but goodwill and made many great friends. In fact a number of my Irish friends have married English people and there have been no issues whatsoever.

Q: **You've lived in Dublin, London, and Paris. What do you think the primary differences in culture are between Ireland and England? How does Paris differ from both of them? How would your characters and storylines be different if they were set in London or Paris instead of Dublin?**

A: Cultural differences are what make life interesting. The French and the English and the Irish are very different breeds. A small example is this: an Irish person will always say yes even if they mean no. A French person will always say no even when they mean yes. An English person will say maybe, and leave you guessing.

I have thus far set my books in Ireland because I love the

way Irish people express themselves—it's so colorful and witty.

Q: **Emma is warned repeatedly about how drastically her life will change when she has children. Was this true for you when you had your son? How did it change the most?**

A: My life has changed in the most wonderful way since having a baby. My little boy has brought such joy to our lives. My husband and I were very ready to have children and after four years trying, we consider our son a little miracle. Parenthood is tiring and you do have to be organized to allow yourself to keep working and so forth, but it's the most rewarding experience in the world. Sorry to sound smug . . . I'm besotted.

Q: **How did your single life and how does your married life mirror the lives of the characters you have created in your novels? In what ways are they different?**

A: I try—in so far as I can—to distance my life from my characters. However, there is always part of you that sneaks into a book, no matter how hard you try. I'm not going to reveal which parts!

Q: **Do you have close female friendships like Emma, Lucy, and Jess? Do you rely on your friends as the characters in your novel do?**

A: My girlfriends are my support group and my cheerleaders. They are extremely important to me and we have all known each other more than twenty years.

Q: Will we be seeing more of Emma, James, and the rest of the cast from *The Right Fit* and *The Baby Trail* in a third installment or at the cinema?

A: I have just finished the third and final book in the Emma and James story. I hope that my readers will like the ending. As for a movie . . . we will have to wait and see.

Questions for Discussion

1. How do Emma's fantasies of what adoption will be like at the beginning of *The Right Fit* differ from the reality of what she experiences later?

2. Why do you think Emma sometimes isn't all that child-friendly, i.e., she's not fond of her nephew and does not make much of an effort to have relationships with her friend Jess's children. In fact, on more than one occasion Emma expresses her aversion to children. On the other hand, she adores her godchild. Why do you think this is? And do you think Emma will be a good mother to her own children?

3. At one point, Emma fumes at her mother, saying, "All I keep hearing is how when you have children your life changes so much and it's so hard and you never get time alone, blah blah blah. I'm ready for change. I'm so ready it's a joke. Not having

kids is bloody hard work too. My life as I knew it hasn't been the same since I started trying to have children. . . . It's so patronizing to be told how hard it is all the time. I don't go around telling people what a nightmare it is to be infertile." (165) Do you think people with children are patronizing to people without children? Why can't Emma rant about what a nightmare it is to be infertile—what is different about society's views toward infertility and parenthood?

4. Describe Emma's and her siblings' relationships with their mother. Why are they reticent about telling their mother about major life decisions? In what ways does Emma resemble her mother?

5. At one point, Jess and Emma get into a row about the insensitivity they feel the other has shown her. Who is right in this argument and why? Did it seem like the sore feelings were fully resolved in the end? How are women's arguments different from men's?

6. Were you surprised that Emma does not tell her best friend Lucy about Donal's sexual indiscretion? Would you make the same decision if you were in Emma's place? Would you want to know about Donal's infidelity if you were Lucy?

7. Babs is matter of fact about her one-night stands and other sexual escapades. Emma slept with James the night they met. She also references wild nights she spent with men throughout her twenties. Do the attitudes about casual sex from these Irish women differ from attitudes of typical American women? How are they the same?

8. Throughout the trials of the adoption process, Emma always manages to find the humor in the situation. What did you think were the funniest scenes in the book? How does Emma's sense of humor reveal the absurdity in her own behavior, her relationship with James, and the way people behave in the adoption sessions?

9. In *The Baby Trail,* Emma endured grueling fertility treatments, including hormone shots, a laparoscopy, and in vitro fertilization. In *The Right Fit,* she goes through an excruciating adoption process during which every facet of her life is painstakingly scrutinized and dissected. Which process is more difficult for her to endure and why? Which process would be more difficult for you?

10. After years of trying to conceive and more than a year trying to adopt, Emma and James experience a twist of fate at the end of *The Right Fit.* Was it believable? Why or why not?

Book Club Tips

1. Read both of the Emma and James books and discuss how the characters develop and change as the stories build upon each other. What do you think will happen next with each of the characters?

2. Much of recent women's literature has been made into major motion pictures recently, such as Jennifer Weiner's *In Her Shoes* and Helen Fielding's *Bridget Jones' Diary*. If *The Right Fit* were made into a movie, discuss who should play each of the characters.

3. At one point in *The Right Fit*, Emma, Lucy, and Jess indulge in a spa day. Start your book club meeting with a trip to the nail salon for a manicure and pedicure for some female bonding like the characters in the novel share.

4. Emma and James are determined to adopt a Russian baby. They study Russian and prepare Russian food for the adoption sessions. To help get in the spirit of Emma and James's efforts, serve a Russian feast of caviar, blintzes, borscht, vodka, and other Russian specialties for your meeting.

1-12

CPSIA information can be obtained at www.ICGtesting.com
Printed in the USA
LVOW120324140112

263879LV00001B/24/P

9 780743 496780